THIRD TIME'S A GHOST

HAUNTED EVER AFTER
BOOK THREE

CARRIE PULKINEN

This is a work of fiction. Names, characters, places, and incidents are either the product of the author's imagination or are used fictitiously, and any resemblance to actual persons living or dead, business establishments, events, or locales, is entirely coincidental.

Third Time's a Ghost

Contact Information: www.CarriePulkinen.com

Edited by Victoria Miller

ISBN: 978-1-957253-16-9

Originally published as To Free a Phantom

CHAPTER ONE

A proud smile curved Erica Miller's lips as Amber, her star theater student, delivered the last line of her monologue. She'd spent weeks perfecting the character, putting the right inflection on the words, and timing her delivery perfectly to create a heart-wrenching scene that was sure to win her a spot at the Yale School of Drama.

Erica rose from her seat in the auditorium and clapped, and the rest of her students followed suit. She shuffled onto the stage and pulled Amber into a hug. "That was amazing. With an audition like that, you're sure to get into Yale."

A pink blush spread across Amber's cheeks. "Thanks for all your help, Ms. Miller."

"I didn't do a thing but give you time to practice. That was all you, sweetie."

The rest of the class filed onto the stage, offering their congratulations and wishing her success at the upcoming audition. Jason wrapped his arm around Amber's shoulders. "I know we're not supposed to say good luck, but I just can't bring myself to wish anything bad on you. I hope you do great."

Caitlyn brushed her brown hair from her shoulder and crossed her arms. "Careful, Jason. You'll jinx her. I hope you break a leg, Amber. Literally."

"Caitlyn..." Erica's sharp tone caused the girl to shrink into the crowd. "That was uncalled for." She crossed her arms and glared at her class. Caitlyn had been nasty to her classmate since Amber earned the lead in their production of *Carrie*. Erica needed to nip this in the bud now, before it got out of hand. "I will not tolerate any kind of negativity in my theater. This is a safe place, where we can all learn and grow as actors and people. If you decide to make acting your career, there will be plenty of off-stage drama in the real world. While you're here, save it for the stage. Understand?"

Caitlyn lowered her gaze. "Yes, ma'am."

Erica raised her voice, looking each student in the eyes as she spoke. "I'm talking to everyone. Do you all understand?"

The rest of the students muttered their agreement.

"I know Mrs. Spencer didn't allow that kind of talk when she ran this place, and she taught me everything I know. Don't think for a minute that you can walk all over your new director."

Daniel, a brown-eyed boy who'd been taking classes there for years, flipped a hand in the air. "That crazy old lady didn't know upstage from down."

Heat flushed through Erica's veins at the way the students dismissed her former mentor. She put her hands on her hips. "She was not crazy."

"She strangled her husband and slit her own wrists." Daniel mirrored her posture.

Her throat tightened. "She was…ill." When she'd first heard the news, she hadn't believed it. She *still* couldn't believe the woman who had played such a pivotal role in her life would do such a thing. Mrs. Spencer had meant everything to her.

She fisted her hands at her sides. "Everyone get in your places for act 2, scene 3. Let's run it from the top."

As the students shuffled across the stage, a loud *pop* sounded from the back of the auditorium, and then the lights went out, casting the entire room in darkness. Caitlyn squealed and latched onto Jason's arm, while several students activated the flashlight features on their phones.

"That's probably Mrs. Spencer's ghost," Caitlyn said. "She doesn't like you talking about her."

Erica sighed and hopped off the stage. "It's not her ghost. There's something wrong with the light board." She'd seen and communicated with plenty of spirits in her lifetime, so if Mrs. Spencer—or any ghosts—were haunting this theater, surely they would've shown themselves by now. "If it is you, Mrs. Spencer," she whispered under her breath, "I'd love to talk to you."

She fiddled with the wires connecting the computerized board to the house and stage lights. She'd only been away from the theater for ten years, but in that time, the system controlling the lights and sound had gotten so high-tech she struggled to operate it. The user manual was so complicated she'd given up reading it a quarter of the way in. She'd have to buckle down and watch some YouTube videos on how to operate the darn thing tonight. If her students suspected her even a third as incompetent as she felt, she'd never get this business off the ground.

Not that she wanted to run a business in the first place, but that was another story.

None of the wires appeared out of place. Hopefully, a reboot would be all the system needed.

A sudden chill in the air made the hairs on the back of her neck rise. It could have been a draft or a reluctant spirit; it was hard to tell the difference. She smoothed her thick braid over her shoulder, running her hands along her cheek to be sure her hair still covered the side of her face. This was the fourth time the lights had gone out in the six weeks she'd been teaching here. If her technical incompetency wasn't to blame, then there was either something seriously wrong with the light board or the theater really was haunted. Though, if it was haunted, why hadn't the ghosts made themselves known?

She'd almost rather the problem be ghosts. Having a technician out to fix the system didn't fit in her nearly-nonexistent budget. If ghosts were to blame, she might be able to convince them to stop if they'd show themselves to her.

She inhaled deeply and pressed the power button. "Please turn the lights back on."

The machine beeped. A line of red and green LEDs flashed on the keyboard as the system hummed to life. She turned the dial for the house lights, and brightness flooded the room. Adjusting the sliders for the stage lights, she doused the students in blue, red, and yellow. They relaxed, returning their phones to their pockets, but Caitlyn kept a firm grip on Jason's bicep.

Erica let out a slow breath. Everything seemed to be working for now. "See?" She made her way to a middle seat in the auditorium. "It's just these darn computers.

They're great when they work. A pain in the tush when they don't."

"Tush?" Jason peeled his arm from Caitlyn's grasp. "C'mon, Ms. M. We're all almost-grown-ups here. Tell us how you really feel."

She arched an eyebrow at her student. "They're a pain in the ass. Happy?"

He grinned. "Yes, ma'am."

"All right." She lowered herself into the seat. "We've wasted enough time. Act 2, scene 3. And…action."

Gage Dawson sauntered into Angelica's Café at ten-thirty-five a.m. Four blondes waited for him at their usual table near the back of the restaurant, and that would normally be the highlight to any man's day. Too bad all four of these women were his sisters.

"You're late," Abigail said.

He eyed his oldest sibling. "Thanks. You told me that three texts ago."

"We started the mimosas without you." Becky tipped her head back and chugged what was left in her flute.

He chuckled. "I'm sure there's plenty more."

As if on cue, the waiter set another pitcher on the table and took everyone's order. Gage asked for his usual: a three-egg omelet with cheese and tomatoes.

"You always order that." Chelsea, his youngest sister, handed her menu to the waiter. "Don't you want to try something new for a change?"

Gage shrugged. "What can I say? I'm a creature of habit."

"Most men are." Deanna, the second youngest, placed her order and looked at Gage. "Why were you late?"

"He had a hot date last night, remember?" Chelsea elbowed Deanna. "Pay attention."

"Ouch!" Deanna rubbed her arm.

Gage shook his head. His little sisters had started bickering the moment Chelsea had learned to talk, and they hadn't stopped since. "My date was three days ago. I was on a ghost hunt last night."

Chelsea's shoulders drooped. "It was three days ago?"

"Pay attention," Deanna mocked.

"I'm sorry." Chelsea held her left hand in front of her sister's face. "Ever since I got engaged, I've been so busy planning my wedding, I lose track of time."

"Oh, rub it in." Deanna slapped her hand away. "Mark is taking his time. He'll propose soon enough."

Gage leaned back in his chair and listened to his sisters' banter. Being the only boy, born smack in the middle of four girls, he'd gotten used to listening. They barely let him get a word in most of the time.

"Anyway…" Abigail gave the younger women the stink eye before turning to Gage. "How did the ghost hunt go?"

He covered his mouth to hide his yawn. He'd been late to brunch because he didn't get to bed until seven that morning. Two and a half hours of sleep wasn't nearly enough for his brain to keep up with the conversations of four sisters. "The investigation was good. We got some compelling evidence, but the client wants the ghosts gone. And we can't do that without our psychic."

Becky drained another glass of mimosa. "Is something wrong with Allison?"

"Nah. She's on vacation with her husband. Fiji, I

think. I gave them a list of some of the other psychics we've worked with and told them if they don't work out, we'll come back when Allison's home."

Chelsea swung her hand through the air as if waving off the conversation. "I want to hear about your date. How did it go with...what was her name? Roxanne? Rihanna?"

Gage groaned. "Rochelle." Of course there'd be no avoiding this conversation, but a guy could hope. One of these days, he'd learn to keep his mouth shut and not tell his siblings about his personal business. He shook his head. Who was he kidding? His family was so close that Chelsea started a group text every time someone so much as sneezed. "It was...fine."

"Uh-oh." Deanna crossed her arms. "What happened?"

"Nothing. I said it was fine."

"We all know what fine means, little brother." Becky gripped his shoulder. "Tell us."

He dragged a hand down his face. He really needed to learn to keep his mouth shut. "We had dinner, and she told me all about her ex-boyfriend and how he cheated on her. It was pretty much all she talked about."

"Awe." Chelsea stuck out her bottom lip. "You're too nice. That's what it is."

He laughed dryly. "Oh, it gets better. I took her home, and she invited me in."

Chelsea straightened her spine and leaned forward. "And?"

"And then she asked me to fix her Wi-Fi."

His youngest sister's mouth dropped open. "Please tell me you didn't."

He lifted his hands palms up.

"You did! Gage!" Chelsea pointed a finger at him. "See? This is exactly what I mean. You're too nice."

"What? I was already there, so I reset it. It's not like I went out of my way." Not too much anyway. "I couldn't leave the poor woman with no Internet connection."

Chelsea narrowed her eyes. "And did you at least get laid for that?"

"Of course he didn't," Deanna chimed in. "Look at his face. That's the face of a man who hasn't been laid in a long time."

"I'm just tired. I…" Gage closed his eyes for a long blink and let out a sigh. He could think of a million different ways to spend Saturday morning that would be better than talking about his sex life with his sisters. Then again, what could he say? Deanna was right. He'd never had much luck in the romance department. "This conversation is over. Let's talk about something else."

"Mom and Steven are going to Cuba next month." Abigail gave him a conspiratorial wink. Though she'd done plenty of instigating when they were kids, he could always count on his oldest sister to be the voice of reason.

He focused his attention on Abigail. "How'd they manage that?"

"It's not that difficult anymore. I hear they have beautiful beaches."

"Is it safe?"

"As long as you stay in the tourist areas."

His mom had been dating Steven for a few years now, but ever since his dad left them when he was eight years old, Gage had considered himself the protector of the family. He'd fought off bullies and taken care of his sisters and his mom for as long as he could remember. Now that none of them needed him anymore, he felt a little…well, useless.

The waiter brought their orders, and thankfully, a few moments of silence ensued as they ate their food.

Becky poured the last drop of mimosa into her glass. "Who's taking me home?"

Abigail patted her arm. "You rode with me, remember? Mom's got the kids."

"Right." Becky turned to Gage, sloshing the contents of her glass onto the white linen tablecloth. "You know what you need, little brother?"

He eyed Abigail. "How many of these has she had?"

"Enough." Abigail took the glass from her sister.

"What you need is a good woman to take care of you. Why don't you have a girlfriend yet?"

Abigail rolled her eyes.

Gage groaned. *Not this again.*

"You need to stop being so nice," Chelsea said. "That really is your problem."

He shrugged. "I am who I am." And he wasn't about to start acting like a dick just to land a date.

"Exactly. You're smart. You're attractive." Chelsea tapped a finger against her chin. "You have no problem *meeting* women, right?"

He crossed his arms. "I suppose."

"Your bad luck happens once they get to know you."

"Great. It's my personality. Thanks for the vote of confidence, Chels."

"No, no." She waved her hands in the air. "Your personality is great too, but women like a challenge. If you play it cool, like you aren't that interested in the beginning, they'll be falling all over you. Trust me."

Abigail shook her head. “Don’t listen to her, Gage. The *right* woman will want you the way you are.”

He laughed dryly. Would the right woman ever come along? With his luck, he wouldn’t even recognize her if she did.

Deanna’s eyes brightened. “Isn’t your ten-year high school reunion in a couple of months? Maybe you’ll meet someone there.”

“I’m not going to that.” Small talk with a bunch of people he hadn’t spoken to in years? No thanks. There was only one person from his past he’d be interested in seeing again, and he doubted she’d fly clear across the country for a reunion.

“You can’t go to your reunion without a date,” Chelsea said. “Everyone will think you’re gay, like they did in high school.”

He narrowed his eyes at his little sister. “Just because I never had a girlfriend, everyone did not think I was gay.”

“A lot of people did,” Deanna said.

“Okay. This discussion really is over now.” He pulled a twenty from his wallet and laid it on the table. “Thanks for the company, sisters. The conversation was riveting, as usual.”

“Where are you going? I want to help you have a better life.” Chelsea reached for his hand as he rose from the table, but he yanked it away before she could grab it.

“I don’t need your help. My life is fine the way it is. Now, I’m going home and going back to bed. I’ve got hours of evidence to go through this afternoon, and I need some sleep.”

Abigail lifted a hand. “See you next month.”

He waved goodbye to his sisters, turned on his heel, and then strode out of the restaurant. What the hell had he been thinking telling his little sister about his date? She'd been meddling in his social life since she was old enough to know what a social life was. They all had, really, but Chelsea was the worst.

And it didn't help that every one of them was either married, engaged, or in a long-term relationship. Even his mom had found someone after all those years of raising five kids on her own. So, what the hell was his problem? They weren't going to leave him alone until he found someone.

He climbed into his Jeep and leaned his head against the headrest. Maybe Chelsea was right. Maybe he was too nice. Being himself seemed to land him in the friend zone ten times out of ten, but he didn't know any other way to be. If being in a relationship meant he'd have to be an asshole, he'd rather stay single.

Grumbling under his breath, he started the ignition and drove home. It didn't matter. If he met the right woman, so be it. If he never did, he was okay with that too.

He pulled into a parking space and trudged up the stairs to his apartment before falling face-first into bed. He was too damn tired to think about this shit now. His phone buzzed in his pocket, so he dug it out and glanced at the screen.

Chelsea. *If you go out on another date, you better call me first. I want to help.*

He rolled his eyes and pressed the Do Not Disturb button. The last thing he needed was dating advice from his baby sister.

Armed with a mug of black coffee and a few squares of dark chocolate, Erica sank onto her living room sofa and opened her laptop. Having this much caffeine at two in the afternoon would probably keep her up all night, but weekends were her only time to work on getting her theater up and running full-time. Come Monday, she'd have to go back to her real job.

She stared at her reflection in the blank computer screen and smoothed her hair down the side of her neck. The dim image barely revealed the revolting scar marring the right side of her body. She almost looked normal. Almost.

Who was she kidding? Not even a pound of stage makeup could make her look normal in real life.

She blew out a dry breath and powered on the laptop. Then, she opened her graphic design program and tweaked the newspaper ad she'd created for the theater. Ad space didn't come cheap, but the flyers she'd posted around town to announce the reopening of the Cornerstone Community Theater hadn't brought in much business. The class fees her cast of seven teens had paid weren't enough to cover the cost to purchase the rights to perform the play, much less pay for the first and second mortgages on the building.

She'd have to live on a diet of beans and Ramen noodles for a while, but she'd manage. The theater—and Mrs. Spencer specifically—had given her so much; she owed it to her former mentor to keep the place afloat.

The sound of tapping on glass drew her attention to the window. A pale, translucent face stared back at her from the other side of the pane. Her heart stuttered at the sight of the woman floating outside her second story apartment, and she nearly dropped her laptop on the floor.

She took a deep breath to calm her nerves and tiptoed toward the window.

The ghost smiled as Erica approached. Most spirits were thrilled to meet someone who could actually see them, though how they knew she possessed that talent, she wasn't sure. The only living person who knew about her ability had been Mrs. Spencer, but that was because she'd shared the talent too.

Erica lifted a hand to wave, and the ghost floated through the glass and into her living room. "Can I help you?" As soon as the question left her lips, she wished she hadn't offered. There was rarely anything she could do to help a ghost. She had no control over her ability. Sometimes spirits showed themselves to her, and sometimes they didn't.

"Help me go home." The voice rang in Erica's ears. How she could hear a spirit speak when a person standing next to her couldn't, she had no idea. The whole thing was a mystery she didn't know how to solve.

"You need to cross over. I hear there's a light or something you're supposed to go toward." Why did spirits think that just because she could see them, she should be able to help them cross over? She'd been asked for help like this so many times, she'd lost count.

The figure faded, becoming more and more translucent as she stared at Erica with heart-wrenching sadness in her eyes. "I can't find it."

"You will, but you can't stay here." A familiar ache clenched in her stomach. What was the point of having this gift if she couldn't do anything with it? "Please…go look for it. I'm sorry I can't help."

The ghost dissipated, taking her buzzing, static energy with her.

Erica plopped onto the couch and leaned her head back. This time had been easy. A few times, when she'd told ghosts she couldn't help, they'd gotten angry with her. One had even tried to push a bookshelf on top of her, but she'd managed to right the shelf and calm the ghost down before it hurt anyone. If this one kept bothering her, she'd have to salt her apartment. That was the only trick she knew for dealing with ghosts. But right now, she had more pressing matters on her mind.

Pulling the computer back into her lap, she stared at the screen. "Oh, Mrs. Spencer. If your spirit is hanging around, I could sure use some guidance. I don't want to fail at this too."

She set the computer aside and flipped open the Saturday morning *Gazette*. She'd bought a spot to run on page twenty of the Arts and Leisure section in two weeks. Hopefully it would be enough to drum up a little business. Add another Saturday class to the lineup. Maybe some elementary-aged kids. It never hurt to start building self-confidence at an early age, and the theater was the perfect place to do it. If she could figure out the business side of things, she'd be okay.

With the classifieds section spread out on the couch, she scanned the columns for garage sale announcements. They'd need props if her cast of seven was going to pull off a decent show, and garage sales were cheap places to find them. Estate sales were even better.

Her finger paused at an entry, and her heart thrummed. 1147 Sycamore Street stared back at her like a beacon of hope. Mrs. Spencer's son was finally parting with her possessions.

A sob lodged in Erica's throat.

It had been three months since the alleged murder-suicide. Well, the case was closed, so she couldn't really call it alleged. It happened, but she couldn't wrap her mind around how such a kind, loving woman could strangle her husband to death with his necktie. Then to slit her own wrists four hours later?

She shivered and took a sip of coffee, allowing the bitter liquid to chase away the chilling image in her mind. If Mrs. Spencer's spirit was hanging around, she obviously wasn't interested in talking to Erica about it. Even though she'd offered her the theater in her will.

Taking on the burden had been optional. If Erica had refused, the theater would have gone to Mrs. Spencer's son, Johnny, along with the rest of the estate, which he was now selling. With the building's prime location, whoever bought it would've torn it down and put in retail shops. But Mrs. Spencer *wanted* Erica to run the theater, so she'd taken the gift, debt and all, and she was determined to make it work.

If Mrs. Spencer's spirit did linger in this realm, her house would be the perfect place to look for her. She checked the clock. Two-thirty p.m. The sale had ended at noon, but they would open the house next weekend to sell off what was left.

She crossed her fingers and said a little prayer. If she couldn't get guidance from her former teacher, someone else residing in the house could help her. Hopefully the mirror—and what it contained—was still there.

CHAPTER TWO

Gage sat at his desk repairing a damaged motherboard and trying to ignore Chelsea's latest text. Ever since brunch four days ago, his baby sister had taken it upon herself to send him every blog post and magazine article she could find on dating. The latest addition to the collection of nonsense he refused to read: an article titled "Why Nice Guys Always Finish Last."

He had to admit, that one was tempting. Better than the previous two she'd sent: "Work on Your Mojo and She'll Fall into Your Arms" and "Sex Appeal, Schmex Appeal, Women Want a Man with Moxie."

Moxie? Mojo? *Oh, no. No thanks.*

"Yo, Gage." Adam handed him a work order ticket. "Sixth floor. Rush job."

He chuckled. "They're all rush jobs, aren't they? I'm not zoned to floor six. Give it to Paul."

"He's hung up with the sales director's computer right now, and this is a priority one."

Gage let out a grunt and rose to his feet. "He's hung up with her computer, or with her?"

Adam laughed and slapped him on the back. "You'll survive."

"It's graphic arts, man. Those people know just enough about computers to get themselves into trouble, and they always think their problems are more important than everyone else's."

"Thanks, Gage. I owe you one."

He picked up his bag and shoved in a new power supply unit before shuffling toward the elevator. A spare mouse, extra power and USB cords, screwdrivers. Generally, all he needed to fix a computer and save someone's day could be found in his bag. Every now and then someone would end up with a failed motherboard or crashed hard drive, and those would require a trip to his office for repair or replacement. But, half the time, they'd kicked the cords under the table and something had come unplugged.

He checked the name on the ticket. Miller. Didn't ring a bell. Then again, nearly eight hundred people worked in the Detroit office alone, and he'd only met a handful of them. He didn't venture out much. His office. The second and third floors—the zones he did repairs for. The elevator and the exit. That was all he needed to see.

The location on the ticket read G-27, but that didn't mean anything. People were constantly changing desks, moving around. They were supposed to contact IT and have a technician move their equipment, but that rarely happened anymore. People were too damn impatient these days. Everyone was in a hurry, and waiting for someone qualified to get them up and running proved too much of a hassle.

He shuffled down the hall toward the graphic arts department. The windows on the east side of the building offered a dazzling view of the city park. The little man-made lake in the center of the green sparkled like diamonds danced on the surface. A man threw a ball and laughed as his Golden Retriever bounded after it. A group of moms pushed baby strollers around a walking trail, and Gage couldn't fight his smile. He paused and gazed wistfully out the glass.

A gorgeous day, and he was stuck inside. Maybe this weekend he could head out to the real lake and do a little hiking. Maybe some climbing. Get in a little nature. He stood at the window, letting the morning sun seeping through the pane warm his skin. Nature was exactly what he needed.

Stepping from the hall, he pushed open the double-doors leading to graphic arts and paused in the entry. Thirty-plus cubicles took up most of the vast floor space, and G-27 sat in the far corner near the window. He sauntered toward the workstation and nodded at the burly, bearded guy occupying the desk. "Miller? You have a problem with your PC?"

The man grunted and shook his head.

It figured. Hopefully, Gage could find Lindsay somewhere in the maze of workstations, and she could point him to the right person.

He found his friend and fellow paranormal investigator hunched over her keyboard, nudging a block of text to line up with an image on the screen. She wore a dark-green silk blouse, and her shoulder-length blonde hair swung forward, hiding her face as she hovered over the computer. He tapped on her shoulder and waited.

She held up a finger and finished aligning the graphics

before pressing control-S and turning around. "Hey, Gage. What brings you out to our neck of the jungle?"

"I'm here to fix a computer that's supposed to be at G-27, but it's been moved without authorization." Not that he should've expected it to be in its proper place. They never were.

Lindsay rolled her eyes and pushed her bangs off her forehead. "We're human beings, not bingo balls. Who are you looking for?"

He glanced at the ticket. "Miller. Possible PSU failure. Most likely only user error."

"Oh, that's Erica."

"Erica?" His heart gave a thud. He'd known an Erica Miller once, but the chances of this woman being the Erica from his past were roughly zero. She'd moved on and never looked back a long, long time ago.

Lindsay stood and peeked her head over the dividing wall. "Erica, your techie is here."

Gage slung his bag over his shoulder and shuffled around the desk.

"Thank goodness. Aaron needs this presentation before he leaves for the conference, and..." Erica turned around, her eyes growing wide in recognition. "Gage? Oh, my God." She flung her arms around his neck before his mind could catch up with what was happening.

His high school next-door neighbor had moved to LA with her boyfriend right after graduation, taking a piece of his heart along with her. And now she was here, working in his building?

She released her hold, but kept her hands resting on his shoulders. "Look at you." Running her palms down his arms, she squeezed his biceps. "You've changed. You're all grown up now."

He gazed into her deep, brown eyes and struggled to form words. It had been nearly ten years since he'd seen her, but his mind flooded with memories. Theater Arts class. Drama club. She'd been so comfortable on stage, in her element. Every time she got into character, her self-consciousness slipped away, and she shined. The highlight of his high school career had been tech theater, operating the lighting and sound for the cast. Watching Erica. Getting to know her.

Get it together, man. He smiled and adjusted the strap on his shoulder. "You haven't changed a bit."

Tall and slender, she wore her long, light brown hair woven into a thick braid over her right shoulder, covering most of her cheek. The scar she never talked about, except to him. Her long-sleeved, peach shirt hugged her feminine curves and concealed the rest of the disfigured skin she so desperately tried to hide. Always long sleeves and pants, even in the summer.

Her smile made his heart race. "Surely, I've grown up a little too."

"You're still as beautiful as ever."

A pink blush spread across her cheeks, and she smoothed the hair down the side of her face. "And you're still full of it."

If only she could see what he saw. "How long have you been back in town?"

"Six months."

He set his bag on her desk and paused. He could understand her not keeping in touch while she was off in Hollywood, trying to be an actress. Her Michigan friends probably rarely crossed her mind in all the excitement of Tinsel Town. But she'd been home for six months, working a few floors above him… "Why didn't you call me?"

She lowered her gaze to the floor and drew up her shoulders. "I didn't…"

"He leaves in an hour, Erica." A woman in a dark pantsuit tapped a pencil on the cubicle wall and strutted into an office.

"Right. Could you, uh…" Erica gestured toward her computer. "I'm on a deadline."

"Yeah. No problem." He pulled the chair away from the desk. "Did you check all the cables? Everything is plugged in?"

"I tried everything I could think of."

He knelt on the ground and shined a flashlight under the desk. That was always the first question he asked, and he always got the same answer—yes, they'd checked everything. Half the time, though, he'd find an unplugged cable dangling behind the desk.

"So far, so good." He stood and checked all the wires on the back of the workstation. Everything seemed to be in place. He pressed the power button.

Erica crossed her arms. "You think it's going to magically turn on just because you're here?"

He chuckled. "You wouldn't believe how many times that's happened." He tested the power outlet and the cables. He tried every trick he knew to get the damn thing to power on without taking it apart. Nothing worked. Rummaging through his bag, he pulled out his screwdriver set and removed the cover from the machine.

Erica drummed her nails on the desk. Gage glanced at her hand, and she jerked it away. A tiny bit of her scar peeked out from her sleeve on the pinky side of her hand. She'd always been self-conscious about it. It seemed she still was. "Is this going to take long? I have to give Aaron the presentation on a flash drive before he leaves for the conference."

Gage tested the power supply unit. Dead. He'd found her problem. "Working for the VP after only six months? You must be good at your job." She'd been busy. That was why she hadn't bothered to call her high school best friend in the six months since she'd been home. Sure, he'd go with that excuse since she didn't seem to have one of her own.

"This'll be the last time I work for him if I can't get the presentation done."

"Why don't you pull it up on Lindsay's computer and finish it there?" He glanced at his friend peeking over the divider. "Looks like she doesn't have anything better to do than pretend she's not watching us."

Lindsay narrowed her eyes and sank behind the cubicle wall.

Erica smoothed the braid over her shoulder. "The file isn't on the network. It's on the hard drive."

Gage shook his head. "Company files are supposed to be saved on the server. We back it up every night."

"I know, but the server is slow, and my presentation is graphics heavy. It was taking too long to load, so Aaron told me to move it to the hard drive so I could work faster. I was planning to move it back to the server as soon as I finished it."

"You don't have another copy anywhere?"

"Not a recent one."

He arched an eyebrow at her before installing the new PSU. Luckily, her problem was an easy fix. If her hard drive had failed, she'd be in a bind. Recovering lost data took time she didn't have. He put all the pieces into their proper positions and pressed the power button again. The machine hummed to life, and he reattached the cover. "There you go. Good as new."

"Thank you. You're a life saver." She hugged him again, and he couldn't help but breathe in the sweet scent of her hair—flowers with a hint of vanilla.

He could've held onto her like this all afternoon, but he forced himself to let her go. "You're welcome. Try it out and make sure everything works. Then I'll be out of your way."

"You've never been in the way, Gage." Her gaze held his for a moment, and a strange energy danced between them. He couldn't recall her ever looking at him like that before. Then again, she was probably just happy he fixed her computer. She clicked the mouse a few times, opened a file, and flipped through the pages. "This is great. Thank you."

"My pleasure." He loaded his gear back into the bag and slung it over his shoulder. "I'll see you around."

She spun in her chair to face him. "Hey, if you want to get together sometime, so we can catch up…you know where I work."

"That I do. Bye, Erica. Good luck with your presentation."

She smiled. "Bye, Gage."

Aaron stood at Erica's desk, tapping his foot and counting down the minutes as she put the finishing touches on the presentation. She could've been done ten minutes ago if her impatient boss hadn't hovered over her, his gaze boring a hole into her back as she worked.

"Time's up, Emily. Is it done?" He held out his hand.

"It's Erica." She handed him the flash drive.

"Thanks." He turned on his heel and strutted away.

Erica collapsed into her chair and sighed. At least he'd shown a little appreciation this time. Thank goodness Gage had been able to fix her computer. An image of her old friend flashed in her mind, and she smiled. He was still the same sweet boy she knew from high school, with his goofy smile and bright aqua eyes. But then again, he wasn't. His musculature had finally caught up with his six-foot-three height. He'd filled out in all the right places… probably from working out, by the feel of his biceps. The lanky, nerdy boy-next-door had grown into an incredibly attractive man.

He was like Gage 2.0.

"Hey." Lindsay peered over her cubicle. "What are you smiling about?"

"I'm not smiling." She tried to flatten her mouth, but her lips wouldn't budge from their grin.

"Yes, you are."

"I finished my presentation. I get to keep my job."

"Uh huh." Lindsay slid around the divider and perched on the edge of Erica's desk. "How do you know Gage?"

Her smile widened. "He's a friend from high school."

"Did you date him in high school?" Her curiosity lilted in her voice.

"Gage? No. My dad and I moved in next door to him when I was a sophomore. He was just a friend. A good friend." The best friend she'd ever had.

She'd done all she could to avoid everyone from her past since she'd returned home. Luckily, in a city this big, it wasn't hard to do. But seeing Gage again had stirred up some strange emotions she hadn't expected to feel.

Lindsay laughed. "Oooh, so you were the girl-next-door. I'm intrigued."

"There's really nothing to be intrigued about. There was never anything between us."

"But *now* you want to date him."

"I..." A flush of warmth spread through her body, something she wasn't used to feeling when talking about Gage. Could she date him? He knew her too well. Knew all her dreams and ambitions that she'd failed miserably at achieving. If they ever did catch up, and he learned the truth about why she'd returned to Michigan, whatever romantic interest he had in her would shrivel before it had a chance to bloom. Not that he ever had any interest in her. She was a screw-up. And an ugly one to boot. "No, I don't want to date him."

Lindsay eyed her skeptically. "Don't deny it. When he was up here before, you two had a moment."

"We did not have a moment."

"Yes, you did. You looked at him. He looked at you. You both felt sparks. You had a moment. I saw it."

Erica rolled her eyes. "We did not feel sparks; he was fixing my computer." Her heart may have fluttered a bit, but that was a normal reaction. Gage had been her best friend. It was natural to feel excited to see him again after ten years.

"Maybe not sparks...not yet...but you felt something, and the sooner you quit denying it, the happier you'll be. You should ask him out."

"No. He knows me too well. It would be...weird."

Lindsay shrugged. "So, you get to skip the awkward

finding out if you're compatible stage. You already know you get along."

Erica picked at the pale orange polish on her nails. She hardly knew Lindsay. Aside from happy hour once a week, which Erica forced herself to go to, she never saw her outside the office. This was the most personal conversation she could remember having with her coworker. With anyone lately. "If you think he's so great, why aren't you dating him?"

She looked thoughtful for a moment before scrunching up her nose. "Nah. That would be too much like dating a cousin. I've never felt sparks about Gage. Not like you do."

"I do not feel sparks." Maybe a few glowing embers, but they'd surely die down as soon as this awkward conversation ended. "How do you know him, anyway?"

Lindsay grinned. "We share a hobby."

"What hobby?"

"Call it research."

Erica arched an eyebrow. "Your hobby is research? Sounds…fascinating."

"Sometimes it is."

"What do you research?"

She tapped a finger to her chin. "You should ask Gage about it when you go on your first date."

"We're not going on a date."

"You told him you wanted to catch up."

Erica sighed. How much of her past was she willing to share to get Lindsay off her back? "When I graduated high school, I moved away to…do something stupid. Gage tried to convince me not to go, and he was right. I wasted years of my life chasing someone else's dream, and now here I am, twenty-eight years old, in an entry-level position, doing graphics for an asshat that can't even remember my name." She picked up a paper clip and stretched it out, trying to straighten it into a rod.

"Better not let Aaron see you doing that. He gets pissed when people waste office supplies."

She tossed the mangled metal into the trash. "Once Gage finds out what a failure I am, any sparks he felt in our *moment* will fizzle out."

Lindsay waved a hand in the air, dismissing the statement. "Everyone makes mistakes. I don't know what Gage was like in high school, but as an adult, he's one of the nicest men I know. He won't hold it against you."

Erica shut down her computer and pulled her purse from a drawer. "He wasn't interested in me then. Why would it be any different now?"

"Maybe he was, and you didn't know it. Men aren't always good at expressing their emotions." Lindsay stood and gathered her things. "Either way, feelings can change. Yours did. Have a good night."

Erica stayed at her desk until Lindsay disappeared through the double-doors into the hallway. If Gage had been interested in her in high school, he'd done an excellent job of hiding it. Or maybe she'd been blind. Accepting the fact that any man would want her was a hard pill to swallow. She hadn't believed Carter, her first and only boyfriend, when he flat-out told her he wanted to date her. Then, she'd realized ten years too late that he'd been more interested in having an acting coach and someone to support him than a girlfriend.

Gage had certainly changed in a good way. Unfortunately, Erica was the same incompetent wreck she'd always been. Sparks could never fly between them, but it would be nice to have her friend back. She rose from her desk and headed to the parking lot. As she hit the unlock button on her remote, her gray Saturn made a *chirp-chirp* noise and the headlights flashed. She followed the sound and slid into the driver's seat before making the half-hour trek to her apartment.

At home, Erica assumed her usual evening position on the couch to watch her favorite talent competition on television. Since she'd screwed up royally in making her own dreams come true, she loved watching other people get a chance at achieving their own.

She still had a dream. While it was too late for her to become a Broadway star, she adored teaching theater. One day she'd have enough classes running to generate the income needed for her to quit her thankless graphics job and focus on helping kids achieve their dreams full-time. If she could ever figure out the business end of things.

Really, all she wanted to do was teach, but it seemed she'd have to figure out how to run the place, too, or she'd be stuck in a cubicle for the rest of her life.

She turned up the volume as an eight-year-old girl belted out a Celine Dion song. Her voice was so rich, so beautiful; Erica teared up. She grabbed her phone, opened the program's app, and gave all her available votes to the little prodigy. This girl was going places—as long as she didn't follow her jerk boyfriend off to somewhere she didn't belong and then get the degree her father wanted her to have.

A tapping sound on the window drew her attention from the television. The same translucent spirit woman floated outside, her sad eyes boring into Erica's heart, pleading for help. She rose from the couch and approached the window. This ghost was getting insistent, so she didn't dare invite her in this time. Not that she actually could have kept her out, but still. "How did you find me?"

The spirit tilted her head to the side. "I felt you. Please help me."

Sadness creeped into Erica's heart, tightening her chest and bringing another round of tears to her eyes. But this emotion wasn't her own. The spirit was projecting her own state into her. Feeding her the despair and hopelessness she felt at being lost between worlds.

Though the emotions were much more intense than her own, they felt sadly familiar. "I'm so sorry. If I knew how to help you, I would."

CHAPTER THREE

Gage drummed his fingers on his desk and checked the clock for the twentieth time this morning. He'd promised himself he'd wait until ten o'clock before going upstairs to talk to Erica, but time seemed to be crawling.

He closed his eyes and rehearsed what he would say when he got to her desk. He'd tell her he was checking to be sure her computer was running okay. That was believable. He'd checked on people before.

He wiped his sweaty palms on his pants. Why the hell was he so nervous? This was Erica. She'd called him her best friend back in high school. He shouldn't have been nervous to talk to her, but there he was, his leg bouncing uncontrollably beneath the table, nausea churning in his stomach.

He'd lied when he'd said she hadn't changed a bit. She was as beautiful as he remembered. More so. But something about her was different. Something in her eyes. The way she'd looked at him yesterday had made his heart thud. She'd never looked at him like that before. Ever. For the first time since she'd moved in next door all those years ago, it felt like the attraction he felt toward her might be mutual.

He glanced at the clock again. Nine fifty-five. "Screw it." He hopped to his feet and jetted toward the elevator before anyone could ask him where he was headed.

He found her at her desk, her loose, light-brown braid cascading over her shoulder, a few stray strands spiraling down the back of her deep purple shirt. When he caught her gaze, her face lit up, and she spun around in her chair to face him.

"Hi, Gage. What brings you to the sixth floor?"

He grinned. "You, of course."

A strange look flashed in her eyes. Surprise? Excitement? He wasn't sure. "I came to make sure your computer was still working. Have you had any more problems with it?"

The look faded to what he could only call disappointment for a brief second before she composed herself. "Everything's fine. I gave the flash drive to Aaron, so my job is safe for now." She let out a dry chuckle.

He considered her for a moment. She'd seemed excited he came to see her, but disappointed when he asked about her computer. Did that mean…? He shifted his gaze to her monitor and scratched behind his ear. *Stop trying to read into it and talk to the woman.* "Why'd he insist on a flash drive anyway? He could've downloaded it himself."

She glanced around as if making sure no one was listening. "Because he's a stubborn old asshat with a my-way-or-the-highway mentality."

"Glad I don't work under the guy." He shoved his hands in his pockets and glanced at Erica's hands folded in her lap. She wasn't wearing a wedding ring. His heart beat a little harder. "So…when you came back, did Carter…?"

"He stayed in LA." She looked into his eyes. "That's over."

"I'm sorry."

"I'm not." She pressed her lips together and held his gaze a bit longer.

The silence stretched into awkwardness, something he'd never experienced with her before. She finally broke eye contact, and her gaze traveled down the length of his body and back up again. Though she didn't lay a finger on him, that one look felt as if she had caressed every inch of him.

He cleared his throat. "Do you want to go to lunch today?"

Her eyes brightened for a split second before she slumped her shoulders and blew out a breath. "I can't. I have a working lunch planned with Brian. He asked me to help him with an ad he's designing."

Gage ran a hand through his hair. "That's okay. I understand." Maybe her comment yesterday about catching up had been a formality. Something nice to say to someone from her past, even though she really didn't mean it.

As he turned to go, Lindsay popped her head over the cubicle wall. "But we're all going to happy hour at Molly's Place after work. You could always join us there." She glanced between Gage and Erica, a smug grin curving her lips.

"Yeah." Erica straightened her posture. "You should come. It would be nice to see you outside of work."

His immediate response would have been "Thanks, but no thanks," but the expectant look in Erica's eyes had him thinking twice. Still, spending an hour at a bar with a bunch of people he didn't know didn't sound much like a "happy" time to him. "I don't know anyone in graphics."

Erica giggled. "You know me."

"And me," Lindsay said.

He glared at his friend, and she sank into her chair behind the divider.

As much as he wanted to spend some time with Erica, doing it in a crowded bar with loud music and a bunch of drunks wasn't exactly what he had mind. He wanted to talk to her. To find out what she'd been up to the past ten years. To figure out if that strange look in her eyes meant it was possible she might feel something more than friendship for him. No, happy hour wasn't the way to go.

He'd give her his number. Put the ball in her court. If she really did want to catch up, she'd call him. And if she didn't...he'd go back to life as he knew it and forget about her. *Yeah, right.* "I think I'm going to pass. Happy hour really isn't my thing."

Her shoulders drooped. "Okay. I understand. But... I'll be there at five-thirty if you change your mind."

"Here." He handed her the business card he'd scribbled his personal cell number on earlier. "If you have any more trouble with your computer, text me. It'll get fixed faster that way."

She took the card and ran her thumb across the ink. "Thanks, Gage. I will."

He turned and shuffled out of the graphic arts department, and probably out of Erica's life. If she'd been back in town for six months and hadn't tried to contact him, she must've had a reason. She'd outgrown her friendship with the boy-next-door and moved on. Hell, he'd moved on too, until he saw her again. The ball wasn't in her court. She'd probably already shoved it into the supply closet.

The elevator chimed for the second floor, and he made his way to his office. As he sat at his desk, his phone buzzed. A text from a number he didn't recognize lit up the screen, and he swiped it open.

Thanks again for fixing my computer. I hope you'll change your mind about tonight, but if you don't, I understand. You've got my number now. I hope you'll use it.

The corner of his mouth pulled into a grin as he saved Erica's number to his contacts. It looked like she wanted to play ball after all. Still, happy hour wasn't the court he wanted to play on.

He busied himself by rebuilding a computer that was past due for an upgrade. It wasn't a rush job. In fact, he didn't have to have the project completed until next week, but it was easy to lose himself to the methodology of the task. The order. The structure. As long as he kept his hands and his mind busy, he could keep his thoughts away from Erica and the futile emotions stirring in his chest. She'd never been interested in anything more than friendship. He shouldn't expect anything more now.

As five o'clock rolled around, he packed up his project and shut down his computer. He looked at the text Erica had sent him and shook his head. If the woman wanted to see him, who was he to tell her no?

Adam stopped at his desk on his way out the door. "Chris and I are going to the bowling alley tonight, if you want to join in. Half-price beer and nachos."

Gage shoved his phone in his pocket and pulled out his keys. "No thanks. I'm going to happy hour."

Erica sat on a barstool at Molly's Place and scanned the faces in the crowd. Close to twenty people from her department showed up today, and many of them were already on their second or third drinks. The entire sixth floor walked on egg shells when Aaron had a big meeting to attend, so it wasn't surprising so many felt the need to let off a little steam now that the boss had gone.

A lone musician stood on the small wooden stage at the opposite end of the room, crooning Ed Sheeran covers while strumming an acoustic guitar. Sports paraphernalia from the local Michigan teams decorated the walls, and the scent of French fries wafted in from the restaurant behind the bar. Lindsay slid onto the stool next to her and ordered her second beer. Erica had barely drained half of her first Dos Equis.

"Looking for someone?" Lindsay grinned and took a swig of Miller Lite.

She chewed the inside of her cheek and swept the crowd again. "He's not coming, is he?"

"Gage?"

Erica nodded.

Lindsay pursed her lips, looking thoughtful. "Probably not. Big crowds aren't his thing. He sucks at small talk. But…" Her grin returned, and she took another sip of beer.

Erica took a drink from her own bottle, but the once-crisp, effervescent liquid had warmed to room temperature. "But?"

"After that moment you two had, it wouldn't surprise me if he showed up."

"Please." She picked at the label on her bottle, but she couldn't deny the flutter in her stomach at the thought that he still might come.

Lindsay leaned her elbow on the bar. "You had another moment this morning. Right before you rejected him."

"I didn't reject him. I had to help Brian with his ad."

"And did Brian really need help?" She eyed her over the beer as she took a swig.

Erica peeled the small label from the neck of her bottle and smoothed it onto the bar. "He tried to pretend like he did." But the way he'd kept leaning over her, trying to guide her hand on the mouse, brushing his shoulder to hers every time he pointed at the screen...he obviously wanted *something* from her, though she didn't know why. Well...she had a pretty good idea, and the reason sat sour in her stomach like expired buttermilk.

"Look at you. Two men chasing after you."

Erica smoothed the hair down the side of her face. "Men don't chase after me." They occasionally tried to conquer her, assuming she'd be an easy lay due to low self-esteem. Preying on the weak. Only, Erica wasn't weak.

"Apparently, they do." Lindsay rose to her feet. "I'm going to mingle. You coming?"

"I don't think I'm going to stay much longer. You have fun."

Lindsay shuffled away, and Erica focused her attention on the musician. He had a nice voice, though he sounded a little throaty. But he couldn't have been more than nineteen. His voice would mature when his body did.

Her mind drifted to Gage and the way his body had matured. She could tell by the way his clothes fit he was pure muscle beneath all that fabric. When she'd hugged him, his body had been hard, but his embrace was warm and soft.

"What are you smiling about?" Brian attempted to sit

on the stool next to her, but he missed, landing half a butt cheek on the cushion and tumbling off before catching himself on the bar.

"Jeez, Brian, we've only been here half an hour. How much have you had to drink?"

He clutched the edge of the bar and slowly slid onto the seat. "I snuck out of the office early. Did a few shots with Toby before everyone else got here."

"Nice." She focused on the big label of her beer bottle, picking at the edges with her fingernails, loosening the paper from the glass.

"Listen, Erica." He grasped her hand, pinning it on the bar. "I think you should reconsider going to dinner with me."

She tried to gently tug her hand away, but he pressed it harder into the wood. "You do, huh?"

"Yeah. I mean…a girl in your condition isn't going to get many offers."

"In my condition?" She yanked her hand from his grasp. "What condition is that, Brian?" She knew exactly what he was talking about. He never could look her in the eyes without his gaze traveling to the side of her face, lingering on her scar. But if he was going to be an ass and point out the obvious, she wasn't about to make it comfortable for him.

He fidgeted in his seat. "Well…I mean…you do a pretty good job at hiding it, but that scar…What happened to you?"

"None of your business."

"Look, all I'm saying is that you should consider yourself lucky you found a man who's willing to look past it to see the real you."

A flash of anger ignited in her chest. This wasn't the

first time she'd heard that line, and she would never fall for it again. She crossed her arms. "You're not looking past it, Brian. You're looking right at it."

Gage parked his Jeep at Molly's Place and marched toward the door before he could talk himself out of it. The bar swarmed with people, most of them young professionals like himself. Unlike himself, they mingled and laughed, chatting with each other about nothing important. Most of these people were nothing more than shallow acquaintances. He shook his head. He'd rather have a few close friends he could talk to about important stuff than fifty so-called friends he hardly knew.

He spotted Erica on a barstool, and his stomach fluttered. But the butterfly sensation quickly turned sour when the guy sitting next to her took her hand. Tall, dark hair, attractive. This must've been the dude she had lunch with. And it looked like their *working* lunch had turned into a lunch *date.*

Lindsay stepped beside him and nudged his shoulder with hers. "Go talk to her."

He shook his head. "She's busy."

"That's Brian. He's got a new girlfriend every month. Believe me, she's not interested in him."

The look on her face was one of annoyance. And when she jerked her hand from his grasp and crossed her arms, the guy had obviously said something wrong. Gage sauntered toward them, but they were both so engrossed in their conversation, neither seemed to notice him.

"Come on, Erica." The guy slurred his words. "With a face like that, you're not going to do any better than me."

Her gaze hardened. "I'll pass."

"I'm sorry, baby." The man clutched her arm. "I don't mean to be rude, but you need me. And I know you want me."

Gage placed a heavy hand on the man's shoulder. "Leave the lady alone, man. She said she's not interested."

The guy swung around and swayed as he focused on him. "Who the hell are you?"

Erica hopped out of her seat and stood next to Gage. "Brian, this is my friend Gage."

Brian stood. "Hey." He cast a glance at Erica. "Man to man…tell her the truth. As ugly as she is, she should take what she can get."

The heat of anger seared through Gage's chest as he pulled his arm back and landed his fist squarely against Brian's jaw. The man spun, landing face first on the bar and catching himself before he could crumple to the floor.

Someone gasped, and the people closest to them backed up, making room for the possible fight about to ensue.

Brian turned back around, rubbing his hand against his face. "What the hell, man?"

Gage shook his hand out, his knuckles stinging where the skin had made contact with Brian's tooth. Starting a bar fight was a dumb move that could land his ass in jail, but it would be worth it. The guy deserved more than a busted lip for saying that about Erica.

"Come on." Erica tugged on his arm, and he followed her toward the exit, the crowd parting for them as they passed. She pushed open the door and dragged him onto the sidewalk. As she whirled around to face him, he braced himself for the tongue lashing sure to come.

But as her gaze caught his, she smiled. Then she laughed. "You didn't have to hit him."

He clenched and unclenched his fists. How could she be so casual? How could she brush off such hateful comments? "No one deserves to be talked to that way."

She smoothed her braid over her shoulder. "I've gotten used to it."

He gritted his teeth, flexing his jaw as he tried to quell his anger at the asshole who insulted her. "You shouldn't have to get used to it. It's wrong."

"It happens. Come on." She took his hand and led him around the side of the building.

The anger began to flush from his system, but the feel of her soft hand in his kept his pulse racing. "Where are we going?"

"To the patio. I owe you an apology."

They cut around the back corner and climbed three steps to a concrete landing. Two wooden picnic tables sat side-by-side on the small rectangle, and a deep irrigation ditch stretched out behind the restaurant, separating it from the neighborhood lying fifty yards away. Off to the west, the sun hung low against the horizon, painting the sky in deep shades of red and orange.

She sat on top of one of the tables, resting her feet on the seat, and patted the space next to her. "Sit with me."

"I didn't know Molly's had a patio." He climbed onto the table and settled next to her, sitting so close, his shoulder brushed hers.

She didn't pull away. Instead, she leaned into him and took his hand in hers again. Just like she used to do in high school. "I don't think it's open to the public. I found it by accident when I was looking for the restroom."

"Oh." He stared out over the water, holding her hand

and letting the warmth of her touch calm his nerves. He was still pissed at the way Brian had treated her, but if she could let it go, he could too.

She rested her head on his shoulder, and the scent of her hair stirred in his senses, unearthing bitter-sweet memories he'd buried long ago. "I'm sorry I didn't call you when I moved back."

He continued staring at the water. Though he wanted say it was okay, deep down, it really wasn't. If he was honest with himself, he'd admit he was hurt. His best friend ran away and basically disappeared for ten years. Then she came back and didn't bother trying to contact him. And now, here she was sitting with him, holding his hand like they were kids again. Like the last ten years never happened.

When he didn't respond, she squeezed his hand. "In my defense, I haven't called anyone. Well, besides my dad."

"So, none of your old friends matter anymore? You run off and get a taste of Hollywood, and now you're too good for us?" He tried to pull his hand into his lap, but she held on tighter.

"No, Gage. That's not it at all. I..." She sighed. "I failed in Hollywood. Miserably. Just like I fail at everything, but this was worse."

He looked at her. "You don't fail at everything."

"Everyone told me not to go. I was a stage actress. New York was where I was meant to be. But Carter wanted to be in the movies, and he convinced me I could be in the movies too." She laughed dryly. "Me. With this." She gestured to her scar.

"Erica..."

"I remember you, especially, not wanting me to go,

even though you only mentioned it once. You told me Carter was using me, and you were right. After we got there, I learned quickly that Hollywood is all about beauty. I went to a few auditions, and they wouldn't even let me speak. They took one look at my face and told me there wasn't enough makeup in the world to make my skin look normal in high definition. The stage is much more forgiving than the screen."

Her eyes shimmered, and he wrapped his arm around her shoulders. "I'm so sorry."

She shook her head. "I should have come home then, but I stayed for Carter. I got a barista job and supported him while he went to audition after audition. After a while, I took out a loan and went to college to get this stupid graphic design degree because I failed at my dream. Years went by, and it was too late for me. I couldn't go to New York; I had student loans and credit card bills to pay. So I stayed. And stayed." She swallowed hard, looking out over the water, and his heart ached for her.

She'd been trapped, living her life for someone else's dream, going through the motions, but not really living for herself. She'd overcome it, though. She'd gotten out, and she hadn't failed.

"And then, one day, it happened. Carter got cast in television series." She folded her hands in her lap. "He came home and told me he'd finally gotten his break, and if he was ever going to make it big, he couldn't be seen with a freak on his arm."

Gage stiffened. "He said that to you?"

She nodded.

The anger he'd felt in the bar barreled through his chest with a vengeance. Where did these guys get off thinking they could treat another human being this way?

Especially someone as vibrant and kind as Erica. "After you supported him for ten years, he called you a freak?"

"And he left me. He moved in with a woman from one of his acting classes. I think he'd been seeing her for a while. He'd just stayed with me because I was paying the bills."

"Oh, Erica." He wrapped his other arm around her and squeezed her tight. "I always thought Carter was an asshole."

"You were right, but I didn't listen. He was the only guy who ever paid me any attention, so I thought he was the best I could do."

He blew out a hard breath. She really had no idea... "He wasn't the *only* guy."

She pulled from his embrace. "Yes, he was."

He held her gaze, willing her to understand so he wouldn't have to say it out loud. He couldn't bring himself to tell her how he felt back then, and it wasn't any easier now.

She opened her mouth to speak, but the words seemed to get stuck in her throat.

He sighed and looked out over the water.

She followed his gaze. "Well, if you ever liked me, you didn't let me know."

He'd wanted to so many times, but then she'd started seeing Carter, and... "Would it have made a difference?" He leaned his elbows on his knees.

"No, I guess it wouldn't have."

Which was exactly why he'd never told her. Not outright, anyway. He may have been a kid, but he hadn't been an idiot. "You needed a friend. I was happy to be that for you."

She stared straight ahead. "And now?"

"What do you need me to be?"

Biting her bottom lip, she turned to him, her gaze dancing around his face, lingering on his mouth a moment before returning to his eyes. "I don't know."

He nodded and stared out at the water. They sat side by side, silently watching the sun dip behind the roofs of the houses across the way. As the palette in the sky faded from red to purple, she finally spoke. "How's your family?"

"They're all good."

"Your mom? I saw a man there when I visited my dad a few times."

"That's Steven. He's a cop. They're going to Cuba in a few weeks, I hear. Abigail and Becky are both married with kids, Chelsea's engaged, and Deanna has had the same boyfriend for two years."

"Sounds like everyone's happy."

"We are."

Sighing, she laid her head on his shoulder. "I missed you."

He had to laugh at that. "No, you didn't."

She lifted her head and cast him an accusing glance. "Yes, I did."

"If you missed me, you would have tried to contact me when you came back. My number hasn't changed since high school. Our parents are neighbors. I'm not that hard to find."

"But I told you why I didn't call. I was embarrassed. I didn't want you to know how bad I'd messed up."

"When have I ever judged you?" He couldn't mask the disappointment in his voice. He'd always been her safe place. The person she could tell anything. What happened to her over the years to make her lose faith in him?

She lowered her gaze to her hands. "You haven't."

"Why would I start now?"

"I'm sorry."

He fisted his hands on his knees. Damn it, he still had feelings for her. Could he rein them in and be her friend again? Or should he tell her? See if she possibly felt the same.

She took his hand again, uncurling his fingers to slip her palm into his. "I did miss you, Gage. I just didn't realize it was you I was missing."

"What's that supposed to mean?"

"From the moment I left, I had this awful ache in my heart that never went away. I thought I was homesick for ten years, but then, when I came back, the ache didn't go away. I started spending more time with my dad, but that didn't help. Being back in Michigan didn't feel right either. And then I saw you. Sitting here next you, talking like we used to do…I finally feel like I'm home again."

A strand of hair fell out of her braid, and he tucked it behind her ear. "I'm glad you're back."

"Me too." She looked at him with a strange intensity…a look that sent his heart racing.

He cleared his throat before he could do anything stupid like give in to the overwhelming urge to lean over and kiss her. "I guess you're not going to the reunion?"

She let out a dry chuckle. "So everyone there can know what I failure I am? No, thanks."

His heart ached at her words. "You're not a failure. Your life is moving in a different direction than you planned, but you're making the most of it. There's nothing wrong with changing course."

A tiny smile tugged at her lips. "Thank you for saying that, but, no, I'm not going to the reunion. Are you?"

"Didn't plan to." He'd considered enduring the shallow

small-talk, cheap drinks, and ten-year-old pop music on the off chance she might've attended. Now that she worked in his building, though, he could avoid the whole ordeal.

The door behind them clanked open, and a cook in a dirty white apron dragged a trash can out the door. "Hey, you guys can't be out here. Staff only." He pointed to a sign above the door.

"Sorry, man." Gage hopped off the table and held his hand out to Erica. She took it, and they strolled to the parking lot together.

"This is me." She pointed to a dark gray Saturn. "I better get home." She opened the door, but hesitated to get in. Instead, she turned and pulled him into a hug. "It was good talking with you again."

Damn, she felt good pressed against him. "Yeah, it was."

She touched her lips to his cheek, a friendly gesture she'd done many times when they were kids. But this time, she didn't pull away. Her mouth lingered near his jaw, her breath warming his skin. She pulled back ever-so-slowly, her nose brushing against his cheek as her lips neared his own.

His heart pounded in his chest. She glanced into his eyes and lowered her gaze to his mouth. Leaning toward him, she brushed her lips to his. Softly. Cautiously, as if she wasn't sure kissing him was the right thing to do. She pulled back slightly to catch his gaze, and then, cupping his face in her hands, she kissed him again, this time, like she meant it.

The taste of lime on her lips made his head spin, and he fought the urge to crush his body to hers and kiss her harder. He'd let her take the lead for now. Rushing her into something she wasn't sure she wanted was bound to backfire.

She inhaled deeply and pulled away, a smile curving her lips as she looked into his eyes. "Hmm." She lowered her gaze and blinked up at him. "That was nice."

"Yeah."

She slid into the driver's seat. "I hope I'll see you again soon."

"Me too."

She closed the door and waved as she drove away.

Gage shoved his hands in his pockets and watched until her car disappeared around the corner. What had happened there? Had she really kissed him? He played the moment over in his mind. The way her breath felt against his skin. The softness of her lips brushing his. That had been way more than a friendly kiss.

"So, you and Erica hit it off." Lindsay grinned at him from the sidewalk, pulling him from his thoughts.

He sauntered toward her. "We're just friends from high school."

"*Just friends* don't kiss each other on the mouth."

He chuckled. "No, I guess they don't."

"Do you know what happened to her?" She adjusted her purse strap on her shoulder. "I've been afraid to ask."

"She was burned in a house fire when she was a kid."

Lindsay grimaced. "How awful."

"It was." Way more awful than she most likely imagined, but it wasn't his story to share. Erica rarely talked about it when they were young, but she'd trusted Gage enough to tell him the whole guilt-ridden story.

"Did you know her then?"

He shook his head. "We met sophomore year."

"If you like her, you need to tell her. Don't let this turn into what you had with Allison."

He furrowed his brow. "I never had anything with Allison."

"You might have, but you never told her how you felt. And by the time you got up the nerve to flirt with her, she had no clue you were serious. Don't screw this one up too."

He pulled his keys from his pocket. "Thanks for the vote of confidence."

She grinned. "I guess I'll be seeing more of you at work now, eh?"

"I may venture up to the sixth floor a little more often."

"Good. I'll see you tomorrow." She clicked a button on her remote, and the headlights on a Toyota Camry switched on. "Bye, Gage."

Shuffling to his Jeep, he slid into the driver's seat. *Don't screw this one up.* No pressure there. He'd screwed up every relationship he'd tried to start. How could he possibly *not* screw this one up too?

He pulled up the text thread from Chelsea on his phone. It looked like he had a lot of reading to do.

CHAPTER FOUR

As Erica lay in her bed, she pulled the blankets up to her chin, fighting the chill that seeped all the way to her bones. Fluttering her lids open, she squinted to focus through the haze. She blinked as a face came into view, floating directly above her head.

"Jesus Christ!" She flopped out of bed, tangling her legs in the sheets and plopping onto the floor with a *thud.* Grinding her teeth, she took a deep breath to slow her pulse and glared at the ghost in her bedroom. "What the hell are you doing?"

The spirit hovered above her bed. "You have to help me."

She kicked the covers off her legs and stumbled to her feet. "Look, ghost lady…What is your name anyway?"

"Sandra."

"I don't know how to help you, Sandra. I don't even know why I can *see* you." She marched to the kitchen and pulled a container of salt from the cabinet. "I want you out of my apartment. Go." She waved her arms in the air as if she could shoo the spirit from her space.

Sandra looked at her with sad eyes, her translucent shoulders drooping as she floated near the sofa.

"Get out."

The ghost dissipated, and Erica grumbled as she sprinkled salt around the perimeter of her entire apartment. Hopefully it would be enough to keep the annoying ghost away. Why on Earth this spirit thought she could help her, Erica had no clue.

She finished salting her apartment and put the almost-empty canister back in the cabinet. She'd have to add extra salt to her next grocery list. Tossing the tangled mess of sheets onto her bed, she glanced at the clock. Six a.m. She wasn't due at work until eight, but if she got there early, she might be able to avoid seeing Brian. She'd dragged Gage out of the bar before the situation could get out of hand last night, but she was dreading what Brian might have to say this morning.

She smiled. The way Gage had laid into him had been impressive. No one had ever stuck up for her like that, and she had to admit it was kind of…hot.

And the way Gage's lips felt pressed against hers… Her stomach fluttered as she replayed the memory in her mind. She hadn't planned to kiss him. Nothing more than a peck. But as she'd touched her lips to his cheek, his warm, masculine scent had drawn her in. Held her there. His soft, full lips were impossible to resist.

Had Gage really changed that much? Or was she finally able to see something in him that had been there all along?

She finished her morning routine and stepped out the door. A wispy fog clung to the grass in the field behind her building. The sun hadn't fully peeked over the orange horizon, but in another hour, its heat would burn the moisture away. She paused to take in the beauty of the sunrise before turning to the staircase. Sandra waited for her on the landing.

Erica sighed and stepped around the spirit. "If I knew how to help you, I would." She started down the stairs.

"Please." The ghost rushed her, passing through Erica's body like stinging, icy wind clawing at her insides.

Erica stumbled. Her foot missed the next step, and she toppled down the rest of the concrete stairs. She caught herself with her hands on the sidewalk, scraping the skin from her palms. "Damn it, Sandra."

The spirit dissolved, leaving Erica looking like a fool talking to herself. Luckily, no one was around to see her tumble. Her braid had fallen to her back, exposing her mangled neck, so she did her best to smooth it back into place with her fingertips.

Back inside her apartment, she washed the dirt from her bloodied palms and patted them dry with a paper towel. The concrete had only scratched the surface, and after a few minutes, the bleeding stopped on its own. She cleaned herself up and made it to the office half an hour early. Thankfully, no spirits tried to stop her along the way. Whether Sandra had injured her on purpose or not, she didn't know. But she was going to have to do something about that ghost.

Brian got to work at eight and shuffled to his desk with his head down, avoiding eye contact. He had a scab on his lip where Gage had hit him, and his ashen pallor and bloodshot eyes screamed hangover. He sank into his seat, disappearing behind the cubicle wall, and Erica let out a breath.

"Morning." Lindsay dropped her purse on her chair

and shuffled around to Erica's desk. "Have you seen Brian today?"

Erica grinned, putting a finger to her lips to shush Lindsay. "He doesn't look so good. What did he do after we left?"

"His friends stroked his ego, and he kept drinking. Found someone else to hit on."

"Good for him." She turned back to her computer, hoping to avoid the next question she could sense bubbling on her coworker's tongue.

Lindsay sat on the edge of her desk. "Where did you and Gage run off to?"

She pressed her lips together and turned around. While it was none of Lindsay's business, it had been so long since Erica had a girlfriend to talk to like this, why not share a little? "We went outside and talked."

"And kissed."

Warmth spread across her cheeks. "Did he tell you that?"

"I saw you in the parking lot. You had another moment, didn't you?"

Erica's heart fluttered. "I think the entire evening was a *moment.* Did he say anything to you?"

"Not much. He's a good guy, you know?" Though she said it matter-of-factly, a trace of warning edged her words.

As if Erica would ever do anything to hurt her best friend. "I know."

"Do you have lunch plans?"

"Not yet."

Lindsay looked at the clock. "I bet he'll be up before ten. I better get to work."

A swarm of butterflies took flight in her stomach, a

sensation she wasn't used to feeling about Gage. But she couldn't sit there and watch the clock, hoping he'd show up and ask her to lunch. If she didn't hear from him by ten-thirty, she'd call him. Why not?

Tomorrow would most likely be a day straight from hell. She might as well have had an IV of dread attached directly to her arm from the way it trickled slowly through her system. It wasn't enough to cause an outright panic, but the constant chill flowing through her veins stirred the sickening thoughts the anniversary would bring. She tried to push them aside. Today would be a good day, and having lunch with Gage was exactly what she needed to keep her mind off tomorrow.

She busied herself with her next project, losing herself to the monotony of the work until her desk phone rang, jerking her back to the present.

She lifted the receiver. "Erica Miller."

"The file you gave me is corrupt." The growl in his voice sent another chill flushing through her body.

"Aaron?"

"Yes, it's Aaron. Who else would you have given a corrupt file to? I need you to e-mail the presentation to me right now."

She cradled the phone between her ear and her shoulder and pulled up her e-mail account. "Sorry about that. Okay. It's sent. Anything else?"

"No."

Silence.

She hung up the phone. "Well, goodbye to you, too, asshole." How did a man with manners like that make it so high up in the ranks? Surely, he didn't act that way toward his superiors. The phone rang again.

"Erica Mil—"

"This one's corrupt too."

"What? That's not possible. I haven't opened it since I copied it to the flash drive for you." She navigated to the file on her hard drive and double-clicked the icon. The presentation software started up, but a big blue box that read *Error - Unknown File Type* hovered in the center of the screen.

"Send me the backup from the server."

Her stomach dropped. "Umm…"

He let out an irritated grumble. "I don't have time for this. Send me the backup now."

"There is no backup…sir." She wound the phone cord around her finger as her mind raced to find a solution. She had an older version from last week on the server. She wouldn't have to start from scratch, but it would take time to redo the presentation.

"What do you mean, there's no backup? The server is backed up every night. Has there been a problem with IT I don't know about?"

"No, IT is doing their job." The last thing she needed was to drag Gage and his department under the bus with her. "The file wasn't on the server."

Silence.

She continued. "Remember? You told me to move it to the hard drive because the graphics were slowing it down?"

"I expected you to move it back when you were finished."

Her heart raced. She wound the phone cord so tightly around her finger the tip of it turned purple. "Well, I forgot."

"You forgot." She'd expected his voice to grow a few decibels louder with his anger, but it got softer, which was way, way worse.

"You were standing over my shoulder rushing me to get it done before you left." The words tumbled from her mouth before she could rein them in. "I'll fix this. I'll make a new one. How much time do I have?"

"My presentation starts in fifteen minutes."

Fifteen minutes? There was no way she could recreate the entire presentation in fifteen minutes. "I…"

"When I give my employees an assignment, I expect my orders to be carried out." He enunciated each word like he was talking to an idiot.

"Your *orders?* Aaron, is this the first time you've tried to open the file?"

"Yes."

"The file I gave you two days ago?"

"I expected it to work."

She closed her eyes for a long blink. "So, you rushed me through it, insisted you have the file before you left, and then you didn't even open it?"

"I expected you to do your job. I thought you were a competent employee." He inhaled sharply and blew a hard breath into the receiver. "Apparently, I was mistaken."

Unwinding the cord from her finger, she gathered it into a ball in her tightly clenched fist. "Aaron, you're as much to blame for this as I am. If you had opened the file when you got there, I would have had time to redo it for you."

"If you had done your job properly, I wouldn't have this problem."

She released the cord and rubbed her hand on her forehead. "Can you postpone it? Give me two hours, and I'll have something ready for you."

"No."

"Well, what do you want me to do then?"

"Nothing, Erica. I don't want you to do anything."

Silence.

"Crap." She slammed the phone down. "Crap, crap, crap. *Now* he remembers my name."

Lindsay peered over the divider. "What happened?"

"I screwed up. Royally." She explained what happened with the file, the trickle from her IV of dread turning into a full-speed flush. "I guess I can kiss this job goodbye."

"He's not going to fire you over one mistake. And like you said, he's as much to blame for not opening the damn thing when you gave it to him. He must realize that."

She shook her head. "This is Aaron we're talking about. He's never to blame for anything."

"I'm sure it'll be okay." Lindsay flashed an unconvincing smile and disappeared behind the divider.

Erica tried to focus on her work, but a sense of impending doom hovered over her head like a storm cloud. How could the file have gone corrupt? Aaron had been standing right there when she'd loaded it onto his flash drive. She'd had the presentation open. She'd saved it, closed it, and copied the file. How could it have corrupted in the five seconds after she'd closed and copied it?

She leaned her elbow on the table, resting her head in her hand. As much as she wanted to blame Aaron, this whole fiasco was one hundred percent her own fault. She should've moved the file to the server. Or at least left a version of it there while she was working on it. Even after Gage reminded her to move the damn thing, she still didn't do it.

She sucked in a breath. Maybe Gage could help. Maybe he could uncorrupt the file. She glanced at the clock and sighed. Not in five minutes, he couldn't. And anyway, he'd already come to her rescue twice in two days.

She didn't need to make a habit of being the damsel in distress.

She'd just make sure she did a fabulous job on her next project and hope that would be enough to redeem herself. And honestly, she'd be thrilled if she never had to work directly under Aaron again.

She worked for another hour, but the guilt gnawing in her gut was about to consume her whole. Maybe she should shoot Aaron an e-mail and apologize. Trying to convince him to share blame probably wasn't the smartest move she could've made. She opened her e-mail program and entered her password. The screen read *invalid user name and/or password.* Maybe she'd typed it wrong.

She tried again.

Invalid username and/or password.

"Well, which is it? My username or password?" She tried a third time and still couldn't access her account. "Damn it."

"What's wrong?" Lindsay wheeled her chair around the desk.

"There is something majorly wrong with this computer. Now I'm locked out of my e-mail."

Lindsay grinned. "Sounds like a job for a certain hot, blond IT guy, if you ask me."

The butterflies she seemed to be storing in her stomach lately came back to life. "Maybe. He'll probably think I did it on purpose though."

"So what? Call him."

She pressed the home button on her phone, and the screen lit up. No, she should reboot the whole system before she called. That's the first thing he'd do anyway.

"Erica Miller?" A lanky man with dark hair and blue eyes paced toward her.

Her heart sank. This guy worked in Human Resources. And if HR was looking for her…

"Right here." She stood and waved a hand in the air.

He handed her an envelope and scurried away.

Erica sank into her chair and slid her finger under the flap. The thin edge sliced into her skin, sending a stinging sensation shooting into her hand…a prelude to the stab in the heart sure to come. She sucked on the end of her finger until the pain subsided, and then she focused on the letter. A single sheet of tri-folded paper awaited her inside the envelope. She held her breath and unfolded the page. Her stomach dropped with a sickening plop as all the blood drained from her head.

"What is it?" Lindsay asked.

"A termination letter. My exit interview is in fifteen minutes." She tossed the paper onto her desk and squeezed her eyes shut. "HR moves quickly when a VP wants someone fired."

"Oh, sweetie. I'm so sorry."

She yanked open her desk drawer, pulled out her purse, and shoved her belongings inside—a solar-powered dancing flower, a quartz paperweight, a picture of the Tuscan countryside, where she longed to go one day. Her hands trembled as she picked up her phone and dropped it in with the rest of her things.

Lindsay put a hand on her shoulder. "Are you okay?"

"I'll be fine." She sniffled. "I didn't like working for that asshole anyway."

"No one does."

She rose to her feet, and her head spun. Why today? Why did she have to screw up and lose her job on the eve of the anniversary of the worst mistake she'd ever made? Tomorrow was going to be hard enough on its own. Now she had no job. No income. How the hell was she going to pay the mortgage on the theater? Her rent?

She'd figure something out. She had no choice. Inhaling deeply, she pushed in her chair and swung her purse over her shoulder. Pressure mounted in the back of her eyes, but she would not allow tears to fall. Not here. "I guess I'll be going then."

"Call me if you want to talk."

"Thanks."

"Or if you feel like getting hammered tonight, count me in." Lindsay tried for a smile, but her eyes held so much pity, Erica almost choked on a sob.

She nodded and hurried out of the office. If she could keep it together for her stupid exit interview, she might make it out with her dignity.

Gage drummed his fingers on his armrest and stared at his phone. His leg bounced incessantly beneath the desk as his nerves twisted his stomach into a knot. He'd read every goddamn dating article his sister had sent him, and now he was more confused than ever.

Act like you care. Act like you don't care. Buy her flowers. Whatever you do, don't buy her flowers. He'd read so much conflicting information last night, he couldn't tell his head from his ass anymore.

But one thing he did know was that he needed to see Erica today. Screw the relationship experts. He was asking her to lunch. Popping a wintergreen breath mint into his mouth, he strode to the elevator and punched the button for the sixth floor.

As he rounded the corner and pushed open the door

to the graphic arts department, he nearly plowed into Lindsay. He stopped short of knocking her down, but the papers she carried scattered on the floor.

"Sorry." He knelt to help her pick them up.

"It's okay." She furrowed her brow. "What are you doing up here?"

He handed her a stack of papers and straightened. "I was going to see if Erica wanted to go to lunch."

She scrunched her forehead until two lines formed between her eyebrows. "You haven't talked to her today?"

"Not yet. Why?" He started toward Erica's desk, but Lindsay caught him by the arm.

"Erica got fired."

Coldness spread through his chest, and his hands instinctively clenched into fists. "What? Why?" If that asshole Brian had anything to do with it, he'd gladly make his lower lip match his upper.

She pulled him to a corner and lowered her voice. "That presentation she was working on for Aaron…the file was corrupt, so he fired her."

He blinked, his mind trying to catch up with the news. Erica had been fired over a damaged file? "Couldn't she send him the backup?"

Lindsay shook her head. "She forgot to move the file to the server. There was no backup."

"Shit."

"I thought she would've told you."

"Well, she didn't." He clenched his jaw. Was he more upset over Erica losing her job or the fact that she didn't tell him? "When did it happen?"

"Two hours ago."

"Thanks." He turned on his heel and marched back to his office. It only happened two hours ago. She was probably still processing it herself; he shouldn't have expected her to call him immediately. If this had happened ten years ago, she'd have told him the first spare second she had. He was always the first person she called when anything...bad or good...happened to her. Even when she was dating Carter, she'd always talked to Gage first. But that was ten years ago. She still might need a shoulder to lean on, though, and he needed to let her know his was available.

He slid into his desk and dialed her number. Straight to voicemail. "Hey, Erica. It's Gage. Call me when you get a chance."

CHAPTER FIVE

Erica's exit interview wasn't much of an interview. They reminded her she wasn't allowed to share company secrets...as if she knew any...and told her to expect her last paycheck to be deposited in two weeks. She somehow managed to hold herself together through the entire ordeal because all she felt was numbness.

Numb was better than hysterical.

Numb could stop for an iced latte—probably the last one she'd have for a while—on her way home. Hysterical couldn't be seen in public.

She ordered a coffee cake to go with her drink, paid the cashier, and almost tripped over the four-year-old boy standing behind her. Her cake, still tucked safely inside its paper bag, slid across the floor.

"I'm so sorry, sweetie." Erica bent down to retrieve her cake, lost her balance, and fell on her butt. Sharp pain shot from her tailbone up to her neck, and she grimaced. Her braid swished behind her back, revealing the scar on her cheek.

The boy clutched his mother's leg. "Mommy, what's wrong with her face?"

The mother's eyes widened in horror. "I am so sorry." She looked at her son. "That's not nice, Jamie."

Erica smoothed her hair back into place and rose to her feet. "It's okay." She smiled at the boy but didn't approach him. "I was burned in a fire a long time ago."

He buried his face in his mother's pants.

The mom patted his head. "I'm sorry."

"Really, it's okay. Most adults just stare; at least he had the courage to ask. Have a good day." Clutching her bag tightly in her hand, she shuffled out the door and headed to her car.

The sun shone high in the sky, warming her face as she trekked through the parking lot. Cars sped by on the street in front of the coffee shop. People meandered along the sidewalk on their lunch breaks, preparing to return to their jobs. The world moved on, while Erica's life fell apart around her.

She climbed into her car and devoured her slice of cake in three bites. The sweet, cinnamony goodness should have lifted her spirits a little bit, but she hardly tasted it. *What a waste of calories.* It wasn't the cake's fault, though. She'd have eaten the whole damn thing if she'd thought to buy it all.

She took a sip of her latte and leaned her head back on her seat. *What now?* She could go home and sulk. But she'd be doing enough sulking tomorrow. How she was going to make it through her rehearsal with the kids, she wasn't sure. She'd been debating canceling the class all week. Lord knew she'd be a mess tomorrow.

But the class would go on as planned. It had been twenty years, for goodness sake. She was strong enough to function. The kids were depending on her. Their parents had paid for a summer production, and Erica intended to give it to them.

A little guidance would've been nice, though. She couldn't go to her dad. He might have already started drinking. Tomorrow would be hard for him too, and she'd caused enough disappointment in his life. Gage had called, and he was always happy to listen.

But what would she say? She'd failed again. Cry on his shoulder. Let him comfort her. Then what? She needed to have some sort of a plan in place before she called him back.

If only Mrs. Spencer were still around.

She started the car and drove aimlessly for a while. As she passed her tiny theater, she considered going inside. The place brought back so many fond memories. But the theater was supposed to be her future, and at the moment, she couldn't see past tomorrow.

She kept driving, passing her old high school, and turning down a familiar street. Mrs. Spencer had turned one of her bedrooms into a rehearsal room, and Erica had taken private lessons every week for two years. If her ghost were around, she might be attached to something inside the house. Of course, after committing a murder-suicide, who knew what kind of state her spirit would be in. What kind of state had her living mind been in to commit such a horrendous act?

Maybe if she parked on the street, she'd be close enough to talk to Mrs. Spencer's spirit. It was worth a try. She would look like an idiot talking to the air if she waited for the estate sale tomorrow morning. At least this way, she wouldn't have an audience.

She pulled up to 1147 Sycamore Street, and her heart

hammered in her chest. A car sat in the driveway, and the lights inside the house burned bright. Maybe her son was there, preparing for tomorrow's sale. She parked in the driveway and made her way to the front porch before she could talk herself out of it.

A tall, dark-haired woman with hazel eyes answered the door. "Can I help you?"

Erica straightened her spine. "Hi, I'm Erica Miller. Is Johnny here?"

The door opened wider, and Johnny appeared behind the woman. "Hey, Erica. This is my wife, Sarah." He put his hand on Sarah's shoulder. "Erica is the one who took the theater off our hands."

Sarah smiled. "Oh. Would you like to come in?"

"Sure." As she stepped into the foyer, a strange heaviness settled in the air. Solemn. A stark contrast to the once-cheerful atmosphere the house used to hold. She followed Johnny and Sarah into the living room, and a thickness formed in her throat. She'd heard the details. She'd attended the funeral. But being here, in the house where it happened, brought on a whole new onslaught of emotions she wasn't prepared for.

Tears pooled in her eyes. If her teacher's ghost was here, she wasn't showing herself. "I'm sorry. It's hard to believe…"

Sarah slid her arm around Johnny's waist. "What can we do for you, Erica?"

Erica pulled a tissue from her purse and dabbed at her eyes. She inhaled deeply, making certain her voice wouldn't fail her as she spoke. "Mrs. Spencer had a mirror in the rehearsal room. An oval one with an ornate metal frame. Have you sold it yet?"

"I think we have it." Johnny motioned for her to

follow him down the hall.

The tightness in her chest released as she entered the room and found the mirror hanging on the wall. But her stomach sank when she saw the price tag. "You're asking a hundred dollars for it?"

Sarah entered the room. "It's an antique."

"I know." It was so much more than an antique, and its…special properties…rendered it priceless. They'd have been justified in asking a million for it if they'd known what it could do.

Johnny blew out a hard breath. "Go ahead and take it."

"Really?"

He shrugged. "You were her star pupil. I'm surprised she didn't will it to you along with the theater." Though he sounded resigned, the slight hint of venom in his voice came as a surprise.

When Johnny had contacted her about the will, they'd had a long, heart-to-heart discussion about the theater. Erica wasn't family, and she wasn't about to take anything that wasn't rightfully hers, whether Mrs. Spencer wanted her to have it or not. But Johnny had assured her she'd be doing him and his family a favor by taking the theater off his hands. Was he having second thoughts about it now? She'd gladly return the place to him if he wanted it. It hadn't taken her long to figure out she'd bitten off more than she could chew.

"I'm so sorry I bothered you. I'll come back tomorrow during the sale and bring enough cash to pay for it. It was nice to meet you, Sarah." She bowed her head and shuffled toward the door.

"Wait." Johnny touched her elbow. "I'm sorry. Being

in this house again after everything...my nerves are shot. Please, take it."

"Are you sure?"

He laughed dryly. "The thing's hideous. If you don't take it now, I'm sure it'll end up in the dumpster tomorrow afternoon."

Ice flushed through her veins at the thought of that mirror—and what it contained—being thrown away like common garbage. "I can bring the cash by tomorrow."

"No worries. It's yours. It's heavy, though. I'll carry it to your car." He grasped the mirror by the metal frame and lifted it from its hook on the wall.

Erica peered into the silver, but only her own face reflected back at her. Apparently, Johnny didn't know about the mirror's special properties. Both Erica and Mrs. Spencer had been sworn to secrecy when they'd discovered it. It appeared her teacher had taken the secret to her grave.

She followed him to the driveway and opened the back hatch of her car.

He gingerly laid the antique inside and closed the door. "I am sorry I snapped at you in there."

"It's okay." She waved off his apology.

"You were one of the few who came to the funeral. Who actually acted like you cared."

"Of course I cared. She was the closest thing I had to a mom." A sob lodged in her throat, and she swallowed it down.

He shoved his hands in his pockets. "I know." Though he was five years older than Erica, he'd been around the house when Mrs. Spencer gave her private lessons. He'd even joked about adopting Erica as his little sister because she'd spent so much time there. "After it happened...most people were ready to write her off as a monster. They forgot all about the good things she'd done. The people she cared about." Tears pooled in his eyes. "I can't believe she did it. I don't want to believe it. But the evidence is all there, isn't it? My mom's a cold-blooded killer."

"Oh, Johnny." She pulled him into a hug. "I didn't want to believe it either. I still don't. But we don't know the whole story."

He patted her back. "And we never will." Straightening, he wiped beneath his eyes and stepped back. "Good luck with the theater. I'll see you around."

"Bye, Johnny."

He shuffled into the house, and Erica climbed into her car and drove home.

It seemed Mrs. Spencer's ghost had moved on. Her husband hadn't shown himself to Erica, so he probably wasn't around anymore either. But that mirror had been in the house when it happened. And if Erica could convince the spirit trapped inside it to talk, maybe she could glean a little more information about what had happened to her favorite teacher.

And if the spirit would talk, maybe Erica could finally get her theater up and running to full capacity.

She hauled the twenty-pound mirror up the stairs to her second-floor apartment. The weight wasn't so bad, but with the oval shape, and the awkward way she had to carry it, her arms where shaking by the time she got it to the landing.

Sandra appeared by her door. "Don't take that into your house. There's a spirit attached to it."

She shoved her key in the lock. "I know. That's *why* I'm taking it into my house." Opening the door, she ran her foot through the salt line, breaking it at the entry, and turned to Sandra. "*You* stay outside." She stepped through the threshold, and using the toe of her shoe, she spread what was left of the salt to connect the circle again. The mirror nearly slipped from her hands, but she caught it with her knee and readjusted her grip. That would have to do for now. She'd add some more salt to the entryway later.

Balancing the mirror on her desk and leaning it against the wall, she settled into the chair and stared into the silver. She smoothed her hair farther over her face to conceal her scar and examined the hollow expression staring back at her.

Dark circles ringed her chocolate eyes, and her pallor had taken on a sickly, pale appearance. She looked even worse than she felt. But things were looking up now. She had Mrs. Spencer's mirror, and hopefully the ghost that came with it. She'd finally done something right.

"Colette? Are you in there?" She held her breath and waited for the shimmering image of the woman to appear. Nothing happened. "Colette?" She knocked on the glass.

Nothing.

Was there a special way she was supposed to call to the spirit? Every time she'd rehearsed at Mrs. Spencer's house, Colette was already there, in the mirror waiting for her. She'd never considered that there might be some magic ritual that needed to be performed to summon the ghost.

She sighed and shook her head. How was she ever supposed to learn how her ability worked if she wasn't allowed to tell anyone she could see ghosts? "Colette, if you can hear me, I could really use some guidance right now."

No response.

"Mrs. Spencer is dead, but I guess you know that. I

was hoping you could tell me what happened." She traced her fingers along the frame as a sob bubbled from somewhere deep in her chest. "She left me the theater in her will, but I lost my job today, so I have no way to pay the mortgage. I've only been able to find seven kids willing to enroll, so I'm not making enough money on tuition to feed myself much less pay all the bills."

Tears flooded her eyes, and she let them spill down her cheeks. "And tomorrow is…I don't even want to think about what tomorrow is." She laid her head on the desk. "What am I going to do, Colette? I fail at everything. How do I expect to make this theater work when I can't even keep a job?"

She straightened and wiped the tears from her cheeks, determined to get the spirit to talk. "I summon the ghost of Colette. Show yourself to me."

Her own mascara-streaked face stared back at her.

"Damn it, Colette, I need help. Abracadabra. *Voilà.* Where are you?" She stood and took one last glance in the mirror. "This is pointless. I'm going to bed."

CHAPTER SIX

Erica sat in the small auditorium as Amber stood in the center of the stage, singing her solo. The girl's voice melted in the ears like butter. Smooth. Soft. She had talent for miles, and there was no doubt she'd do well for herself with the right guidance.

But this song needed something Erica couldn't quite put her finger on. It was good, but it would be great if she could figure out how to coach her pupil. If Colette would appear, the spirit could tell her exactly what was missing.

Colette had been a Broadway star in the 1940s. She knew the ins and outs of making a great production…of making a great actress…better than anyone. She'd been Mrs. Spencer's advisor for years, and when Erica revealed her ability to see the ghost, Colette became her mentor as well.

But she was stuck inside that damn mirror, and Erica had no clue how to summon her. She rolled her neck to stretch the stiff muscles. She must've gotten up sometime in the night, because when she'd woken this morning, she'd found herself sitting in front of Colette's mirror, head down on the desk.

Amber finished her song, and the cast seamlessly acted out the rest of the scene. Just as Jason escorted Amber to the center of the stage for the finale, the lights brightened, blinding the actors, before shutting off one by one until only a few remained, casting the stage in an eerie blue haze.

The kids stopped and stared at Erica. Caitlyn used the opportunity to attach herself to Jason's arm again. "It's Mrs. Spencer. She doesn't like the way you cast the show."

Erica shook her head. "It's not Mrs. Spencer." She marched to the back of the auditorium. "It's this stupid light board. I need to have it looked at."

The house lights dimmed, darkening the auditorium.

"Damn it." As her eyes adjusted to the darkness, Erica fumbled her way to the light controls and jiggled the knobs. "Please turn the lights back on."

The dimly-lit LEDs across the board appeared to be getting power…just not enough. She checked the cord where it attached to the wall and to the device, but everything was in its place. "I don't know, guys. Let's keep rehearsing, and we'll worry about the lights later. We've still got two hours of practice left."

Jason peeled himself away from Caitlyn's grip. "What if this happens during a show?"

"It won't. I'll call someone to fix it this afternoon."

They ran through the scenes the rest of the morning, the lights dimming and changing colors several times before finally going back to normal. With the erratic behavior, Erica wanted to agree with her students that a ghost was messing with the lights. But nothing showed itself to her, no matter how hard she tried to see a spirit.

It definitely wasn't Mrs. Spencer, and Erica had never seen a ghost in this building…not even when she was a pupil here herself.

She dismissed her students and dropped into a chair. With no source of income, she couldn't afford to pay a technician. She might be able to cancel the ad space she'd bought in the newspaper, but that wouldn't be enough to cover the cost of repair.

She closed her eyes and let out a sigh. Gage could fix it. He had a way with mechanical things. Electrical. Computers. The man was smart and sexy.

Her stomach fluttered. She hadn't returned his call from yesterday; she couldn't ask him for a favor now. But she didn't have another option she could afford. At least she had her emotions under control today. She'd managed to keep her mind away from thoughts about today's date all morning. Maybe Gage could distract her enough to get her through the rest of the day.

And she wouldn't mind seeing his bright aqua eyes again. Maybe even tasting his soft, full lips. She dialed his number before she could change her mind. He answered on the first ring.

"Hey, Gage. I'm sorry I didn't call you back yesterday."

"Are you okay?" Concern emanated from his voice. No doubt he'd heard she'd been fired, but she didn't want to talk about it. Not over the phone.

"I had a rough night, but I'm fine. I will be, anyway."

"That's good to hear."

An awkward silence stretched between them. He was obviously waiting for her to say something. To steer the conversation away from her job loss or to gush about it. When she said nothing, he cleared his voice.

She took a deep breath and forced out her request. "I

was wondering…when Mrs. Spencer had the theater renovated, she installed this new, fancy, computerized light board. It's been on the fritz lately, and I thought…well, lighting was always your thing…"

He chuckled. Was it a humorous chuckle or a perturbed one? "You want me to come have a look at it?"

"Would you? If it's not too much trouble."

"It's no trouble at all." He paused. "Can you give me two hours?"

"Yeah. Two hours is great. Thank you."

"Any time."

As she hung up the phone, her stomach did flip flops. She'd get her light board fixed and get to spend some time with a hot guy. Her lips tugged into a smile. It felt weird to think of Gage that way, but there was no denying his hotness. Gage 2.0 had a sex appeal she'd never noticed before. The question was, what was she going to do about it?

Gage sat on his sofa, tapping his fingers against his knee. His first instinct had been to drop everything and head to the theater right away, but if he'd learned anything from the scores of dating articles Chelsea had sent him, it was that he shouldn't make himself look desperate. Waiting two hours made it seem like he was busy…so she knew he had a life too.

Still, he couldn't help but notice the sinking feeling in his stomach. He shouldn't get his hopes up. She'd only asked him to fix something for her. The last woman he'd dated brought him home and asked him to fix her Wi-Fi. Then he never heard from her again.

He couldn't let that happen with Erica. It *wouldn't* happen with Erica, but he needed to be sure he did everything right with her. He groaned and dialed his baby sister's number. He would probably regret this.

"Hey, big brother. To what do I owe the pleasure of hearing your voice this afternoon?"

"Hi, Chels. I need some advice."

"Really?" Damn, she sounded way too excited. "Shoot."

Pressing his thumb and forefinger into his brow, he squeezed his eyes shut. "Erica's back in town."

His sister paused for a moment. "Please don't get your heart broken again."

He let out a breath. Chelsea was always the most observant one. No matter how hard he tried to pretend he wasn't crazy about Erica in high school, his little sister had always seen the truth. "She never broke my heart to begin with. Anyway, I think she might be interested in me now."

The slight sucking sound of the refrigerator door opening drifted through the phone, followed by the *thud* of a drawer opening and closing. "What makes you say that?"

He stood and paced the room. "She kissed me."

"What kind of kiss are we talking about?" She spoke around the food in her mouth. "A peck on the cheek? Don't read too much into it."

"It was on the mouth."

She swallowed. "With tongue?"

He stopped, closing his eyes for a long blink before pacing again. Why had he decided to call his sister about this? Oh, right. Because if he'd asked a guy friend for advice he'd have told him to man-up and ask her out.

Maybe that was what he should do. "There was no tongue, but it was a real kiss. It meant something."

She took another bite of whatever she was eating. "How do you know it meant something?"

"Because I could feel it, and I know she felt it too." She *had* to have felt it.

Chelsea finished chewing before she spoke again. "How do you know she felt it?"

The look in her eyes. The way her gaze lingered on his lips as she pulled away. He exhaled an exasperate sigh. "I just do. Never mind. I'm sorry I called you."

"Wait, Gage. Assuming she is interested, what are you going to do about it?"

Pausing in the living room, he dropped his arm to his side. "That's why I called you. I don't want to screw this up."

The sound of his sister's nails drumming on the countertop filled the silence before she spoke. "When are you going to see her again?"

He plopped onto the couch. "She bought the old theater, and she asked me to go by and look at the light board. It's broken."

"And you told her no, I hope."

"Why would I tell her no? I said I'd be there in two hours."

She sighed. "Oh, Gage. Don't you see the pattern here?"

Yes, he saw the pattern, but this was Erica. She was different. "It's not going to be that way."

"It's already that way. Don't do it. Call her back…no, even better…text her and tell her something came up, and you can't go."

He switched the phone to his other ear. "Something came up?"

"Yes. Don't tell her what. Be mysterious about it. Then wait and see if she calls you again."

Yep, he definitely regretted making this phone call. "I'm not doing that."

"Please don't go. You know what? I bet even Abigail will agree with me. Let me add her to the call."

He groaned. "That's not necessary." But she had already dialed their oldest sister's number.

"Hey, Abby, guess what?" Chelsea sang. "Erica Miller's back in town."

"Does Gage know?"

She giggled. "He's on the phone."

"Hey, Abigail." He lay on the couch and propped his feet on the arm. "Sorry to drag you into this. I had a brain fart and decided to call *Chelsea* for dating advice."

Abigail laughed. "You must be desperate."

"I'm not desperate."

His niece squealed in the background, and Abigail shushed her. "Are you wanting to ask Erica out?"

"Yes, but—"

"He already kissed her," Chelsea interrupted. "And now she's asked him over to fix something for her. Tell him not to do it."

"Why wouldn't he do it? They were best friends."

"And then she moved away and broke his heart." Chelsea sighed. "Don't you remember him sulking in his bedroom after she left?"

He clenched his teeth. "I did not sulk."

"You blasted Secondhand Serenade over and over all day long," Chelsea said. "You were sulking."

Sure, he was sad to see Erica go. And so what if he'd

found some music that fit his mood? He wasn't sulking. He'd graduated and hadn't started college yet. He didn't have anything better to do at the time. "Anyway..."

"I think you should do it," Abigail said. "And then ask her to dinner. And *talk* to her. If you still have feelings for her, you need to make sure she knows this time."

"I guess that will work too," Chelsea said. "But don't act too needy. And don't be clingy. Be cool."

"Be yourself," Abigail said. "Let us know how it goes."

"Thanks, I will." He pressed end and tossed his phone on the coffee table. Abigail's advice made sense. If he told her how he felt, the absolute worst that could happen would be for her to never call him again. And while that was the last thing he wanted to see happen, he'd lived the past ten years without her in his life. He'd survive.

He read his newest demonology book to occupy himself for the next hour. While he hoped to never come into contact with another creature from hell again, he couldn't deny his fascination with them. It had been almost a year since he'd helped his friends fight off the shadow demon living in their attic, and if he hadn't studied the creatures as much as he had, they'd probably all be dead. Paranormal investigators had to be prepared for the worst, and sometimes human spirits could be as awful as demons. What would Erica think about his hobby? Most people didn't give a second thought to the existence of ghosts...until they encountered one themselves.

He showered and changed and then headed to the theater to meet Erica. She'd said the light board was on the fritz, but he had to wonder if the problem could have a paranormal source. Two spirits that he knew of haunted Erica's theater, but there was no sense in scaring her by mentioning it over the phone. They were harmless as far as he knew, and the problem could still be electrical. He'd find out soon enough.

He pulled into the parking lot next to Erica's Saturn and wiped his clammy palms on his jeans. Fix her light board. Ask her to dinner. Tell her how he felt. He could do this. No sweat.

He pulled open the front door and stepped into the lobby. Pale sunlight filtering in through the windows provided the only light in the small space. A heavy, black door separated the entry area from the auditorium. Finding it unlocked, he pushed it open and stopped by the last row of seats.

Erica stood on stage, straightening a vase of fake flowers on a prop table. She moved a chair into place and stepped back to eye the position. A flood of memories came rushing through Gage's mind as he watched the bright lights glisten off her light brown hair. How many days had he spent in the light box at school watching her perform…shining the spot light to make her hair appear as if it were glowing?

He could've stood there watching her all afternoon, but he had a mission. Fix the lights. Ask her to dinner. Tell her how he felt.

He cleared his voice.

She turned around, and her whole face brightened. "Hi. I didn't hear you come in."

"You should keep the front door locked when you're here alone."

"I usually do." She descended a short set of steps and glided up the aisle toward him. "I unlocked it for you." She stopped two feet in front of him and wrapped one arm across her stomach to rub the other. The hint of a blush spread across her cheeks. "Thank you for coming."

He shoved his hands in his pockets. "No problem. How are you? Lindsay told me what happened at work."

She lowered her gaze to floor. "She did, eh?"

"It's a shame I had to hear it from her. Why didn't you tell me?"

She shrugged and raised her gaze to meet his. "I was… embarrassed."

"Why?" She'd never been embarrassed to talk to him before. What had changed?

"I had just told you about how badly I'd failed in LA. I didn't want you to know I'd screwed up yet again."

"I could have helped you. I might have been able to recover the file."

She shook her head. "Not in fifteen minutes."

"I would have tried."

"What's done is done." She shrugged. "It doesn't matter."

"No, I suppose it doesn't." He chuckled, though he couldn't force a bit of humor into his laugh.

"What?"

"It's nothing. I…back in high school, I was always the first person you turned to. But we've lost ten years between us, so I guess I shouldn't expect things to go right back to the way they used to be. I do wonder what's changed to make you not trust me anymore. I haven't changed."

She leaned forward, shifting her weight to her toes. "But you have changed, Gage. We both have. And I do trust you, but something is different now. I don't know what it is about you…about us, but *something* has changed."

There was that look again. That fire in her eyes that

wasn't there before. She was right; something had changed, and he'd be damned if he was going to let it slip away.

He stepped toward her. Screw telling her how he felt; he'd show her. Cupping her left cheek in his hand, he lowered his mouth to hers. Her lips were warm and soft, and she responded to his kiss, opening her mouth to let him in. He slid his other hand to the small of her back, pulling her close as she wrapped her arms around his waist. A soft moan escaped her throat as her tongue brushed his. God, she felt good in his arms. Her taste. Her scent. The feel of her soft curves pressed against him. He closed his eyes, allowing his body to memorize the contours of hers.

As the kiss slowed, she placed her hands on either side of his face, stroking his cheeks with her thumbs as she pulled away. "Yeah. That's the something I was talking about."

His heart hammered in his chest. "Change is good."

"In this case, I agree." She kissed him again before resting her head on his shoulder and letting out a satisfied sigh.

He stood there holding her for a while, enjoying the way she felt in his arms. He'd hugged her plenty of times, but an undeniable energy danced between them now. This moment felt too good to be real. Too good to last. Chelsea's advice rang in his ears: *Don't read too much into it.* How could he not? He slowly released his hold and ran his hands up and down her arms. "You have a light board you need me to look at?"

She smiled and gave him a curious look before nodding at something behind him. "It's right over there."

"Show me what it's doing." With his hand on the small of her back, he guided her toward the computer system. She didn't seem to mind the close contact. In fact, when he stopped in front of the board, she sidled next to him, sliding an arm around his back to rest it on his hip. Something between them had definitely changed, and he couldn't fight his smile. "Do the lights go out completely or do they blink?"

"Both. What's so funny?"

His smile widened. "Nothing. I'm glad you called me back."

She returned his grin. "Me too."

He leaned over the board, toying with the dials. "You know, I could charge you seventy-five bucks to take a look at this thing. Then another eighty-five an hour to fix it."

She crossed her arms, shifting her weight to one foot. "You *could.*"

"But I won't." He continued messing with the dials. "I think you should let me take you out to dinner instead."

She laughed. "*Let you* take me out to dinner? That sounds like you're asking me on a date."

He straightened and turned to face her. "That's exactly what I'm doing."

She blinked and furrowed her brow. "I would…love to go on a date with you."

"You look surprised."

"I kinda am."

"Surprised I asked or surprised you said yes?"

"Both, actually. But…when?"

His sister's advice swam in his mind. *Don't be clingy. Don't be needy. Try not to look desperate…Fuck it.* He shrugged. "Are you free tonight?"

"I'm free now." She held his gaze with her deep, brown eyes, and he was tempted to say screw the lights and take her home with him right then. But the lights were the reason she'd called him.

"I've got a job to do right now." He winked. "But I'll be free as soon as I'm done."

She smiled and sat on the arm of a chair. "Okay."

He checked the cables connecting to the machine and to the walls, making sure everything was in place. Erica probably checked it all already, but in all his years working in IT, he'd learned the easiest fixes were often the ones most overlooked. He glanced up every now and then to find her watching him, a tiny smile tugging at the corners of her pink lips. What he would've given to know what she was thinking…

He couldn't find anything wrong with the mechanics of the system. That left three possible causes: the building's electrical system, the software, or the paranormal. The latter two he could handle, but if the building's electrical was the culprit, Erica would have to call someone in to rewire the place.

He tapped a few keys on the keyboard to get into the system, and a frigid breath on the back of his neck made his arm hairs stand on end. He shivered but tried to ignore the spirit manifesting behind him.

The air around him grew colder until goose bumps pricked at his skin. He hovered his fingers above the keys, not touching anything, and the house lights flickered.

Erica covered her mouth and gasped, her eyes growing wide as she focused her gaze on something behind him. Could she actually see the spirit? One way to find out.

He rubbed the back of his neck to chase away the chill. "Is it Leroy or Stanley?"

Her mouth hung open. She rose to her feet and shuffled toward him tentatively, rubbing her arms as if she also felt the chill. "You can see it too?"

"No, but I can feel it. Tall and thin or short and round?"

She blinked rapidly. "Tall. But how…" She tilted her head to the side and looked past Gage. "Have you been doing this to the lights?" Crossing her arms, she tapped her foot on the floor. "Well, I would appreciate it if you would stop. I've got a show to produce."

The buzzing energy around him dissipated, and the air warmed to a normal temperature. He closed the computer and turned to Erica. "I didn't know you could see ghosts."

"I didn't know you could feel them."

"Everyone can feel them. Most people don't recognize what they are. You saw him, though. Have you always had that ability?" Maybe he didn't know Erica quite as well as he thought he did.

"Since I was a kid."

"Why didn't you tell me?"

She dropped her gaze to the floor. "I couldn't. I…it's a long story."

He leaned against the table. "I've got time."

Looking into his eyes, she furrowed her brow as if unsure of how much she should share. "This is the first time I've seen one here. Where did they come from? And if you can't see them, how do you know their names?"

"Sounds like we have a lot to talk about. Want to go get dinner?"

She shivered. "I do."

CHAPTER SEVEN

Erica's heart pounded as she pulled into the parking lot of her apartment complex. She slid out of her seat and met Gage at his Jeep. The thought of asking him to come inside briefly crossed her mind, but she dismissed it. She was about to confess the secret she'd been keeping from him…from everyone…her entire life. If they were alone inside her apartment, she might fall apart. At least in a public place, she'd be forced to keep it together.

She slipped her hand into his and allowed the familiar warmth of his skin to calm her nerves as they strolled toward a small Italian restaurant three blocks away. "I've never talked about this with anyone but Mrs. Spencer."

He squeezed her hand. "She could see them too."

"How did you know that?"

He grinned. "I'm an IT genius by day, paranormal investigator by night."

"Really?"

"I work for the Detroit Area Paranormal Society. D.A.P.S. for short. When Mrs. Spencer did the renovations a couple of years ago, she woke some spirits who'd been in the building for decades. She wanted physical evidence to show her family, so D.A.P.S. investigated for her."

They made a left and shuffled down the sidewalk under a canopy of oak branches. The setting sun filtered through the leaves, dappling the sidewalk in light and shadows. Erica paused by the restaurant. "I didn't know ghosts slept."

He opened the door for her, and they followed the hostess to a table in the back. As soon as Erica slid into her seat, with a light puff of breath, she extinguished the single candle burning on the table.

Gage glanced at the wick. "I guess woke isn't the right word. Leroy and Stanley had been there all along, but they were quiet. Content to sit back and observe the living without making a fuss. As soon as the renovations started, it stirred them up. Their home got a makeover, and they weren't happy about it at first."

The waiter arrived to take their order, and Erica asked for a long pour of cabernet with her meal. She'd managed to avoid thinking about the significance of the date for most of the day, but the explanation Gage needed…that he deserved…for why she'd kept her ability a secret wouldn't be an easy one to give.

"Are the ghosts dangerous?" Her stomach sank. Was she putting her students in danger by holding classes?

"Nah. They're harmless. Probably just wanted your attention. Say hello every day, and they shouldn't bother you."

"I wonder why they didn't show themselves to me before."

"That, I don't know. I don't have the ability to

communicate with spirits. I run tech on the team. Cameras, EVP, EMF detectors…" His eyes brightened as he talked about his side job.

"I've seen the TV shows."

"Most of the time, it's not nearly that exciting. Sometimes we come across a nasty one, though." Gage sipped the beer the waiter set in front of him.

Erica ran her finger up and down the stem of her glass. "I'm glad Leroy and Stanley aren't nasty."

"They told the psychic on our team they were happy there, so we let them be. You can cross them over if they bother you."

Cross them over? She couldn't even see them until they wanted to be seen. How was she supposed to force them out? She took a long sip of wine. "I don't have that ability."

"Sure you do. If you can see spirit energy, you can help it find its way to the other side." He said it matter-of-factly, like it should have been the easiest thing in the world.

"I don't even know why I can see them."

"I know someone you can talk to about it. Her name is Allison. Strongest medium I know. She'd be glad to help you develop your gift."

Gift. She had to chuckle at that…but talk to a medium about her ability? She couldn't do that. Aside from promising her mom she'd never tell anyone she could see ghosts, she'd also sworn her secrecy with Mrs. Spencer. When her teacher had discovered Erica could see Colette, the ghost in the mirror, Colette had made them both swear never to tell anyone about her. Never to talk about spirits. She'd been keeping her secret since she was a child, so Colette's request didn't seem strange.

But now, sitting here with Gage, who didn't question her ability…who accepted her as she was…she wanted to share her secret. She wanted to tell him everything.

She reached across the table to hold his hand. "I'll think about it."

Their food arrived, and Erica ordered another glass of wine. The first one had finally taken effect, spreading a pleasurable warmth from her stomach to her limbs. Her body relaxed, but the man sitting across from her had her heart thrumming. A comfortable silence stretched between them as they ate. Though the curiosity in his eyes was evident, he didn't pressure her to spill her secrets.

She sat up straight and grinned as she watched him take the last bite of his manicotti. She had feelings for Gage, and he liked her too. At least she had one good thing happening in her life.

He caught her gaze and returned the smile. "What?"

She shook her head. "Nothing. You're…"

"Different?"

"But the same." She finished her second glass of wine. Or was it her third? She couldn't remember. Whichever it was, it had finally given her the courage to talk about her secret. "I never told you I could see ghosts because I promised my mom I wouldn't tell anyone."

"Why would she make you promise that?" He paid the tab and offered her a hand to stand.

She rose to her feet. "It's a long story."

"I've got time."

She paused and considered him for a moment. He did have time…because he *made* time. For her. The butterflies took flight in her stomach again as a warm ache spread through her chest. She'd missed this. Missed *him.* "Want to sit at the bar for a while?" Another glass of liquid courage might be enough to get her through the story.

They found two seats at the end of the bar, and Erica ordered her third glass of wine before excusing herself to the restroom. Gage ordered a beer, but he didn't intend to drink it. Whatever story she was about to tell sounded like it wouldn't be easy for her to share, and he wanted to make sure he caught every word.

Erica rarely talked about her mom, and he understood why. But having the ability to see ghosts had to be scary for a child. Not being allowed to talk about it would've made it worse.

She returned from the restroom and slid into her seat, flashing him a small smile before turning to her drink. She took a long sip, draining half the glass before setting it on the bar and tracing her finger up and down the stem. "Thanks for dinner."

"You're welcome." He took her hand and held it in her lap. He needed to get her talking before the wine clouded her thoughts. "Why didn't your mom want you to talk about your ability?"

She inhaled deeply, tightening her grip on his fingers, focusing her gaze on the glass. "When I was a kid, my dad was an alcoholic. Now he only drinks once a year, but when I was little, it was pretty bad."

"Yeah, you've told me that." He moved his other hand on top of hers.

"When I was eight, he forgot about my mom's birthday. Spent the day passed out on the couch." She pulled from his grasp and chugged the rest of her drink. Lifting a hand to the bartender, she pointed to her glass, and he refilled it.

"Hey." Gage rubbed a hand across her back. "You've already told me this story. You don't need to relive it." He couldn't begin to imagine the pain, the fear, an eight-year-old child would have felt in such a horrific event. Why would she want to tell him about it all over again?

"I didn't tell you everything." Tears glistened in her eyes.

"Come here." He wrapped his arm around her shoulders and pulled her into his side. If he'd have known his questions would lead to this godawful memory, he'd have kept his damn mouth shut.

"I knew my mom was sad my dad forgot, even though she tried to play it off. So, when she was in her bedroom, I shook my dad awake and begged him to take me to buy her a cake. He told me to make her one myself."

His heart ached for her. Why was she torturing herself by reliving this memory? "You don't have to talk about this."

She wiped a tear from her cheek. "I need to."

"Okay." If she needed to tell him this story, he'd listen. As much as it tore him up to hear it, her pain had to be a million times worse.

"I had one of those Kinder Cookin' Ovens, but the old kind from the 1980s. My mom got it from a garage sale. I wasn't allowed to use it upstairs, but I wanted to surprise her, so I set it up on the floor in my bedroom. I plugged it in to heat it up, and my mom came upstairs. I threw a blanket over it, so she wouldn't see." She sat up straight and took another drink of wine. "A blanket. On an oven, Gage. How could I have been so stupid?"

"You were eight. You weren't stupid." He rested his

hand on her thigh and gave it a squeeze. She'd told him her mom died in the fire, but she'd only given him the condensed version of the story. This detail was something new.

"She told me to come downstairs for ice cream. My dad was passed out on the couch, but my mom and I celebrated her birthday, and I was so excited I forgot all about the cake. Until I went to bed."

Running her hands over her hair, she smoothed it down the side of her face. "The fire started with the blanket, but my room was a mess, so it spread quickly. By the time I woke up and screamed for help, the entire upstairs was ablaze. My bed…"

A sob bubbled up from her throat, and she covered her mouth. "My mom came bolting through the flames like a superhero. She scooped me out of my bed, but it was already on fire. The pain was…" She shivered. "The last thing I remember is my mom tossing me out the window. Then I woke up in the hospital a few days later." She buried her face in her hands.

He rubbed her back, trying desperately to think of the right words to take her pain away. If he could have reached into her chest, pulled out the agony, and endured it himself, he would have done it in an instant. But this was an ancient pain that was so much a part of her, there was nothing he could do to separate her from the torture. "I'm so sorry."

Lifting her head from her hands, she glanced around the room as if suddenly remembering they were in a public place. She wiped the tears from her cheeks and finished off her fourth glass of wine. "The fire was my fault. I killed my mom."

No wonder she rarely talked about her mother. The

guilt must have been eating her alive all these years. As an eight-year-old, she probably did believe she'd killed her mom. He held her hand. "It was an accident."

"It was still my fault."

"You didn't kill her."

She sucked in a shaky breath. "I can't believe I'm telling you all this. I've never told anyone this story."

He motioned to the bartender to close out their tab. If she drank any more wine, he'd have to carry her home. "We don't have to talk about it."

"Yes, we do. I want you to know the truth."

Would she be telling him this if she were sober? Or was her sudden openness merely a side effect of the alcohol? It didn't matter. He'd listen for as long as she needed him to. Whatever she wanted to tell him.

"I had a point in telling you this story. Oh, right…the ghosts. When I woke up in the hospital, my mom was there. She stayed with me the whole time while my dad went to rehab. He quit drinking after that." She let out a dry chuckle. "I guess I would have too."

"I thought your mom died in the fire." He signed the check and slid his credit card into his wallet.

"She did. The firefighters were able to rescue my dad, but by the time they got to my mom, it was too late."

"Her ghost stayed with you."

She bit her bottom lip and nodded. "It was the first time I'd ever seen a spirit. Maybe the trauma of the fire triggered something in my brain to jumpstart the ability. I don't know. When my mom figured out I could see and hear her, she made me promise never to tell anyone. She said it was dangerous, and people would either call me crazy or try to take advantage of me."

That must have been why she couldn't see the ghosts in

the theater until today. She'd never developed her ability, so she had no control, no idea what kind of power she possessed. "That had to be hard keeping a secret like that for so long. Especially for a child."

"It was. Walk me home." She stood and swayed on her feet.

He jumped up and caught her by the arm.

"Sorry." She squeezed her eyes shut. "I don't usually drink this much. My head's spinning a little."

"Let's get you home." Gage held her by the arm to steady her and led her out of the bar. "You told Mrs. Spencer about your ability, right?"

"She found out the same way as you. She had a…" She clamped her lips together and glanced at the sidewalk. "I reacted to a spirit at her house. I didn't tell her about my mom. We didn't talk much about our abilities at all, but it was nice just knowing someone else could see what I could see. I'm sorry I never told you."

"I understand why you didn't."

She sighed and leaned into his side, so he wrapped his arm around her and guided her home. She stumbled on the steps, but he managed to get her to the second-floor landing safely. Sliding the key into the lock, she paused and turned to him. Her tears had dried, and a tiny smile played on her lips. "Thanks for listening."

"Anytime." He reached for her, planning to hug her and say good night, but the air temperature around him plummeted. Goose bumps pricked at his skin, and a chill ran down his spine.

Erica shook her head. "Not now, Sandra."

"You have a ghost at your apartment too?"

She glanced at the door before placing her finger on his lips. "Shh…I don't want to talk about ghosts anymore tonight." Trailing her finger down his chin, she rested her hand on his chest. "It's early. Do you want to come in?"

His heart dipped into his stomach. "Is that you asking me, or the wine?"

She giggled. "Probably both." Stepping through the threshold, she waited for him on the other side. "Come on."

He shifted his weight to the balls of his feet, ready to follow her in, but he stopped. Temptation urged him on, but he couldn't…even though he really, *really* wanted to. He shoved his hands in his pockets. "You've had a lot to drink, and I don't—"

"Oh, Gage." She grabbed his arm and yanked him inside. "Don't you see? This something different that's happening between us…I like you. And I really want to kiss you right now."

Oh, hell. He wanted to kiss her too. To do a whole lot more than kissing, but he couldn't gauge her soberness. Could the alcohol be fueling her desire? She'd had four glasses of wine. He'd be able to think straight after that amount of alcohol, but how well could Erica handle her drinks?

She placed her hands on his chest, and electricity pulsed through his body. She blinked up at him, gliding closer, erasing the space between them. "Please kiss me, Gage."

He touched his fingers to her cheek, and she closed her eyes. As he slid his gaze to her plump, pink lips, the memory of the way they'd felt pressed to his came rushing back. Tender. Warm. Just a kiss. He'd indulge in one brief brush of the lips, and then he'd say good night. He leaned in and took her mouth with his.

A soft moan emanated from her throat as she snaked

her arms behind his neck and melted into his embrace. She felt so damn good in his arms; if she'd been sober, he'd have scooped her up and carried her to the bedroom. She roamed her hands over his body, slipping them beneath his shirt. Her soft fingers danced over his skin like velvet, the intimacy in her touch hardening him with desire. But as her caresses neared the waistband of his jeans, he had to put the brakes on before they did something she'd regret.

He grasped her hands. "I should probably head home." Giving her fingers a squeeze, he released them and stepped back.

She dropped her gaze to the floor and smoothed her hair over her scar. "I understand. It's hard to get excited about someone who looks like a monster."

"Whoa. Where did that come from?" He reached for her shoulder, but she jerked away.

"It's okay, Gage. I'm ugly. I know that. I shouldn't have expected anything more than rejection." She tucked her scarred hand into her sleeve and angled her face away from him.

"I'm not rejecting you. Erica…" He hooked his finger under her chin, raising her gaze to his. How could she say such horrible things about herself? "I think you're beautiful."

She scoffed. "Beautiful?" She tossed her braid behind her back and tucked her hair behind what was left of her scarred ear. Gesturing to her face, she let out a sardonic laugh. "This can never be beautiful. And no one will ever want me." Tears shimmered in her eyes as she stared at him, challenging him to disagree.

This had to be the alcohol talking. How else could they go from making out to her accusing him of being repulsed? Wasn't it obvious he wanted her? She was all he'd thought about since she'd come back into his life. "I don't care about your scar. Honestly, I hardly notice it. When I look at you, all I see is you. And I am incredibly attracted to you; I just don't want to rush things."

She laughed again, without a trace of humor. "If you're attracted to me, it's only because you haven't seen it all."

He reached for her again, but she took a step back. Letting his arms fall to his sides, he sighed. "I haven't seen it all because you keep it covered."

"For good reason." She shoved her sleeve up her arm and held it out to him. "Look."

The scar extended from the pinky side of her hand up to disappear into her shirt. The warped, discolored skin shone in the light in the smooth places. In other spots, bumps and ridges marred her arm, the flesh puckering and dipping in a random kaleidoscope design. His heart ached for her. The pain she'd endured must have been unbearable. And at eight years old…

She stared at him, waiting for a reaction. He kept his expression neutral, but he needed to say something. What could he say, though? No words could convey the sympathy he felt for her, and at this moment, he doubted sympathy was what she needed.

"Well? Say something."

He looked into her eyes. "It's your arm."

"It's hideous." She yanked her sleeve down.

He wanted to reach for her again, but he refrained. She'd only back away. If she would let him hold her, he'd take her in his arms and hug her until the hurt went away. "Your arm is scarred, yes. What happened to you is tragic, but I don't care about how it looks. It doesn't define you."

"A lot more than my arm is scarred, Gage." Anger tinted her words, but he couldn't tell if she was mad at him or her condition. "If you saw it all, you wouldn't be able to say you're attracted to me. You definitely wouldn't say I'm beautiful."

"You *are* beautiful."

"You haven't seen me." She yanked her shirt over her head and dropped it on the carpet. "Look at it. Look at this hideous scar, and then look me in the eyes and tell me you're still attracted to me."

His gaze never straying from her eyes, he knelt to retrieve her clothing from the floor. "Let's not do this. Please put your shirt back on." He held it out to her, and she snatched it from his hands.

"Not until you look at me. *Really* look at me."

He sighed and allowed his gaze to travel to the side of her face. He'd seen this part of her scar plenty of times. Aside from the first time he'd met her, he'd never given it a second thought. It was simply what her skin looked like. The same pock-marked pattern, smooth in some places, rough and ridged in others, extended down her neck and across her shoulder to cascade down the entire right side of her body. His heart wrenched at the sight, but the pain in her eyes tore his insides to shreds. Her scars ran deeper than what he could see.

He reached for her, and she stepped back again. "You don't have to touch me."

"I want to touch you." Closing the gap between them, he took her face in his hands and ran his thumbs across her skin. Both sides—the scarred and the smooth.

She stiffened. "Why?"

He held her gaze, staring deep into her dark-brown eyes, willing her to believe him. "Because you're beautiful." Leaning in, he touched a soft kiss to her lips. When she didn't pull away, he kissed her again. The faint taste of cabernet still lingered on her tongue, and as she slid her arms around his waist, he couldn't stop the moan from rumbling in his chest nor the blood from rushing to his groin.

He kissed her forehead and trailed his fingers down her arms. "Believe me now?"

"Yes." Her voice came out as a whisper. She released her hold and turned her shirt right side out to clumsily pull it over her head. "I'm sorry." She smoothed her braid back into place, covering her scar. "The wine is making me say things I'd normally keep to myself."

"I'm glad you told me." He wrapped his arms around her and pressed his lips to her head. They stood there in her living room holding each other, her head nestled against his chest, the sweet scent of her hair tickling his senses, and he lost himself to the moment. He could have held her like this all night. He would have if she needed him to.

She sniffled and looked up at him. "Do you remember that time junior year, when you sneaked into my window and stayed with me all night?"

"Yes." How could he forget?

"It was the anniversary of the fire...of my mom's death. I'd spent the morning at the cemetery with my dad. By the afternoon, he was wasted. He came in my room and apologized. I know he felt as guilty as I did, but...he told me he was sorry for making me ugly."

He held her tighter. She'd called him in tears that night, and he'd sneaked out of his house to comfort her. He hadn't planned on staying all night, but the way she'd clung to him, snuggled into his side as he lay next to her in her bed...he couldn't have left her alone.

She pulled away to look into his eyes. "Do you remember the date that happened?"

He shook his head. "It was sometime in the summer."

"It was June twenty-sixth. Eleven years ago, today."

"Oh, Erica. I didn't realize." No wonder her emotions were such a mess. It was the anniversary of the most horrible day of her life, and he'd tried to treat it like any other day. If he'd used his brain, he would have remembered; she'd told him the date years ago. But he'd been too concerned with taking her out on a date…with his own emotions…than with the pain she must have been enduring. *Jackass.*

She chuckled. "Look at me. Wasted like my dad. The apple doesn't fall far from the tree, does it?"

"You aren't wasted. And so what if you had a little to drink? You're allowed to drown your sorrow every now and then."

"You were always there for me when I needed you." She held his face in her hands and rose onto her toes to kiss him. "Will you be here for me now? I don't want to be alone."

His heart pounded in his throat. "You want me to stay the night?"

"I promise I won't try to make a move on you."

What if I want you to? No…he couldn't think like that. "Good, because I don't think I could resist you if you did." Dear Lord, he was going to do this. Was he insane or a glutton for punishment?

She led him by the hand to her bedroom and switched on a lamp. A deep-purple duvet covered her queen-sized bed, and an ornate, oval mirror sat propped against the wall on a desk in the corner.

Erica slipped off her shoes and glanced at the mirror. "Probably best if we keep our clothes on, huh?"

"Probably so." He groaned inwardly. Keeping his clothes on was the last thing he wanted, but in her condition and with the significance of the date, doing anything more wouldn't be right.

They climbed into bed, and she snuggled into his side like she did all those years ago. With her head resting on his shoulder, she draped her arm across his chest, and he held her tight.

"When I called you that night, back in high school, and you came over…I was fully prepared to lose my virginity to you, but you never made a move. Thank you for that."

His stomach tightened, and he squeezed his eyes shut. God, how he'd wanted to make a move that night. Like he wanted to make one now. But when he made love to Erica, he wanted it to be for the simple reason that she wanted him. Not because she was hurting, and not because alcohol had lowered her inhibitions. "You needed a friend. I was happy to be that for you."

"You're the best friend I've ever had."

He stared at the ceiling. A shaft of moonlight cut through the room, illuminating two of the ceiling fan blades. How different would his life have been if he'd had the courage to tell her how he felt all those years ago? If she had offered herself to him that night, would he have had the nerve to take her? Probably not, and it didn't matter anyway.

She was here now.

The woman of his dreams lay in his arms, and he wasn't doing a damn thing about it. He needed to tell her how he felt. To let her know friendship wouldn't be enough this time. He wanted her to be his and his alone.

He swallowed the thickness from his throat. "Erica?"

Her only response was the soft rise and fall of her chest as she slept on his shoulder.

CHAPTER EIGHT

Bright sunlight painted the back of Erica's eyelids red. She rolled to her side, and the dull ache in the base of her skull spread to the front. Clutching a pillow, she inhaled deeply, filling her senses with Gage's masculine scent, and her stomach tightened. She blinked her lids open and ran a hand down her side. Still fully dressed.

She sat up. The sound of something sizzling in a skillet and the rich aroma of brewing coffee beckoned her. She smiled. After everything she'd put him through, Gage hadn't left yet.

Sliding out of bed, she tiptoed to the bathroom mirror and glanced at her reflection. Mascara stains streaked her cheeks, and her braid had matted itself into the precursor for a giant dreadlock. She grimaced. She'd been a mess last night and all but begged Gage to stay during her breakdown. He'd asked her on a date, and she'd turned it into a fiasco.

She washed her face and rebraided her hair before padding into the kitchen.

Gage slid an omelet onto a plate and smiled. "Good morning, sunshine. How are you feeling?" The cheerfulness in his voice warmed her chest.

"A little headache."

He put the plate down and held her gaze, concern tightening his eyes. "You were pretty upset last night. Are you going to be okay?"

"I'll be fine." She half-smiled. "Thanks for putting me back together when I fell apart."

His eyes softened, and he pulled her into a firm hug. "Any time."

She leaned her face into his chest and breathed in his musky scent, enjoying the way his strong arms felt wrapped around her. He smelled like comfort. Felt like home.

She cringed as the memory of last night flashed through her mind. "Thank you, also, for making me keep my clothes on. I'm sorry for...everything."

"Nothing to apologize for." Kissing the top of her head, he guided her into a chair and then put the other omelet on the table. With two cups of coffee in hand, he slid into the seat across from her. "They're ham and cheese. I hope that's okay."

"This is great. Thank you." The myriad of emotions tumbling through her body had her stomach turning, but she forced herself to eat the food he'd made for her.

Gage took a few bites of his omelet. "I noticed you salted your apartment. Are you having trouble with ghosts here too? The one you talked to before we came in?"

Somehow, she'd managed to drag him through her door without breaking the protective ring last night. Had he been anyone else, she'd have made up an excuse for the salt being on the floor, but she didn't have to with him.

The burden of that heavy secret no longer weighed her down. "No trouble. It gives me some peace while I'm at home."

"Makes sense."

She gazed at the man before her, his blond hair still disheveled from sleep, and her heart gave a squeeze. Gage was sweet, sexy, honest…and he was there for her when she needed him, like he always had been. "I meant what I said last night. You really are the best friend I've ever had."

The corner of his mouth twitched as he took a deep breath. "Had you been sober last night, and come on to me like you did, things would have ended very differently." He pinned her with a heavy gaze as if willing her to understand the meaning in his words.

She did understand. He wanted more than friendship, and honestly, she did too. There was no denying the way her pulse raced every time he was near. Gage was the only person who truly saw past her disfigured skin to the human beneath. But if they weren't compatible as a couple, she could lose him as a friend. Was she willing to take that chance?

"I should go." He rose and carried the plates to the sink. "Sure you're going to be okay?"

"I'm fine." She followed him to the kitchen and put a hand on his arm. "I'll clean this up."

Pausing, he took a deep breath and turned to face her. He opened his mouth as if to speak, but he blew out a hard breath and shuffled toward the door.

She needed to say something. To give him an answer to the silent question hanging between them. Could they be more than friends? Would it be worth the risk?

"Gage, I…" She hugged him. She didn't have an answer.

He wrapped his arms around her and kissed her cheek. "Bye, Erica."

"Bye."

She watched through the window as he shuffled through the parking lot and climbed into his Jeep. What the hell was her problem? The most amazing man she'd ever met just walked out her door, and she'd let him go. He could meet another woman tonight and forget all about his feelings for her. How would she feel if that happened? What would she do if it didn't?

Well, that was a royal fuck up if he'd ever experienced one. Gage put his Jeep in drive and headed home to change into his running clothes. A nice, long jog through the park might clear his mind and help him figure out exactly what he'd done to screw this up.

And maybe how to fix it.

Somehow, they'd gone from her trying to undress him, to undressing herself, to him trying to be a gentleman and not take advantage of her. And in his efforts to do the right thing, he'd landed himself smack in the middle of the friend zone. Again.

He made it home, changed, and then headed to the park. With his sneakers laced tightly and his headphones blasting a classic rock playlist, he jogged along the path around the man-made lake. A family of ducks waddled down the bank, each fluffy duckling plopping into the water and paddling off behind its mother. Thoughts of his nieces and nephews, with their chubby cheeks and high-pitched giggles, curved his lips into a smile.

Coming from a family as large as his, he'd always

assumed he'd have three or four kids of his own someday. He'd be the kind of dad who was always around. Home on the weekends and right after work. Helping with homework and baseball practice, driving to dance classes. Whatever his kids needed, he'd provide it. He'd be the man his own father never was.

But if he couldn't get his act together and convince Erica he was worth her time, he'd never have a chance of seeing that dream come true. Building a future with anyone but her was inconceivable. It had to be Erica. He picked up his pace as he passed the lake and followed the gravel trail into a wooded area of the park.

Erica had feelings for him. That had been obvious at the theater that afternoon. Friends didn't kiss each other the way they had in the auditorium. Maybe she was embarrassed this morning after her emotional display the night before. Maybe she just needed a little time to compose herself.

Cooking breakfast in her apartment might have been overstepping his boundaries. He had made himself at home in her kitchen. Could she have been upset about that?

Who knew? Her emotions had been like an old, rickety, wooden rollercoaster, jerking one way only to spin around and jut in another direction. She'd lost her job. She'd relived the memory of her mother's death, which was way more guilt-ridden than he'd ever known. She was busy trying to run a theater. How could he expect her to want to start a relationship on top of all that?

More than anything, Erica needed a friend...and being friends seemed to be his specialty.

Erica let out an exasperated breath and marched to her bedroom. Add her mixed up emotions for Gage to the long list of problems she needed to solve. Her number one priority should have been figuring out how to make her theater successful, but she couldn't get her mind off the way she'd felt wrapped in Gage's arms.

Plopping into her desk chair, she gazed at her reflection in the antique mirror. Some of the silver had tarnished, leaving dark spots around the edges of the glass. Maybe if she had it re-silvered, the renovation would wake up the ghost sleeping inside it. Haunted or not, the thing was so old it had to be worth at least a few hundred dollars. Lord knew she needed all the money she could get. Her savings account would run dry eventually. "If you aren't going to talk to me, Colette, I think I'm going to list you on eBay."

The image shimmered, clouding her features in a sparkling fog. She straightened, leaning forward to peer into the glass. Her heart raced. "Colette?"

The fog receded, revealing the image of an elegant woman with dark, curly hair piled high on her head. A few shiny ringlets hung down around her face, accenting her delicate jawline, and a black choker with an ivory cameo adorned her slender neck. The spirit narrowed her dark eyes. "You wouldn't dream of it."

"Colette!" Erica grabbed the mirror frame and fought the urge to kiss the glass. "I was afraid you weren't there anymore!"

The ghost flipped a hand in the air. "I'm trapped in here. Where would I go?"

She released her grip on the frame and leaned back in the chair. "I tried to summon you. Why wouldn't you talk to me?"

The spirit arched an eyebrow. "No one *summons* Colette DeVeau. I hadn't decided if I wanted to speak to you. You've been a blubbering mess since you brought me here."

Erica straightened her spine. "I've gotten all the blubbering out of my system." Colette never had patience for weakness or tears. If she wanted her to stick around, she'd have to be strong from here on out. She had so many questions, needed so much help, but the one that had been burning in her mind for months had to come first. "What happened to Mrs. Spencer?"

Colette pressed her lips together and shook her head. "Such a sad ending. The poor girl went nuts. I heard dementia mentioned, but she never confided in me. All I could do was watch her fall apart." She stared off into the distance, a faraway look falling across her features.

Erica chewed her bottom lip. That didn't make any sense. "Do you know why she killed her husband? I didn't think dementia turned people violent."

The ghost's eyes turned cold, pinning Erica with a hard stare. "He was holding her back. Keeping her from her dreams. Men do that, you know? She had the potential to turn that theater into something spectacular. It took three years to convince the man to let her renovate. We were planning a grand performance, but he wouldn't let her invest the money into the show."

"Really?" That didn't sound like Mr. Spencer at all. "He always seemed so supportive."

"Men will always crush your dreams." Her eyes softened, a sympathetic smile curving her cherry-red lips. "But you already know that, don't you?"

Erica slumped her shoulders as a pang of regret for all her wasted years flashed through her chest. "I sure do."

The spirit made a *tsk* sound. "You were my protégé, Erica. You were going to be a star, until you followed that *dreadful* boy off to Hollywood. I'm still not sure I can forgive you for that."

"I'm not sure I forgive myself…but that's over. How can I make it up to you? I own the theater now, and I've got one class going. We have a production scheduled for the end of the summer, and I'm going to start advertising. I just don't have enough kids on board to keep it afloat. Can you help me?"

Colette regarded her and tapped a finger against her chin. "You don't need advertising, darling, you need a grand show. A performance of *Showboat* to rival Broadway. Pull out all the stops. Props, costumes, lighting, a live orchestra. Once people see what kind of show you can put on, they'll flock to your theater."

Erica chuckled. "If I had the money to put on a grand show, I would. Right now, I'll be lucky to afford costumes from a run-down resale shop. What else can I do?"

Colette crossed her arms. "Do you want to be a success, or don't you?"

A successful teacher and director, yes. Being a business owner didn't appeal to her in the slightest, but Mrs. Spencer had wanted her to do it. She'd try to be a success for her. "Of course I do."

"Then you'll do as Colette says."

A sour feeling formed in her stomach. She'd have to start from scratch. New scripts. New sets. The kids would have learned all those lines and blocking for nothing. What would they think of throwing out everything they'd worked on for the past six weeks?

It was risky. Then again, Colette had been a Broadway star in her time. Not just a star, she'd been in with the directors and producers. She knew the ins and outs of the entire business, so her advice was worth its weight. "I suppose I could cancel the ads and get my money back. But that still won't be enough to pull off a show like you're suggesting."

"Beg, borrow, steal. Do whatever you have to do to make it happen."

Erica let out a slow breath, the sour sensation in her stomach creeping its way into her throat. "I don't know, Colette…"

"Well, if you don't want my help, I'll leave." Her image faded as the sparkling fog retreated from the glass.

"Wait."

The translucent image reformed, and the ghost arched a delicate eyebrow, crossing her arms and drumming her fingers against her biceps.

"Okay. I'll see what I can do."

The spirit smiled triumphantly. "Good. And get rid of that boy you brought home last night too."

Her breath caught. "Gage?"

"Men are only good for one thing, and he didn't even give you that. Well, two things, but he didn't look like he had money. Get rid of him."

Now that Gage was back in her life, she couldn't imagine living without him. "He won't cause any trouble. He's just a friend." After the way she'd acted last night… and the way she'd brushed him off this morning…he'd probably already decided she wasn't worth pursuing a relationship with anyway.

"Boys and girls can't be friends. Someone always wants more. Make sure it isn't you."

"I'll be careful." Careful to keep her relationship with

Gage a secret from the spirit. She couldn't afford to lose either of them.

"Go clean yourself up and come back to me when you have a plan." The spirit dissipated with the fog, leaving Erica staring at her own reflection.

Well, now what? She rose from the chair and shuffled to the bathroom to clean herself up like Colette said. Turning on the shower, she dropped her clothes to the floor and stepped under the steady stream of water. The heat relaxed her muscles, but it did nothing to slow the river of thoughts raging through her mind.

Colette wanted a grand show. And *Showboat* of all things. Did the spirit have any idea how much it would cost to produce? Even if Erica had a full schedule of classes going, she wouldn't be able to afford a show like that. The set alone would cost the equivalent of three months' rent. And a live orchestra?

She laughed as she worked the lilac-scented shampoo through her hair. Even if she could pull it off, she'd be in debt up to her eyeballs. And what if it didn't work? What if she put on Colette's grand production and no one signed up for fall classes? What if no one came to the show? Then what?

She rinsed and shut off the water. Colette had never steered her wrong before. The spirit was rigid in her ways, always insisting Erica follow her stage directions exactly. She'd never been wrong about acting. Why should Erica doubt her now?

Anyway, she was an adult, and she was allowed to say no. The live orchestra was out of the question, but surely she could pull off the rest of the production. She didn't have to do *everything* the spirit insisted.

And she certainly didn't have to "get rid" of Gage. Wiping the fog off the bathroom mirror, she gazed at her reflection. Gage hadn't even flinched when she'd taken her shirt off last night. He didn't frown or scowl or do anything to hint at being disgusted by her appearance. Even her own father still grimaced sometimes when he looked at her.

When Gage looked at her, a fire sparked somewhere deep inside her soul. He truly was the nicest man she'd ever met, and she owed it to him—to herself—to explore these newfound feelings. If their friendship could survive ten years apart, it could survive one more date.

That's what she would do. She'd take it one date at a time. Have a nice dinner. Talk about him rather than herself the whole time. Dinner. She could do that.

She threw on a pair of sweatpants and a long-sleeved T-shirt and tiptoed past the mirror. Swiping her phone from the table, she slipped out onto the balcony and dialed Gage's number. He answered on the first ring.

"Hey, Gage. Do you think..." She blew out a breath. All she had to do was ask him out. It was a simple question, so why was she having such a hard time pushing the words over the lump in her throat? "Can I have a do-over?"

"A do-over?" He sounded skeptical.

She picked at a piece of flaking paint on the banister. "Yeah. You asked me on a date last night, and I screwed it up. I was hoping you'd give me another chance. I promise to behave this time."

Silence hung between them. She peeled the chip of paint from the railing and flicked it over the side. A sinking feeling formed in her stomach as she watched the brown flake float to the ground. He was probably thinking of a nice way to let her down. To tell her she'd had her chance, and she'd blown it. Her heart pounded so hard she could feel each pulse of blood as it rushed through her veins. "If you don't want to, I understand." She held her breath.

"I'm free tonight."

She let out her breath in a giggle. *Real smooth. Get it together.* "Tonight's good."

"I'll pick you up at seven."

She bit her bottom lip and glanced through the window at the mirror in her bedroom. If Colette found out what she was doing, she may refuse to help her with the theater. "What if I came to your place, and we can go from there?"

He paused. "Yeah. That's fine. Still seven?"

"Text me your address, and I'll be there."

CHAPTER NINE

Gage shoved the last of the supplies into his backpack and wiped his sweaty palms on his jeans. Certain he'd blown any chance he had of starting a relationship with Erica, he'd jumped at the chance for a do-over on their date. He had one more shot, and he would not screw it up.

The bell rang, and he swung the backpack over his shoulder and opened the door. Erica stood on the porch, her hair glistening in the light of the setting sun. She wore a teal, long-sleeved shirt that hung loose over her hips and the sexiest pair of skinny jeans he'd ever seen. Teal Converse matched her shirt, and her smile made him forget to breathe.

He stepped outside, shutting the door behind him. "You look beautiful."

Casting her gaze downward, she smoothed her braid over her shoulder. "Thank you."

She was obviously not used to hearing compliments. He'd have to change that. He took her hand, running his thumb from the unmarred skin to her scar. "I mean that."

She met his gaze. "I believe you. What's the backpack for?"

"It's dinner." He patted the pack. "Oh, I almost forgot." Yanking the door open, he grabbed a blanket from the sofa and tucked it under his arm. "We're having a picnic."

She smiled. "That sounds nice."

"I hope so." He'd scoured the Internet all afternoon for ideas for a romantic date. They'd tried dinner and drinks, and that had ended badly, so he wanted something different this time. Something more personal. Taking her to see a play had crossed his mind, but he had no idea what she'd already seen and what she hadn't over the last ten years. Plus, seeing a play or a movie would require two hours of silence. He wanted to explore the possibility of a relationship, and that would require conversation.

He drove her to the park and spread the blanket under a willow tree near the lake. The long, drooping branches created a canopy around them, and the deep orange sun painted the sky in shades of red and purple.

Kneeling on the blanket, he unpacked the supplies as Erica settled next to him. "Sandwiches, cheese, fruit, and dessert."

She giggled. "Twizzlers?"

"Best candy ever." He pulled out a box of Godivas. "I brought chocolate too."

"Oh, dark chocolate. That's my favorite."

"I remember." He caught her gaze, and his heart gave a thud. His mom had liked to keep a big bowl of Hershey's Miniatures in the kitchen when they were young. Every time Erica had come to their house, she'd picked out the Special Dark bars and left the rest.

Her smile brightened her eyes. “This is so nice. No one has ever gone to this much trouble for me.”

“It was no trouble at all.” He handed her a sandwich and scooted closer to her. They ate in silence for a while, staring out over the lake, watching the ducklings dip their heads in the water, imitating their mother. They'd pull their bills up and shake their down feathers, turning themselves into little fluff balls floating on the surface. Erica leaned into him, and he let out a satisfied sigh. Their do-over was going well so far.

She finished her sandwich and folded up the wrapper, stuffing it into the bag. “Tell me more about D.A.P.S.”

“What do you want to know? You said you've seen the TV shows.” He bumped her shoulder with his.

She smiled, taking his wrapper and adding it to the bag. “Do you go around getting rid of people's ghosts?”

“Sometimes. But only our psychic can actually get rid of them. Most of the time, we just gather evidence. You'd be surprised how many people want to keep their ghosts once they find out they're harmless.”

“Hm.” She rubbed her hands together. “I'd love to learn how to help them cross over.”

“Allison's on vacation with her husband, but I'm sure she'd be happy to help you when she gets back.”

“Do you ever think about quitting your day job? Hunting ghosts for a living?”

A professional ghost hunter. That would be some job...not that there was much money to be made in paranormal investigation. Unless a team landed its own TV show, they'd never make enough to survive. “I've thought about it, but I like my job. Staying up all night and then going over hours of evidence the following days can take a toll on you. I like the balance I have right now.”

"That makes sense." She nibbled on a piece of cheese.

"What about you? Are you looking for another job, or are you focusing on the theater now?"

She inhaled deeply and let out a heavy sigh. "I haven't decided. I want to make the theater work. I love teaching. It's the business side of it…dealing with budgets and scheduling and trying to increase enrollment. It's not as fun as I thought it would be."

"Maybe you can find a partner. Get someone else to run the business, while you teach the classes."

"I have…someone who's helping me. Her advice is kinda scary though."

"Oh?" He turned toward her, resting a hand on her knee.

She glanced down to where he touched her, and a tiny smile curved her lips. "She thinks I should funnel all my money into putting on a huge production with the kids I have. That once the community sees this grand show, people will be lining up to take my classes."

"Sounds risky." And not the smartest way to get a business running, especially when she had no other income.

"I know. But she's a former Broadway star. She knows what she's talking about. I just… What do you think I should do?"

She definitely shouldn't pour all her resources into one show in hopes that it would be enough to draw a crowd, but it wasn't his decision to make. "I think you should go with your gut. Do whatever feels right."

She looked into his eyes. "That's good advice."

Advice he needed to follow, himself. And with the way she looked at him…like he was the only man in the world...he'd be an idiot not to follow his own gut. "You know what feels right to me?"

Her gaze drifted to his mouth before returning to his eyes. "What?"

His heart pounded. "Being here with you."

She smiled and drifted toward him. "There is a certain rightness here, isn't there?"

"There certainly is." He reached his hand behind her neck and pulled her in for a kiss.

She came to him willingly, parting her lips to let him in. Warm. Inviting. She ran her hand halfway up his thigh and squeezed, sending blood rushing to his groin. He leaned forward, laying her back on the blanket, and she moaned into his mouth. Damn, this felt good. Way better than his teenage mind could've ever imagined. Her taste. Her scent. Her soft curves pressed against him. He'd fantasized about being with Erica more times than he could count, but he'd gotten it all wrong.

This. The real her, clutching his shoulders, searing his skin with her kisses...this was *so* right. If they hadn't been in public, he would've taken her right there on the blanket. Instead, he pulled away slightly, catching her lower lip between his teeth.

She slid her hands into his hair, pulling him back for more, and he planned to give her everything she wanted. He glided his hand up and down her tender curves until something warm and wet plopped onto his shoulder.

"What the hell?" He rolled off her and tugged on his shirt to see what had landed on him. Another drop splattered onto his stomach.

Erica shot to her feet, but it wasn't until three more golf ball-sized bombs splatted on his shirt that he realized what was happening.

He scrambled to his feet and yanked the blanket from beneath the tree. "Shit."

Erica giggled. "Literally."

"What the hell kind of bird is that? An ostrich?"

She peered into the branches. "I think it's a raven."

"No way a raven can shit that big." His shirt was covered in bird crap from the top of his left shoulder, clear down to the hem in front. And the smell… "Dear God, this stinks."

Erica laughed and rolled up the blanket. "I guess that's our cue to leave."

"Apparently." He grasped the back of his shirt and yanked it over his head, carefully avoiding the splattered shit. "Did any get in my hair?" He shook his head, gently running his fingers through his hair to avoid smearing any crap that might have landed on his head.

Erica's eyes widened, the smile fading from her face as she swallowed and licked her lips. "Your hair is fine. Your body is…uh…" She cleared her throat. "You must work out."

He hadn't expected that reaction from her…or any reaction really…when he'd taken his shirt off. He'd just wanted the stinky shit away from his body. But now that he had her attention… He chuckled. "Nah. I don't have time for the gym."

"You must do something to look like that."

He shrugged. "I go rock climbing."

"Fascinating." Her smile returned as she slinked toward him and ran her fingers across his chest. His stomach tightened at the feel of her soft touch on his skin. "My nerdy boy-next-door has grown into an incredibly sexy man."

He slid his free hand to the small of her back. “I’m still a nerd.”

“A sexy nerd. I like it.”

Dear lord, did she have any idea of the fire she lit inside him? If he didn’t get her into his bed soon, he would spontaneously combust. He tossed his dirty shirt into the backpack and wrapped his other arm around her. “I like *you.*”

She rose onto her toes and placed a gentle kiss on his lips. “I like you, too. Want to head back to your place?”

“That sounds like an excellent idea.”

“Let me throw my shirt in the wash real quick. Make yourself at home.” Gage kissed Erica on the cheek and sauntered down the hallway.

She couldn’t help but smile at the fluid way he moved, the way his muscles contracted beneath his smooth skin. Her heart and her stomach seemed to be tangling themselves up in a frantic dance that was both sickening and exhilarating at the same time. She needed to calm herself down before she passed out on the floor.

He disappeared around a corner, and she finally focused on her surroundings. A huge television hung on one wall, and a dark-brown leather sofa sat across from it. An aloe vera plant occupied a small table near the window, and a bookcase full of paperbacks stood adjacent to the sofa. What kind of books did a man like Gage read?

She padded to the bookcase and ran a finger along the spines. Thrillers. Mysteries. Lots of paranormal reference books. Her smile widened. He even had a few romance novels on the shelf.

She picked up a volume on demonology and flipped through the pages. Frightening illustrations of monsters and shadow creatures stared back at her. She shivered and returned the book to the shelf.

"Find anything interesting?"

She jumped at the sound of Gage's voice. "I see you're a Nora Roberts fan."

"Those, uh…" He chuckled. "I'd like to say they aren't mine, but it's kinda obvious they are, isn't it?"

She held her thumb and forefinger close together. "Little bit." She turned toward the bookshelf, and he moved behind her, sliding his arms around her waist and nuzzling into her neck.

He hadn't bothered to put on another shirt. "I have eclectic tastes."

Her heart sprinted. "Those demonology books…is that for real?"

"Unfortunately." He reached for one of the volumes, running his thumb across the spine. "Demons are very real."

She swallowed. Did she really want to know the answer to her next question? "Have you ever met a demon?"

"Twice." He dropped his arm to her waist.

She twisted in his embrace to look into his eyes. "What happened?"

"I vanquished them." A cocky smile curved one corner of his mouth.

"Really?"

He shrugged. "I had help, but, yeah. Nasty little suckers."

"Wow." This sweet man with the bright, kind eyes and gentle touch could vanquish demons. He was smart, hot, brave, nice…everything a girl could want, all wrapped up in a sexy, muscly package.

She ran her hands across his stomach, marveling at the softness of his skin contrasting with hard sinew beneath. Gliding her fingers up his chest, she hooked them behind his neck and brushed her lips to his—a gentle, teasing kiss before she pulled away. She wanted this man like she'd wanted no other. Could he possibly want her too?

She looked into his eyes, frozen by the smolder in his gaze. "Your apartment is nice."

"Would you like to see the rest of it?"

She swallowed the dryness from her mouth. "I'd like to see your bedroom."

Closing his eyes, he inhaled deeply, touching his forehead to hers. "Are you sure?"

She bit her bottom lip. Was she sure? Making love to Gage would change everything. The innocent friendship they'd shared as kids would be forever morphed into something else. Something more.

She wanted something more.

"I'm sure."

He gazed into her eyes, boring into her soul, giving her plenty of opportunity to change her mind. When she didn't waver, he took her hand and led her down the hallway. As he crossed the threshold, he flipped on the light switch and pulled her into his arms.

Her resolve crumbled. What was she thinking? A man as hot as Gage had probably been with dozens of women. With her hideous appearance and lack of experience, he was sure to be disappointed. And then what?

Sex with Carter had been mechanical. Always missionary. He hardly touched her, and when he did, it was only the unscarred side of her body. She'd lie there, mostly clothed, and he'd do his thing, and then they'd be done. Gage had shown her more passion in a single kiss than her ex had during their entire relationship. She'd never even had an orgasm.

She pressed her palms against his chest. "Gage?"

"Hmm?" His breath against her neck raised goose bumps on her arm.

"There's something you need to know."

"What's that?"

"This is…" She pushed him away so she could see his face. She had to be able to gauge his expression. "You'll be the second man I've ever been with."

He held her gaze. "Okay."

"I don't want you to be disappointed."

"Erica." He put his hands on her shoulders. "The only way I could possibly be disappointed is if you changed your mind. And even then, it would be all right. Are you changing your mind?"

"No." The word left her lips so easily. "I'm not changing my mind. I want you." God, did she want him. "I just wanted you to know."

"Okay." He brushed her braid behind her shoulder and took her face in his hands.

His thumb brushed the scar on her cheek as he leaned in to kiss her, and she shuddered. "Will you turn off the lights?"

"Sure." He flipped on a bedside lamp and turned off the overhead light.

But it was still too bright. He'd see too much. "Can you turn that one off too?"

He stepped toward her, sliding his hands over her hips, nuzzling into the unscarred side of her neck. "Then I won't be able to see you."

"I'll keep my shirt on then. It will be hard for you to stay turned on if you have to look at me."

"What?" He pinned her with a heated gaze. "Erica, I *want* to see you."

Heat flushed her cheeks. He couldn't possibly mean that. "It's okay. I understand. Really."

He shook his head. "You don't understand anything. Come here." He tugged her toward the closet and closed the door to reveal a full-length mirror.

She recoiled. "I don't need to see my scars. I know they're repulsive."

"Don't look at yourself. Look at me." He stood behind her and pulled the band from her hair, loosening the braid. Gliding his fingers to her scalp, he lifted her hair from her shoulders and trailed his lips along the scarred side of her neck. "Look in my eyes, Erica. Do I look like a man who's repulsed?"

She caught his gaze in the mirror, and her pulse pounded in her ears as he slid his hands across her stomach, pulling her back to his front. "No." Her voice came out as a whisper.

He grasped the hem of her shirt, and she held her breath as he tugged it over her head, dropping it to the floor. Surely, he'd flinch or at least look at her with pity.

His eyes held nothing but passion. He glided his fingers down her arms and slipped his hands around her waist, touching each side of her body equally, as if she were whole. His touch didn't linger on the rough spots. He didn't pull away at the unnatural sensation her marred skin must have provided to his fingers. "It doesn't hurt for me to touch you, does it?"

Her heart pounded harder in her chest as his gaze traveled up and down her body, his touch caressing her with an intimacy she'd never felt before. "No. It feels different; there's nerve damage, but…no pain anymore."

He unhooked her bra, dropping it to the floor before running his hands up her stomach to cup her breasts. "Does it feel good?"

She sucked in a sharp breath. "Yes." Though not for the reason he probably thought. On her scar, she couldn't feel much more than pressure. As his fingers lightly grazed her chest, goose bumps only rose on the uninjured side.

What felt good was the *way* he touched her. The heat in his eyes as he caressed her as if the scar didn't exist. As if he *liked* what he saw. As if he wanted her.

The warmth of his bare chest against her back sent shivers running down to her toes. He held her as if she were precious, his touch tender yet possessive at the same time.

He unbuttoned her jeans and slid down the zipper, his gaze never straying from hers in the reflection.

Her stomach tightened. "It goes all the way down my leg."

"Have I given you any indication that I'm not completely turned on so far?" He pressed his arousal into her back to prove his point.

She shivered. "No."

As he worked her jeans over her hips, she cringed at the thought of him seeing her granny panties. She didn't own a set of sexy lingerie. She'd never had the need. Never felt sexy before. Never had man look at her, much less touch her like Gage did.

He helped her step out of her pants and sank to his knees as he slipped her underwear down her legs. Running his hands up her thighs, he gripped her hips and pressed his lips into her lower back. A tingle ran up her spine.

Rising, he wrapped his arms around her waist, pulling her close against his chest. The sensation of his firm body against hers had her trembling.

"You're beautiful. Don't listen to anyone who tells you otherwise." His voice held so much conviction she could almost believe him.

She twisted in his arms and took his mouth with hers. A deep rumble emanated from his chest as he opened up to let her in. He held her tight. Kissed her hard. Every feminine urge in her body flared to life as he slid his hands down her back to cup her butt. "I want you, Gage."

"I want you to have me." He released his hold. "Lie down."

As she crawled onto the bed, he rummaged through a dresser drawer, pulling out a condom and then laying it on the nightstand. He dropped his pants to the floor, and her eyes widened at the bulge in his underwear. As he peeled the gray fabric down, his erection sprang out, long and hard. Her fingers twitched with the urge to touch him.

His chiseled body was sculpted to perfection, with muscular arms, a solid chest, and rippling abs. And his dick… Holy moly, she couldn't wait to have it inside her.

He chuckled. "My eyes are up here, sweetheart."

"There's just so much to look at. You're…wow."

"I'm glad you approve." He climbed onto the bed and lay on top of her.

The feel of his lips on her skin as he trailed kisses down her neck had her aching with need. "Make love to me, Gage."

"Oh, I will. After I've memorized every inch of you." He glided his lips lower, running his hands over her body. Touching. Kissing. Tasting her. *All* of her.

Never in her life had she felt beautiful, but the way

Gage held her, kissed her, his teeth and tongue grazing her skin as he worked his way down her body, made tears well in her eyes. She swallowed the thickness from her throat and blinked them back. She would not ruin this moment by crying, even if they were tears of sheer joy.

He spread her legs, settling his shoulders between them, kissing and nipping at her inner thighs as if one of them didn't look like it should have been on a monster. As he neared her center, her stomach tightened. The warmth of his breath on her sensitive parts had her insides twisting with need.

When he slipped out his tongue to taste her, a shudder ran through her body, rocking her very core. A satisfied *mmm* vibrated across his lips as he slid a finger between her folds. The warmth of his tongue, the friction he created inside her…it was unlike anything she'd ever felt. She fisted the sheets in her hands as tension coiled in her body so tight she thought she'd explode.

"Gage. Oh, my God." A soul-shattering orgasm ripped through every part of her, splintering her senses as she frantically grabbed at his shoulders, wave after wave of searing pleasure turning her muscles to gelatin. Dear lord, what had he done to her? Moisture collected in the corners of her eyes, but this time she couldn't stop the tears from trailing down her face. He'd given her so much more than an orgasm. He'd made her feel *wanted.*

As the intensity faded to a pleasurable ache, she wiped the tears away before he noticed. He rose onto his arms, a drunken smile curving his lips, and she reached for him, pulling his face to hers. "That was the most incredible thing I've ever felt."

He chuckled and whisked the condom from the

table. "I'm not done with you yet." Tossing the packaging aside, he rolled the rubber down his shaft. "Are you ready?"

"God, yes." She'd never been more ready for anything in her life. She needed this man.

He pressed against her, pausing to gaze into her eyes, building the anticipation that already had her core coiled into a tight spring. This moment would change everything, and she was *so* ready for it.

He pushed into her, filling her completely, penetrating her very soul. Groaning into her mouth, he kissed her passionately as he moved inside her. "Erica, this feels so good."

All she managed was a primal moan in response. He had no idea how good it felt for her. Wrapping her legs around his waist, she gripped his shoulders, clinging to him. He buried his face into her neck…the damaged side…paying no mind to her scarred skin or mangled earlobe. He simply made love to her. All of her. And it was the most beautiful moment she'd experienced in her entire life. As his rhythm increased, another orgasm built in her core, releasing in an explosion of ecstasy.

He grunted, twisting his hands in her hair, as his own climax overtook him. His body shuddered, a deep moan emanating from his chest to vibrate in his throat. As he relaxed on top of her, she loosened her grip and glided her fingers along his sweat-slickened skin. His breathing slowed, and he inhaled deeply, rising onto his arms to look at her.

She reached for a tangled mass of her hair to pull over the side of her face, but he caught her hand.

"You don't need to hide from me, okay?"

She bit her bottom lip and nodded. He'd seen every

inch of her. Touched and kissed every part. And still he looked at her like she was a treasure.

"Don't go anywhere." He rolled out of bed and tossed the condom in the trash before pulling back the sheets and climbing in next to her.

She snuggled under the covers next to him, resting her head on his shoulder, and he wrapped his arms around her, pulling her tight to his body, kissing the top of her head. She wanted to say something. She felt the urge to thank him for making her feel wanted for the first time in her life. But the words sounded too shallow and flat to describe the emotions swirling through soul.

Instead, she lay there silently, listening to steady rhythm of his heart beating in his chest, basking in the afterglow of making love to her best friend.

He ran his fingers through her hair. "I have to go to work tomorrow."

She squeezed her eyes shut. The reality of her lack of employment was the last thing she wanted to think about now. She was falling for Gage, hard and fast, and if she could stop time and spend forever in this moment, she'd do it in a heartbeat. Unfortunately, she had to face reality and the fact that Gage was asking her to leave.

"If you don't mind—"

She rose onto her elbow. "I understand. I'll get dressed." She tried to sit up, but he caught her arm and pulled her to the pillow.

"I was going to say that if you don't mind getting up early, I would like you to stay the night with me."

"Oh." Warmth spread through her chest. "I don't mind."

"Good." He reached across the bed and turned off the lamp, casting the room in darkness.

She cuddled into his side and draped her arm over his chest, letting the quiet hum of the air conditioner paired with the steady thud of Gage's heart lull her to sleep. There was definitely no going back to the way things were before. She wouldn't want to if she could.

CHAPTER TEN

Gage stared at Chelsea's name on his phone screen and debated pushing the call button. Having his little sister involved in his love life was the last thing he needed, but if he screwed up this relationship with Erica, he'd never forgive himself.

She hadn't said much when she'd left that morning. As soon as his alarm went off, she'd slipped out of bed and gotten dressed. Erica had thanked him for the evening, and he'd said something idiotic like the pleasure was all his and told her he'd call her. Then he'd walked her to the door, kissed her goodbye, and watched her walk away… like a dumbass.

He'd slept with his best friend. He should've said something. Asked when he could see her again. Told her she was the only woman for him. Anything. But, no, he'd let her walk away. *Asshole.*

He hit the little green button before he could change his mind. Chelsea answered on the second ring.

"Oh, my God. You slept with her, didn't you?"

He cringed. "What makes you say that?"

"Why else would you be calling me at seven-thirty in the morning? She just left, didn't she? Or are you leaving her place?"

"She left mine."

"Okay. What's the plan? Wait…dammit. I need to get on the elevator. Meet me for lunch at Antonio's at noon. And *do not* call her before we talk."

"Why not?"

"Promise me you won't. I have to go."

"Okay. Bye, Chels."

Damn. Now what was he supposed to do? Surely Erica wouldn't expect a phone call before lunch today. She knew he had to work. He could play it cool. Hopefully his sister would have some solid advice for him, and he wouldn't screw anything else up.

He shoved his phone in his pocket and headed to his Jeep. Traffic on the way to work did nothing to calm his nerves, and by the time he made it into the office, his fingers itched to dial Erica's number. But he'd wait a little longer.

He couldn't fight his smile as he slid into his desk and powered on his workstation. Making love to Erica last night had been beyond his wildest expectations. Sure, she'd been shy and reserved, but when she'd cried out his name as she came, he'd nearly lost it right then. And the way she'd felt wrapped around him, squeezing him… He needed to stop thinking about it before he gave himself a raging hard-on right there at his desk.

She was still self-conscious about her scars, but he would change that. Hopefully, with time, she'd learn he didn't give a damn about whether or not her skin was smooth. Someday, she'd believe him when he told her she was beautiful.

He busied himself rebuilding a computer, and when lunchtime rolled around, he jetted out the door to meet his sister.

At the restaurant, he found Chelsea sitting at a table by the window, impatiently drumming her bubblegum-pink nails on the red-checkered tablecloth. She glared at him as he approached. "You didn't call her yet, did you?" Typical Chelsea. Straight to the point.

He slid into the seat across from her. "It's good to see you, too. How have you been?"

"We don't have time for chitchat. Your happily ever after is hanging in the balance here. Oh, and I ordered you your usual roast beef sandwich. I hope getting laid hasn't changed your tastes." She smirked and sipped her tea.

"That's fine, and no, I haven't called her. But I don't get why I'm not supposed to." It was all he'd wanted to do all morning.

"Didn't you read any of the articles I sent you?"

"Some of them." He'd read every damn one, and was even more confused than before he started.

"The rule is you need to wait at least a day to call after you have sex."

He laughed. "I thought that was the rule for calling after the first date. This wasn't our first date. And anyway, it's Erica. It's different." Surely all these crazy relationship rules didn't apply to dating his best friend.

"It won't be different if you don't listen to me. You don't want it to turn out like it did with Allison and Roxanne..."

"Rochelle."

"And every other woman you've attempted to date, do you?"

He crossed his arms. "No." She had a point, but

damn. Waiting a full day to call her when he couldn't get her off his mind seemed wrong. They'd connected. The entire dynamic of their relationship had changed overnight. Shouldn't he at least let her know he was thinking about her?

A server delivered their sandwiches and gave Gage a glass of water. As the waiter scurried away, his friend Trent approached the table. He wore a charcoal suit and carried a paper bag in one hand and a Styrofoam cup in the other. He tucked the bag under his arm and reached out a hand to shake. "Hey, Gage. How you been?"

Gage stood and shook his hand. "Good, man. How about you? No more trouble with spirits in your house?"

"Haven't heard a peep."

Gage turned to Chelsea. "This is Trent, he had the shadow entity I told you about."

She cringed. "I'm Chelsea, Gage's favorite sister. You're braver than me staying in that house. I would've moved out the first chance I got."

Gage glared at his sister. "I've told you things aren't that simple."

"I know. I know. Hey, why don't you join us for lunch, Trent?"

He took the bag from under his arm. "I don't want to impose."

"You're not imposing. Come on." She pulled out a chair and practically shoved Trent into it.

Gage sighed. His sister never did know how to take no for an answer.

"I was just telling Gage he shouldn't call the girl he slept with last night." Chelsea grinned and took a bite of her chicken salad.

Gage huffed. "Let the man eat his lunch, Chels."

Trent chuckled. "Oh, man. That's none of my business."

"I want a man's opinion on this," Chelsea said. "He slept with his best friend last night. They didn't talk about it before she left this morning. Tell him he should wait a day to call her."

Trent took a bite of his own food and cut his gaze between Gage and Chelsea as if he wasn't sure he wanted to get involved. Gage groaned inwardly at the thought of yet another person having an opinion on his love life. Then again, Trent was happily married…his advice might be more helpful than his twenty-two-year-old sister's.

"You slept with her, and then you didn't talk about what that meant for your relationship?"

"Exactly." It was a dick move. He should've said something, but he'd been too caught up in the afterglow to think clearly.

"That's a tough one, man. On the one hand, you don't want to seem too needy. It might be good to give it some time to simmer. Let her come to terms with how she feels about it."

Chelsea leaned forward, smiling smugly. "See, I told you."

Trent shrugged. "On the other hand…if you guys were good friends already, you might want to get it sorted out quickly. I don't know what to tell you, except go with your gut."

Gage gave Chelsea a pointed look. "My gut says to call her."

She rolled her eyes. "And going with your gut has worked out so well for you in the past."

Trent rose to his feet. "I've got to get back to the

office. It was nice to meet you, Chelsea." He shook her hand and clapped Gage on the shoulder. "Good luck, man."

"Thanks, Trent. See you."

He turned to Chelsea as Trent strode away. "I want to call her."

"Please don't. Just wait one day. Call her tomorrow afternoon." She took his hand across the table. "Trust me on this. Please?"

He sighed. If waiting a day, giving Erica some time to think, would help him not make an ass of himself, he could do that. It went against everything his gut was telling him to do, but Chelsea was right. He couldn't allow himself to fuck up this relationship too. "Okay. I'll wait until tomorrow. But you better be right about this."

Erica sat at the makeup table in the theater wing, staring at the ghostly image of Colette in the antique mirror. "I can't believe Amber didn't show up for her private lesson." Today seemed to be chock-full of disappointments from people she thought she could count on. "I'm going to call her."

"No, don't." Colette's image solidified in the glass. "I'm telling you, dear, if she doesn't have the drive to show up, she has no business being your lead."

"She's an amazing actress. Wait until you see her perform." Erica had brought the mirror to the theater to get the spirit out of her house. She'd assumed her personal life was about to get much more personal after last night with Gage, but the day was almost over and he still hadn't called.

"I've seen…better, I'm sure." The spirit faded to a translucent mist.

"You keep fading. Do you need to recharge? I should call Amber and make sure she's okay." She paused, a foggy image flitting through her mind. Her student standing on the stage rehearsing her song, Erica pacing through the seats.

She shook her head. Amber hadn't shown up for her private lesson; she'd remember it if she had.

Colette darkened for a moment before fading again. "You need to let it go. Let them both go."

A sharp pain shot through her heart. After the way Gage had made her feel last night…the things he'd done for her…*to* her… She never should have told the spirit what she'd done. "I don't want to."

The ghost rolled her eyes. "You got a night of great sex out of it. If they don't have money, that's all men are good for. That boy is taking up too much of your mind when you should be focusing on the show. Have you bought the rights yet? Have you started looking for costumes? A tech to run the lights?"

She picked at a piece of imaginary lint on her shirt. "I was hoping Gage could run the lights."

The spirit sighed. "When are you going to start listening to Colette, dear? He's a man. They're all the same."

He was probably busy. Maybe the server went down at work, and he'd spent all day trying to get it back online. Or he had a lot of computers to repair. Or maybe he was waiting for her to make the next move. "I should call him."

"Don't." Colette's image solidified as she reached an arm toward Erica. The spirit almost seemed three-dimensional, as if her hand had penetrated the glass she'd been trapped in for decades.

Erica squeezed her eyes shut. When she opened them, the ghost appeared behind the glass like normal. "He was shy when we were kids. Maybe he still is."

"Never put yourself at the mercy of a man. If he really wanted you, he would have called by now. Forget about him."

She had a point. Gage had been shy when they were young, but not with her. Aside from never telling her he'd had a crush on her, he'd always been open with her. And even if he was busy, a text only took five seconds to send. He could've at least done that. Erica straightened her spine. "You know what? You're right. He's obviously not the same sweet guy I used to know."

Colette smiled. "Of course I'm right, dear. I've had ages of experience."

He'd led her on, gotten what he'd wanted, and now he was done with her. Some best friend he turned out to be. She should've known something was up when he didn't mention seeing her again when she'd left his apartment. He'd just given her that dreamy, sleepy smile and kissed her goodbye.

The morning after hadn't felt awkward at the time, but the more she thought about it, the more awkward it became in her mind. He probably regretted sleeping with her. Maybe he'd done it out of pity.

Anger burned white hot in her chest. A pity fuck. That's all it had been to him. "I'm so mad at him."

Colette nodded. "You should be mad. He used you."

She glanced at the ghost in the mirror. "Thanks for talking some sense into me. I'm going to head home."

"Aren't you going to take me with you?"

She considered the heavy, oval mirror. It was awkward to carry, and she'd nearly dropped it coming down the stairs this morning. "I can't keep carrying you back and forth. You'll be better off staying here anyway. You can watch the kids and help me coach them."

The spirit pursed her lips, crossing her arms to tap a finger against her bicep. "True. You will be spending most of your time here now."

"I've got nothing else to do." Her body ached, her stomach growled, and she was so mad at Gage she couldn't think straight. Some food, a hot shower, and a good night's sleep would make her feel better. "I'll see you tomorrow."

A wave of nausea rolled through Erica's body. Her vision blurred, and she swayed on her feet. This was the second time she'd experienced the strange sensation today. Blinking her gaze into focus, her own reflection stared back at her from the antique mirror. She glanced at her watch. Eight p.m. Hadn't it been seven a minute ago?

"Colette?" She tapped on the glass.

A shimmering mist filled the mirror as the spirit's translucent form came into view. "I'm running out of energy, dear. What is it?"

"Weren't we just talking?"

"Yes, and you said you were going home."

"But…" She rubbed her temples. She had said that, hadn't she? But she could've sworn it was seven when she did. She'd been thinking about getting some dinner. Or had she been…? Confusion clouded her mind. What had she been doing? "I think I lost an hour. How long have I been standing here?"

Colette flipped a hand in the air. "A few minutes,

maybe? I don't know. I need to recharge, and so do you, darling."

The ghost faded, and Erica blinked at her own reflection. She shook her head. Some sleep would definitely do her good. All this stress was affecting her brain, and she needed to get it together if she intended to make this theater work. She had enough in her savings account to pay the rent and utilities for three months. That should be plenty of time to pull the show together.

And with Gage apparently out of the picture, she'd have nothing to distract her from her mission. She took a deep breath and blew it out with conviction. She could live without him. She'd made it through the past ten years just fine.

CHAPTER ELEVEN

Gage stared at his phone and gripped a pencil so tight it broke in half in his hand. It had taken every ounce of willpower he could muster to keep himself from calling Erica last night. Hell, he'd had to turn the damn phone off and bury it in the bottom of his drawer, but he'd done it.

And now he felt like the biggest ass on the face of the planet.

Why had he listened to his sister? Not calling Erica had been a mistake. Every cell in his body had screamed at him to call her. To tell her how he felt. That he wanted to be hers and hers alone. Now she wouldn't take his calls.

He'd tried three times this morning. Every one went straight to voicemail.

"Dude, could you stop with the leg bouncing?" Adam called from across the room. "Some of us are trying to work."

"Sorry." He stilled his nervous jitters and checked the clock. Eleven a.m. "I'm going to take an early lunch."

Adam lifted a hand to wave but thankfully didn't look

up from his keyboard. Gage wouldn't have to explain the sweat beading on his forehead in a sixty-eight-degree workroom. If Erica wouldn't take his calls, he'd go see her in person. Apologize profusely. Hell, he'd beg for forgiveness if he had to.

He drove by her apartment complex, but he couldn't find her car in the parking lot. If she wasn't home, she must've been at the theater. It made sense. The place was her only source of income now. Maybe she was there with her friend who was helping her plan that big show she'd talked about. Hopefully she'd be there alone.

He parked in the theater parking lot next to Erica's car and strode to the entrance. Pulling on the front door handle, he found it unlocked. The auditorium door hung wide open. He'd have to talk to her again about keeping them locked when she was here alone. Though the place was located in an upscale part of town, there was no need to tempt the fates.

"Erica?"

He crept down the aisle toward the stage, scanning the rows of seats, but the auditorium sat empty. Eerily quiet. As he reached the front row, the air temperature around him plummeted as if an arctic wind gusted through the room. Every hair on his body stood at attention, saluting the electric buzzing sensation crawling across his skin.

He let out a breath, creating a fog in front of him. "Whoever you are, you've got my attention."

The seat next to him unfolded and popped back into its normal position.

"Are you Leroy or Stanley? Or someone else?" Though the two stagehands were the only spirits he'd met when D.A.P.S. investigated, there could've been more ghosts hanging around. Sometimes when dormant spirits became active again, they drew in other ghosts from the area. Even in death, it seemed humans sought out the company of others.

Another seat flopped down and popped back up. Then another a few spaces down, as if the spirit were leading him toward the right side of the stage. If he'd thought to bring his backpack inside, he could've used an audio recorder to communicate with the ghost. If it had something to say—and it seemed like it did—he might have been able to hear the spirit's disembodied voice on the recorder.

He usually carried a few pieces of paranormal equipment with him whenever he knew he'd be in a haunted location…just in case. But this time, his mind had been occupied with apologizing to Erica. At least he had his priorities straight now, Erica being number one, and all those stupid dating rules not even making it on the list.

Climbing the short row of steps to the stage, he caught a glimpse of Erica in the wing. She sat at a makeup table, the halo of lights shining brightly around her. The antique mirror he'd seen in her bedroom sat propped against the makeup mirror, and Erica leaned toward it, running a brush through her long, loose hair.

Frigid, buzzing energy pressed against him, almost as if trying to keep him away. He stepped through it, and the electricity dissipated. The curtain ruffled, and as he took another step forward, warmth returned to the air.

Erica didn't seem to notice his presence, so he entered the wing and stood behind her. "Hey."

Narrowing her eyes briefly as if she were confused, she tilted her head slightly. "Gage." She said his name as if she were recognizing him for the first time. Rising to her feet, she pushed the chair aside and faced him. Her hair fell behind her shoulders, revealing the thick layer of stage makeup she'd applied to the scar on her face and neck.

She used to apply this type of makeup for the shows in high school, when she'd been an actress herself. From a seat in the house, her skin would've appeared smooth. She'd told him it was the only time she'd ever felt normal. When she could pretend to be someone else, like her past didn't exist. Up close, though, the scar was still obvious. The makeup almost comical.

"What's with the stage makeup? Are you putting on a one-woman show tonight?" He chuckled, trying to lighten the mood.

A strange intensity flashed in her eyes, like she wanted to ravish him and strangle him at the same time. "Why would I do that?"

He couldn't blame her if she wasn't in the mood for jokes. She was probably furious with him. He cleared his throat. "I tried to call this morning a few times."

She tilted her head to the side. "Hmm. I must've turned my ringer off. I was very angry with you."

"Yeah. About that. I'm really sorry I didn't call you yesterday. I was trying so hard not to screw this up, and I took some very bad advice from Chelsea."

She prowled toward him, her gaze raking up and down his body. Slipping her tongue out to moisten her lips, she caught her bottom one between her teeth. "Chelsea?"

His heart sprinted. With the hungry look in her eyes, he didn't know whether to be turned on or scared. "My little sister. Are you okay?"

She touched his shoulder, gliding her hand down his arm, and moved closer to him, her body mere inches from his. Her breath warmed his cheek as she leaned in. "Do you want me, Gage?"

"You know I do. I've always wanted you." He'd do anything to make her understand how much she meant to him.

"Prove it." She slipped her hand between them, rubbing his dick through his jeans.

His stomach tightened. This was a side of Erica he hadn't seen before. It was sort of…sexy…but not quite right. Not really *her.* He swallowed. "Now?"

Pulling back slightly, she moved her hand to his stomach, sliding it beneath his shirt. "Unless I'm not attractive enough for you."

"Erica, you're beautiful. How many times do I—"

She popped the button on his pants and slid her hand beneath his clothes to grip his cock.

"Oh, hell." He hardened in her grasp, and he pulled her closer, planting a passionate kiss on her lips. If this was what she needed, right here, right now, he would give it to her. He'd give her anything.

With a hand on his shoulder, she pushed him away, never releasing her hold on his dick. "If you really want me, you should take me right now." She shoved him into a chair and straddled him, hiking her skirt up around her hips.

Pulling her panties aside, she sheathed him, her wet warmth enveloping him, scattering his thoughts to the wind in a million microscopic pieces. Not that he had time to think. She rode him hard and fast as if she were a completely different woman than the timid angel he'd made love to days before. She gripped the back of the chair and moaned as she came, and his own orgasm ripped through his body, turning his muscles to jelly.

She let out a contented sigh before rising to her feet and straightening her clothes. Turning to the mirror, she ran her fingers beneath her eyes and around her lips to fix her makeup.

Dazed and a little breathless, Gage buttoned his pants and watched her as she gazed at her own reflection in the mirror. "Does this mean I'm forgiven?"

She looked at her watch. "Aren't you supposed to be at work?"

"I'm on my lunch break." He stepped behind her, sliding his arms around her waist. "Have dinner with me tonight?"

"Sure."

He caught her gaze in the reflection, and she flashed a tight-lipped smile. She may have forgiven him, but she hadn't forgotten. "I promise to make it up to you."

She pulled from his embrace. "You better get back to the office. You don't want to lose your job too."

"All right. I'll see you at seven?"

She narrowed her eyes at her purse sitting on the table. "Text me the time. I've got a lot to do here, and I don't want to forget."

"Okay." He eyed her skeptically. She was acting strange, but he obliged and texted her. *I will make it up to you. See you at my place at seven.*

She pulled the phone from her purse and typed a response. *I'll be there.* "Now I'll remember."

"I hope so." What was going on with her? "Are we good now?"

"Of course."

Her half-smile was less than convincing, and when he wrapped his arms around her, kissing her on the cheek, she didn't turn to him. Didn't kiss him back. He released his hold, and she busied herself cleaning the makeup mess. "I've got a lot to do. I'll see you later."

He hesitated to leave. Two nights ago, she'd been afraid she was too inexperienced for him, and now she'd ravished him in an almost animalistic act of passion. Not that he was complaining, but what had gotten into her? "Are you sure everything's okay?"

"Just peachy." She gave him another half-smile. "Bye, Gage."

"Bye, Erica."

He shuffled across the stage and up the aisle to the exit. No spirits tried to get his attention on his way out of the theater. Shielding his eyes against the bright sunlight, he jogged through the parking lot and slid into his Jeep. That encounter didn't go anything like he'd planned. Her behavior had been…confounding. Had she really forgiven him, or was she trying to prove a point?

She had every right to be angry with him. Tonight, he'd make it up to her. He'd make a candle-lit dinner in his apartment, and screw the advice columns, he'd buy her flowers too. Then he'd tell her how he felt, and hopefully she'd say she felt the same. No more rules. No more games. He would follow his gut and get his woman.

Erica opened her eyes and lifted her head from the desk. Had she fallen asleep in the theater? She rubbed the sore spot on her temple and gazed into the mirror. Her skin felt dry and flaky, as if she'd washed it with hand soap and forgotten to moisturize. She glanced at her watch. Six-thirty p.m.

"What the hell? How did I lose seven hours?" She tapped on the mirror. "Colette?"

The ghostly image appeared, though her translucence made her barely visible. "What are you still doing here?"

Erica opened her mouth to speak, but she closed it. What was she doing there? She'd gotten to the theater around ten that morning. Discussed her plans with Colette, and then... What? "I'm not sure. I think I fell asleep."

"I'm not surprised. You were very busy today. You'd best check your messages and go home. The scripts will be here tomorrow, and we've got rehearsals scheduled every night until show time."

She blinked, her mind reeling as she tried to connect the pieces of what the spirit was saying. "Wait. We do? How are the scripts getting here tomorrow? I haven't ordered them." Or had she? A vague memory, as translucent as the spirit before her, flashed in her mind, but she couldn't grab onto it long enough to make it seem real.

Colette shook her head. "You ordered them this afternoon, dear. Overnight shipping. Well worth the cost, if you ask me."

Okay, so that part was real. Why couldn't she hold on to the memory? "And the rehearsals?"

"E-mails sent out to everyone. All the actors are on board. I really must recharge now. Have a good night."

The ghost faded until only Erica's sallow reflection stared back at her. Had she really done all that today? The entire day seemed like a fog in her mind. She rose from the chair and shuffled to her office. Pulling up her theater e-mail account, she found a group e-mail sent to all of her kids requiring rehearsals five nights a week plus Saturday afternoons.

A vague memory of typing the message flitted through her mind, but nothing solid would form. The proof she'd done it stared her in the face, though. Was she going crazy?

What had the kids said about Mrs. Spencer? That she didn't know upstage from down by the time her life had ended. Was something in the theater affecting her? Mold? Asbestos? Maybe the so-called friendly spirits weren't as friendly as Gage thought. She said hello to them every morning, and they hadn't caused her any more problems… Unless they were making her brain foggy.

She could ask Gage, but… An image of him standing in the wing flashed through her mind, and her mouth went dry. Of him sitting in the chair, her straddling his lap. She shook her head. That had to be a dream. She may not remember sending an e-mail, but she would never forget having sex with Gage.

She grabbed her purse and headed for the door. She'd been spending way too much time in this place. Locking the doors as she exited, she pulled out her phone and checked the screen. Her heart fluttered. Gage had messaged her. *I will make it up to you. See you at my place at seven.*

And, apparently, she'd responded. *I'll be there.*

When had she typed that message? Was she going out of her mind? Could he really have stopped by the theater today and apologized? She pictured herself standing in front of the mirror, Gage standing behind her, sliding his arms around her waist.

That couldn't have happened, because that would mean the rest of her dream had happened too. And there was absolutely no way her dream had been real. She was furious with Gage for not calling. She wouldn't have done that.

She glanced at his text again and sat in her car, slamming the door. He had a lot of explaining to do if he planned to make it up to her. Putting the car in drive, she slowly pulled out of the parking lot. Maybe she shouldn't go. Let him see how it felt to be stood up. She could go home, not answer the phone when he called to see why she didn't show.

Then again, what would that prove? That she could be just as stubborn as him? And he hadn't exactly stood her up, had he? He simply hadn't called. Her stomach sank. She hadn't called him either. If he wanted to make it up to her, she at least owed him a chance to explain.

She drove to his apartment and knocked on the door.

Gage grinned as he opened it, sweeping her into his arms and carrying her across the threshold. His masculine, musky scent filled her senses, the warmth of his embrace melting the tension in her muscles. She allowed herself five seconds of pleasure in his arms before pushing him away. "Stop."

He furrowed his brow. "What's wrong?"

The dream she'd had of him in the theater grew clearer in her mind, flushing her cheeks with heat. Fisting her hands at her sides, she chewed the inside of her cheek as she chose her words. "You can't sleep with me, ignore me for two days, and then act like everything's okay. You at least owe me an apology…and an explanation."

He dropped his arms by his sides. "I gave you both this afternoon, but I'll say it again." Stepping toward her, he rubbed his hands on her shoulders. "I was so afraid of screwing this up, of scaring you away, I took some very, *very* bad advice from Chelsea of all people. She convinced me not to call so I wouldn't seem too clingy. She said I should give you time to process what happened between us, and even though I knew in my heart I should have called you, I didn't." He took her hands in his. "It's not an excuse...just an explanation. I'm sorry, Erica. Please forgive me for my temporary lapse in judgement. It won't happen again."

"I..." She stepped back, pulling her hands from his grasp. His words sounded so familiar, like she'd heard this excuse before. Her thoughts scrambled, and she couldn't focus on exactly what she'd heard, but... Had he really been at the theater this afternoon, or was this simply a case of déjà vu? If he was at the theater, did she really...? She rubbed her temples. "I don't know."

"Are you okay?" The corner of his mouth pulled into a crooked smile. "I thought after you pushed me into a chair and had your way with me, all was forgiven."

Her stomach dropped. "I did not have my way with you, Gage. What are you talking about?" She couldn't have. She'd never be so bold. It was a dream. It had to be.

His eyes tightened with concern. "Why don't you come sit down, and I'll get you a glass of water. You're looking a little pale."

"I don't want to sit down."

"I made dinner. Look." He gestured toward the table. A bouquet of pink roses acted as a centerpiece with candles on either side.

The savory scent of thyme floated in the air, and she shuffled toward the table in a daze. She peered at the candles, and her chest tightened. He hadn't forgotten her aversion to open flames; the candles were flickering LEDs.

If she'd been in her right mind, she'd have accepted his apology, sat down at the table, and had a nice dinner with him. But something was very wrong.

She rested a hand on the back of the chair. "You're saying you came to the theater this afternoon?"

"Yes. Don't you remember?"

She backed toward the door. She did remember, but she didn't at the same time. Everything…her memories of the entire day were cast in a haze. "I…don't know."

He reached for her but let his hand drop to his side when she recoiled. "We didn't use a condom. Are you on birth control?"

"I…yes, I am, but…" She fumbled with the door-knob. She needed to leave. To get away from Gage and figure out for herself if the things he said were true. *Please don't let them be true.* The memory grew more vivid in her mind, the haze dissipating like a fog burning off the damp grass in the sunlight. If she had done those things, she hadn't been in control of herself.

"Please don't leave."

She pulled the door open. "I'm sorry, Gage. I need to think."

He caught her by the hand. "What's going on?"

She slipped from his grasp and paused on the porch. "Can ghosts…control you?"

"They can get inside your head if they're strong enough." He stepped through the doorway and lowered his voice. "Are you having trouble with the spirits at the theater?"

Her chest felt like a solid block of ice that quickly spread through her veins. One of the so-called friendly spirits had been controlling her mind. It was the only explanation. "I have to go."

She turned on her heel and darted through the parking lot. Playing the foggy memories of the day through her mind on the short drive home, she still couldn't comprehend what had happened to her.

She'd ordered scripts she wasn't sure she wanted to

order. Planned rehearsals for a play she hadn't yet fully committed to. Had sex with Gage in the theater wing. Nausea churned in her stomach. *What must he think of me now?*

Why would Leroy or Stanley, *male* stagehands who died ages ago, make her do those things? They rarely showed themselves to her, and once she acknowledged their presence, they hadn't messed with the lights or caused any more problems. Unless they were pretending to be someone they weren't. Could ghosts even do that? Or maybe Colette… No, she was trapped inside the mirror. What could she do?

Erica had been able to see ghosts since she was a kid, and they'd never gotten inside her head before. Why would they start now?

She was stressed. That's all it was. People acted out of character in extreme circumstances all the time. Though her circumstances weren't *that* extreme—lord knew she'd been through much worse—surely the stress of the situation was getting to her.

But what she'd done with Gage… Her abdomen tightened as a flush of hot humiliation spread through her body, melting the ice in her veins. How could she face him again?

CHAPTER TWELVE

What the hell? Gage dropped into a chair and leaned his elbows on the table. He'd been able to dismiss Erica's peculiar behavior at the theater for the sheer relief that she'd forgiven him...or so he thought. But for her to not remember him being there, much less having sex with him, was beyond strange. The unexpected way she'd acted. The bizarre look in her eyes as she'd prowled toward him... Erica wasn't the type to prowl.

It was almost as if she'd been...possessed.

Shit. He shot out of the chair and raced to his bookcase. Pulling volume after volume of paranormal references off the shelves, he stacked them on the coffee table and began his research. He scoured the texts, searching for anything that resembled what had happened to Erica that afternoon. After an hour of reading, pausing only to turn the damn oven off before he burned the place down—so much for that candle-lit dinner—he'd come to one conclusion. She hadn't been possessed by a demon.

Too many tell-tale signs of demon possession hadn't been present in Erica. Her eyes hadn't glazed or gotten glossy…they'd been hungry. Her movements had been fluid like whatever was controlling her had experience with a human form. That meant whatever got inside her had been human once itself.

But could a ghost exert that much control over a living being? He'd seen the long-term effects channeling too many spirits could have on a medium, but he'd never witnessed anything like what he'd seen this afternoon. Unfortunately, the one person who could answer his questions was vacationing seven thousand miles away. Allison had told him to call her if anything urgent came up with D.A.P.S…

He checked the clock. Eight-thirty p.m. What time would it be in Fiji? Twelve-thirty tomorrow? One-thirty? It was afternoon, anyway. Hopefully she'd have her phone on her. He dialed her number and prayed the call would go through.

"Hi, Gage." Allison's cheerful voice rang in his ear.

"I'm so sorry to bother you on your vacation."

"It's no problem. We just finished lunch. What's up?"

He let out a hard breath. "I need some psychic advice."

She chuckled. "I can't do readings over the phone. You know my ability doesn't work that way."

He switched the phone to his other ear. "Not that kind of advice. I have this…friend. Her name's Erica."

"Oh? A girlfriend?" Her voice raised an octave as if she were smiling.

"Maybe. I don't know. Anyway…Is it possible for a spirit to possess someone? I'm not talking about channeling like you do. Not communication through a living person, but can they actually make a living person do and say things against their will?"

She paused, the humor draining from her voice. "It's

possible. The ghost would have to be incredibly strong though."

He shot to his feet and paced the living room. "Has it ever happened to you?"

"Logan's ghost got inside my head, remember? I might've jumped out the window if you guys hadn't stopped me. What happened to Erica?"

"Nothing dangerous like that." He plucked a rose from the vase and pressed the soft petals against his nose. The sweet smell tickled his senses, reminding him of the floral scent of Erica's hair. "She was acting…out of character today. She did some things I don't think she'd normally do."

"Like what?"

His face flushed with heat, and he returned the rose to the vase and resumed pacing. "I'd rather not say."

She cleared her throat. "Can I ask *where* it happened?"

"Remember the old theater we investigated on Center Street? She owns it now."

"I remember that place. Leroy and Stanley were the ghosts we encountered there, right?"

He ran a finger over the spines on his bookshelf, pausing on a title by Nora Roberts. "Yeah."

"They aren't strong enough to control someone like that. Maybe the former owner is there now?"

"I don't think so. Erica would have told me that. She can see spirits."

Allison paused. "If she's a medium, she should be able to figure out what happened to her."

Gage sighed. "She's a medium, but she doesn't know how to control it. Says she can only see the spirits if they show themselves to her. She's owned the place for two months and didn't know it was haunted until I told her."

"Oh, wow. Well, I'll be happy to check it out for her when we get back in town. Do you think you can handle it until then?"

He chuckled. "I can handle anything." *Hopefully.*

"Based on what you've told me of the situation, all I can say for certain is that it's *possible* a strong spirit got ahold of her, especially if she can't control her psychic abilities. That makes her more susceptible to possession. But it's also possible she was acting out of character for another non-supernatural reason."

The knot in his chest loosened. "I guess that's true. I do tend to jump to the first paranormal conclusion I can find, don't I?"

"Yes, and you're right a lot of the time. But sometimes things aren't as complicated as they seem. Try not to let your emotions cloud your judgement."

He sank onto the sofa. "Thanks, Allison. You're right, as usual."

"Talk to her about it. If the problem continues, especially if things turn violent, call me. If we need to come home early, we can."

"It won't come to that." No way in hell would he let it escalate into a problem he couldn't handle. "Thanks again, Allison. Tell Logan 'hi' for me."

"I will. Bye, Gage."

Talk to her. That's what he'd been trying to do all day, and damn it, he'd keep trying until she listened. He dialed her number—of course it went straight to voicemail. That left him only one option. He grabbed his keys and headed for her apartment.

Gage climbed the steps to the second floor and knocked on her door. Silence greeted him. He knocked again, harder this time. No answer. She had to be home;

her car sat in the parking lot. He tried one more time, pounding with the side of his fist.

The lock disengaged. Erica peered at him sleepily through the crack in the door. "Gage? What are you doing here?"

"We need to talk. Can I come in?"

"Okay." She opened the door wider, and he stepped inside. She wore blue satin pajama pants, her bare toes peeking from beneath where they skimmed the floor. Her pink, long-sleeved T-shirt clung to her braless breasts, and he could just make out the outlines of her nipples.

He reminded himself to breathe. "First off, I want to say again that I'm sorry I didn't call you."

"It's okay, Gage. Really. I understand." She sank onto the sofa and patted the cushion for him to sit.

He sat down next to her. "I'm worried about what happened earlier at the theater…and you not remembering."

She flashed a half-smile. "I'm on birth control. I should have told you."

"That's good to know. But…it didn't seem like *you*. Not the you I know. And when you came to my house, you acted like you didn't remember doing it. I'm wondering if there might be another ghost at the theater."

Her eyes widened for a moment before she furrowed her brow. "Besides Leroy and Stanley?"

"I called Allison, the psychic I work with at D.A.P.S. She doesn't believe either one of them is strong enough to possess a living person, but…"

She blinked. "You think I was possessed?"

"It's possible. Have you run into any other ghosts there?"

She stared at her hands folded in her lap. "There are no other ghosts there."

"Are you sure?"

"Gage." She put her hand on his. "I wasn't possessed. I remember doing it. I…" She sighed and wrapped her arms around herself. "We shared something the other night that changed our relationship. Things can never go back to the way they were before, and I didn't want them to." She shrugged. "Then you didn't call. I didn't know if you regretted what we did or if you didn't care. I was so angry with you. I was mad at myself, too, for thinking you were different. For believing you."

"I am different, though." He rested a hand on her knee. She didn't pull away. "I just suck at dating."

A real smile brightened her face as she laughed. "Yeah, you kinda do. I'm sorry for coming onto you like that. I don't know what came over me." She placed her hand on top of his, lacing their fingers together. "We both screwed up. Can we forget today happened? And the day before? Let's pretend I left your house this morning."

The tension in his muscles eased. Her words were tempting…and convincing. "But…your memory. You really seemed like you didn't know what happened this afternoon."

She sighed and laid her head on his shoulder. "I was confused. I had so many conflicting emotions running through my mind, I didn't know upstage from down."

A wriggling sensation in the back of his mind told him there was more to it than that, but at this point, he wanted to move on. To forget the whole debacle had even happened, like Erica suggested.

He kissed the top of her head and inhaled the sweet

scent of her hair. He needed to tell her how he felt. He'd been dancing around the subject since she came back into his life, trying to show her and failing miserably. She needed to hear the words. "So, we're good now?"

She lifted her head and kissed him on the cheek. "More than good."

"Because I need to tell you something, and I know it's too soon, and it goes against the rules of dating…but we've already established I suck at dating."

She laughed. "We both suck at dating."

He turned his shoulders to face her. "I don't even know who made up the rules, but I'm tired of following them." He took a deep breath and let it out slowly. This was either going to move their relationship forward or fuck it up royally. She either wanted to be with him or she didn't. Either way, he needed to know. "I don't want you to ever have to wonder how I feel again. No matter what happens, there should never be any doubt in your mind about where you stand with me. I want to be with you. Only you. No more dating. No more games. I want a relationship."

Her eyes brightened, and she slid her hand behind his head to pull his mouth to hers. Her lips were soft and inviting. The faint taste of minty toothpaste lingered on her tongue, making his mouth water for more.

She pulled away far enough to look into his eyes. "I only want you, Gage." She kissed him again, crawling into his lap and running her hands over his body. The once-faint outlines of her nipples beneath her shirt grew more defined as they hardened. His own arousal grew, stretching his jeans tight against his groin.

She tugged his shirt over his head and bit her bottom

lip as her gaze lingered on his chest. "I can't get over how much you've…grown up."

He held her face in his hand, running his thumb across her cheek. "It happens with age."

"You've aged well."

"So have you." He reached for the hem of her nightshirt and peeled the thin fabric from her body.

A shy smile lit on her lips as she reached to the wall behind him and turned off the light switch. She was still embarrassed of her body. He still planned to change that.

Roaming his hands over her sensuous curves as his eyes adjusted to the darkness, he pulled her close, reveling in the feel of her bare skin on his. They belonged together, and now that they'd established their relationship, it felt as if a fifty-pound weight he'd been carrying since he was sixteen years old had lifted from his shoulders. Erica was finally his.

Her breath whispered across his lips. "Make love to me, Gage."

He laid her back on the couch. With one knee on the cushion and one foot on the floor, he glided his fingers down her body, stopping to tease her hardened nipples with his thumbs before continuing down her stomach. Her breathing grew shallow as he slid her pants and panties off and rose to his feet to remove the rest of his clothes.

She raked an appreciative gaze over his body and reached for him, tugging him on top of her. "I need you."

His chest tightened at the sexy sound of her raspy voice. She needed him, and he was more than willing to give himself to her. She could have him every day for the rest of her life, and he still wouldn't tire of giving.

Running a hand down the side of her body, he lifted her thigh and guided it over the edge of the couch so his hips fit between her legs. Her delicate fingers danced up and down his back, sending warm shivers cascading down his spine.

He ran his lips across her collarbone, and her breath hitched as he pressed his tip against her. Her deliciously wet sheath beckoned him to enter, and as he slid inside her, his entire body shuddered in pleasure.

She exhaled a long, slow breath as he filled her, and she tangled her fingers in his hair, pulling his mouth to hers. She kissed him slowly, deeply, moving her hips beneath him to match his tender thrusts. As she held his gaze with her deep, dark eyes, he saw the world in them. *She* was his world.

This was the Erica he'd made love to the first time. Gentle. Affectionate. Cautiously passionate. He took his time with her, roaming his hands over her body, trailing his lips across her skin.

His climax built slowly, from somewhere deep in his soul, but he wasn't about to come unless she did first. Sliding his hand between their bodies, he found her sensitive nub and stroked it gently.

She gasped. Her hips rocked faster, pushing him closer to the edge. He met her passion beat for beat, and just as he couldn't hold back anymore, she found her release, gripping his shoulders as her body shuddered around him. His orgasm ripped through his soul, tearing his insides to shreds.

He held her tight, burying his face in her hair until his ragged breathing slowed.

She turned her face to meet his gaze, a satisfied smile playing on her lips. "I definitely only want you."

"That's good to know."

Rolling to his side, he pulled her close. The narrowness of the couch forced them to lie chest to chest, but he felt like he couldn't hold her close enough. She was the only woman for him. Forever.

She lifted her hips to adjust her position and squealed as she nearly fell backward off the sofa. He caught her by the butt and sat up, pulling her into his lap.

Her laughter danced in his ears. "I guess the couch isn't the best surface for love-making."

"I'd lie on the cold tile floor if it meant I could make love to you."

She kissed him, catching his bottom lip between her teeth and giving it a tug before letting go. "I can think of plenty more comfortable places."

"Like where?"

She grinned. "We already know the couch and your bed work, but we need to try my bed. There's also that chair." She nodded to the accent chair in the corner. "The carpet. The countertop might work if I sat on it. Oh, and the shower."

"Challenge accepted." He'd make love to her in all those spots and more. She only needed to name the time and place.

She smiled and leaned her forehead against his. "I have a confession."

"Oh?"

"Since we're officially in a relationship and everything, I thought you'd want to know..." She bit her bottom lip and trailed a finger down his chest. "Until my first time with you, I had never had an orgasm."

He blinked twice. "Never?" She couldn't be serious.

Her gaze met his, and she shook her head.

"I…wow. I'm glad I could help you experience that."

"Me too." She snuggled into his arms.

She'd never had an orgasm? He couldn't imagine what sex with her jackass ex-boyfriend must've been like if he'd never made her come. Selfish bastard.

It wasn't like getting her to climax was a difficult thing to do. He could tell what she liked by the way her breathing changed when he touched her. The way her muscles tensed, the sounds she made. And, oh, the sounds she made when she came. Watching Erica climax…being the reason she climaxed…was enough to send him over the edge every time. He pressed his lips to her ear. "There are plenty more where that came from."

She giggled. "Promise?"

"Oh, yeah. In fact…" He rose from the couch and scooped her into his arms. "I think you need to have another one."

"Now?"

"Right now." He carried her to the bedroom and made love to her again.

The incessant beeping of the alarm on Gage's phone dragged him from his peaceful sleep. He groaned as he rolled away from Erica's warm embrace to mash the stop button on the screen. With a sigh, he sat up and stretched his arms over his head.

Erica fluttered her lids open. "What time is it?"

He gazed at the beautiful angel lying next to him and leaned down to kiss her cheek. "Five. I have to go to work."

"So early?" She moved her hand beneath the sheets to glide her fingers up his thigh.

He shivered. "I left all that food out last night." He rested a hand on top of hers, stopping her from reaching her destination. "I need to clean it up."

Sitting, she let the blankets fall away from her body, exposing her breasts. She didn't bother to cover herself up.

His chest tightened. Though the room was cast in darkness, enough moonlight filtered in through the window that he could see her. Was she finally finished hiding from him?

She scooted closer and kissed his cheek. "I'm sorry I ruined dinner."

"It's okay. We both suck at dating, remember?"

"At least we suck together."

He laughed. "That's true." He slid out of bed and shuffled to the living room to retrieve his discarded clothes. When he returned to the bedroom, he found Erica still sitting in the bed, sheets draped around her waist, a sweet smile playing on her lips. As she watched him dress, her smile grew wider.

He turned his shirt right side out. "What are you smiling at?"

She dropped her gaze to the bed before blinking up at him. "You. You're so sexy and confident and sweet. Aside from dating, you seem to be good at everything you do."

He chuckled. "I try."

"Promise you're done taking advice from your sister?" She crawled to the edge of the bed and rose onto her knees.

His own knees nearly buckled. Her hair flowed down her back, leaving her glorious front fully exposed. She didn't shy away as he roamed his gaze over her body. The temptation to turn on the light so he could really see her had him reaching for the switch, but he refrained. She was already opening up to him more. No need to push it. "I promise. Chelsea and I are going to have words later, but I guarantee I'll be doing things my way from now on." He moved toward her, taking her in his arms.

She rested her head against his chest. "I like it better when you do things your way."

"So do I." She felt so damn good pressed against him, he was tempted to call in sick and spend the day in her bed. Let the rest of the world fall away for a while and just be with her. But the nagging voice in the back of his mind wouldn't be quiet until he'd fully addressed the issue from last night.

He pulled his shirt over his head. He still wasn't one hundred percent certain her behavior yesterday had been due to her emotions. Dealing with spirits was tricky business, especially when they played with the mind. But would she be willing to let him check the theater out? Honesty and openness seemed to be going well for him so far. No need to stop now.

"Would you mind if I did a mini investigation at the theater with my team tonight? I want to be sure nothing sinister is lurking in the shadows there."

She lowered her gaze to the floor. "Tonight?"

He slipped on his shoes. "I want you to be safe there."

"I'm sure it was nothing." She sat cross-legged on the bed and pulled the sheet into her lap.

"I know, but I've dealt with some nasty entities that were really good at hiding." He sat next to her. "My friends had a shadow demon living in their attic, and they wrote off the activity to their imaginations from stress. It wasn't stress." And he could never live with himself if Erica were injured because he'd let an evil spirit run loose in her theater.

Taking a deep breath, she met his gaze. "Sure. If it will make you feel better."

CHAPTER THIRTEEN

"How could you agree to this?" The ghost in the mirror fumed with anger, her image solidifying and fading in a steady pulse as the sparkling mist surrounding her darkened. "They're going to find me."

Erica shrugged. "So what if they do? They all know spirits are real. There's no need to keep your existence a secret from them."

"That may be true, but you're forgetting one important thing. They get rid of ghosts. They're going to try to vanquish me. I can't help you from the other side, dear. I have to stay here."

"They won't if I tell them to leave you be. They didn't try to vanquish Stanley or Leroy."

The ghost arched a delicate eyebrow. "I'm sure they will now, after your little display yesterday. What were you thinking having sex in our theater after you told me you were done with him?"

Heat crept up Erica's neck. If Colette had seen what she'd done with Gage, the other ghosts probably had too.

Then again, one of the other ghosts could have been what made her do it. The memory of the afternoon was mostly solid in her mind now, but she still couldn't figure out the motivation. "I don't know. I wasn't myself yesterday."

The ghost crossed her arms. "No, you weren't." The corner of her mouth quirked into a grin. "He did have a nice penis, though. I'll give you that."

"Colette, please…" Her ears burned with embarrassment.

"What? I give credit when credit is due. The man is well-hung."

She tried to suppress her smile. She shouldn't have been discussing her boyfriend's penis with anyone, much less a ghost, but she couldn't deny it. Gage did have a nice one.

"Wipe that smile off your face, dear. You need to end it with him."

The hell she did. Gage was everything she wanted in a man…and he wanted *her*. "Why do you say that?"

"He's a distraction, and he'll hurt you. It's what men do."

Erica straightened her spine. What did this ghost know about men? She'd lived in the forties. Things were different now. Gage was different. "He's not going to hurt me."

"As soon as someone pretty shows the slightest bit of interest in him, he'll leave you."

"No, he won't. He thinks *I'm* pretty."

The ghost scoffed. "He lies. It's what men do."

She fisted her hands at her sides as her body flushed with heat. "You keep saying 'it's what men do,' but they don't. Not all of them."

The foggy mist surrounding the spirit darkened. "Yes,

they do. It's their nature."

"You may know everything about the theater, Colette, but when it comes to men…you're clueless. Gage would never lie to me. He cares about me."

The spirit narrowed her eyes as if challenging her to say her next line.

"And I care about him." She crossed her arms. "This conversation is over." She'd idolized this spirit when she was young, but she was done blindly taking orders…from anyone. Gage was the man she was meant to be with, and no one could take him away from her.

The ghost inclined her head, peering down her nose at Erica. "I see. If that's the case, I suppose I'll have to live with it. But please, darling, can we keep my existence here a secret for a while? I've been trapped in this mirror for seventy years. People have tried to free me before. To send me to the other side." She shuddered. "It's painful."

"You can feel pain?"

"More than you can imagine."

She'd had no idea a spirit could feel any sort of physical sensation. They were pure energy, so how could they? They didn't have bodies or flesh to register the feelings of touch or temperature. But it didn't matter in this case. "I really don't think Gage will try to get rid of you. If I explain…"

The image of a tear rolled down the spirit's cheek. "Please. The pain is unbearable. Like being trapped inside a raging inferno. Surely you understand."

A sickening feeling formed in her stomach. She understood far too well the feeling of flesh searing in the flames. As her thoughts drifted back to her terrible accident, she shuddered. "Okay. I won't say anything yet. But I'm going to have to tell him eventually."

Colette smiled. "Give it a month. Once he's satisfied of your safety, you can break the news easily. Let him see how well we work together."

The sound of the auditorium door opening echoed through the building. "Okay. Make yourself scarce."

The spirit's image dissolved, and Erica trotted onto the stage. Gage carried a huge black duffel bag on one shoulder and a backpack slung over the other. He smiled at her as he trotted up the aisle, and her heart raced.

She hurried down the steps and ran to him, wrapping her arms around his neck and pressing a kiss to his lips. He let the bags slide off his shoulders and drop to the ground as he snaked his arms around her waist.

"It's good to see you, too, sweetheart."

Lindsay stepped through the door, followed by a round man with a beard and a tweed jacket. "Hey, Erica. How are you?"

She released her hold on Gage's neck and wrapped her arm around his bicep. "I'm good."

Gage patted her hand. "This is Richard. He's the founder of our little group."

"Hi, Richard. It's nice to meet you." She shook his hand. "Where is your medium?" She'd have to make sure she kept anyone who could actually see spirits away from Colette.

Gage wrapped his arm around her shoulders. "You're playing that role tonight. Allison is still out of town."

"Oh." The tightness in her chest loosened. With Colette trapped inside the mirror, the chances that their equipment would pick up on her were slim. A powerful medium might be able to force the spirit to show herself, but she didn't have to worry about that tonight. At least for now, the secret of her spirit mentor would be safe.

"What do I need to do?"

"Right now, help me set up. Lindsay and Richard are going to take some baseline readings of temperature and EMF around the building so we'll know if we get anything abnormal later."

She followed Gage around the theater as he set up cameras and other gadgets to record movement and changes in the atmosphere. Lindsay and Richard split off to get their readings, and an hour later, they met on the stage.

Gage balanced a laptop on one hand and typed something on the keyboard. "Find anything interesting?"

"Everything is steady for the most part," Richard said. "We got a slight EMF spike around the mirror in the wing over there." He pointed to Colette's mirror.

Erica held her breath. Had they discovered her?

"Yeah, but it faded in and out," Lindsay said. "Probably some residual energy or maybe Leroy or Stanley playing with us."

She exhaled. "I'm sure that's what it is."

Gage closed his laptop and rested his hand on the small of her back. "Let's get this show on the road, guys. Erica, come with me." He grabbed his backpack and led her off the stage to her office.

Closing the door behind them, he set his computer and bag on the desk and pulled her into his arms, roaming his hands down to cup her butt.

She playfully swatted him away. "I thought we were investigating."

He flashed a devilish grin. "I'm trying to investigate what's underneath your clothes, if you would cooperate."

She let him pull her close, losing herself to the comfort

and warmth of his strong arms holding her. "I think you know exactly what's underneath my clothes."

"Doesn't mean I'll ever get tired of investigating it." He took her mouth with his.

A slow heat spread through her body from her lips to her chest to her toes. He held her face in his hands, deepening the kiss until her muscles felt like they'd fall right off the bone. As he pulled away, his intense blue-green eyes bore into her soul, searching for something she hoped he'd find in her.

"If you'd have told sixteen-year-old me that someday I'd be making out with you in the theater office, I never would have believed you."

A sour sensation twisted in her stomach, and she pulled from his embrace as a wave of dizziness made the room spin. Her skin crawled as she sat on the edge of her desk. "Shouldn't we be helping them?"

Gage gave her a quizzical look. "They always do their thing first. Allison and I watch on the monitors while they try to gather physical evidence. After they've done their best to stir shit up, we'll go in and see what you can pick up on."

A little spark of anger ignited her chest at the mention of Allison again, but she ignored it. Where had it even come from? "How long have you known Allison?"

A wistful look flashed in his eyes. "Six or seven years, I guess. Why?"

She clutched the edge of the table as her stomach twisted tighter. "If she's so great and powerful and can communicate with spirits at her will, why do you even bother with all the technical stuff? Can't she go in and vanquish them all and be done with it?"

He put a hand on her knee, and she fought the urge to

pull away. Where was this sudden onset of negative emotions coming from?

"I don't know if vanquish is the right word. If we're dealing with a demonic entity, then yeah, we do our best to send those suckers back to hell where they belong. Ghosts don't necessarily need to leave, unless they're causing trouble for the property owner." He took her hand. "Most people want proof they can see and hear for themselves."

His touch helped ease the strange disquiet rolling through her system, but something didn't feel quite right. "Does it hurt the spirits when they cross over?"

"Hmm..." He furrowed his brow. "I never thought about it before. It doesn't seem to. I mean, I've never caught any screams of anguish on the recorders as they crossed. Allison would be a better person to ask. She's an empath too, so she'd know. She can feel other people's emotions."

She gritted her teeth. If he didn't stop talking about Allison...what? Why was she letting this get to her? She shook her head to rid herself of the strange thoughts flitting through her brain. "What if the spirits don't want to leave? Does it hurt them if you force them to cross over?"

He inhaled deeply. "I can't say we've ever had to *force* a human spirit to cross over. Sometimes they take a little convincing, but in my experience, Allison can convince the orneriest ones it's time to leave. She's good. When she gets back in town, you should meet her. I think you'd get along."

She pulled her hand from his grasp and wrapped her arms around herself. "How long did the two of you date?"

He laughed. "I never dated Allison."

"But you wanted to."

His mouth opened and closed as if he wasn't sure how to answer. "What makes you say that?"

She shot to her feet. "It's obvious. You get this… faraway look in your eyes whenever you mention her name." Didn't he? Or was she imagining it?

He stood and reached for her hand. She let him take it. "I can assure you, sweetheart, Allison and I have always just been friends."

"Friends like you and me?"

"No. Baby, no. The way I feel about you is…I…" He sighed. "I never felt this about Allison. Or anyone for that matter."

"But you liked her."

"You have no reason to worry. Where is this coming from?" He rummaged through his backpack and pulled out a device with red and green lights.

"I…" She swayed on her feet as her thoughts clouded in her mind. What were they talking about? She'd been angry with him a moment ago, but she couldn't for the life of her remember why.

He waved the device in the air around her, frowning at the darkened display. Shrugging, he dropped the tool into his backpack and pulled her into his arms. "Allison is my friend. Nothing more. Okay?"

That's right, she'd been jealous of the way he talked about his colleague. But why? It had never bothered her before. Maybe since she'd made herself vulnerable… sleeping with him, sharing secrets…now her insecurities were surfacing. She'd have to work harder to keep herself in check. She slid her arms around his waist. "I'm sorry. I don't know why I said those things. I guess I got a little jealous."

"I promise nothing has ever happened between Allison and me."

The strange thing was, she wasn't a jealous person. Gage was a smart, sexy, sweet man. His talents in the bedroom proved he'd obviously been with other women. So what if he had? *She* was his present and hopefully his future. Being jealous over something that happened in the past would do her no good.

"Gage," Lindsay's voice crackled over the walkie-talkie. "We're ready for Erica."

He let Erica slide from his arms and reached for the doorknob. He hadn't lied about Allison. Not really. He just hadn't fully answered the question about whether or not he'd had feelings for her.

Besides, how he'd felt in the past was irrelevant. Sure, he'd wanted to take his relationship with Allison past the friendship stage, but it hadn't been mutual. And the feelings he'd had for her paled in comparison to how he felt about Erica.

He'd never felt this way about anyone before. There was no need to complicate their relationship with talk of the past. He led her by the hand to the stage.

"We caught some curtain movement and flickering lights." Lindsay sat in a chair in the front row. "All the same Leroy and Stanley stuff we've gotten before. If there's someone new here, he's not letting us know."

Gage sat on the stage and let his feet dangle over the edge. "Let's do an EVP session and see if anybody wants to show himself to Erica."

She settled on the stage next to him so close their

thighs touched. His pulse raced just being near the woman; he definitely didn't need to complicate things by talking about the past.

Richard pointed a camera at Lindsay. "Go ahead and start with the questions."

Lindsay nodded. "Whatever spirits are here with us tonight; will you please tell us your names?" She paused to give the ghosts time to answer.

Gage looked at Erica, but she shook her head.

"Erica is here with us. Maybe you know her? She owns the theater now." Lindsay set the recorder on the arm of the chair. "If you will show yourself to her, she'll probably be able to see you."

Silence hung in the air for a moment until Erica sucked in a sharp breath. "Leroy is standing by the chair to the right of her." Her voice was a whisper only Gage could hear.

"Our right or her right?"

"Ours. Oh, and Stanley is next to him now."

Gage's heart thrummed, and he instinctively took her hand. "Hey, guys. Were you around when I stopped by to see Erica here yesterday?"

Her ears reddened. "I don't want to talk about that in front of your friends," she whispered. "Did you tell them what happened?"

He squeezed her hand. "I didn't give them any specifics. Did the ghosts answer?"

She rubbed her forehead. "Yes. They were here."

"So you saw what happened?" he asked the ghosts.

"Oh, God." Erica shrank in on herself. "They saw."

He rubbed her back. Though the situation made her uncomfortable, he had to push the spirits for answers.

"Now, I'm not making any accusations, but did either of you have anything to do with it?"

She placed her fingers against her temples. "No, Gage, they didn't. Can we stop now?"

He focused on the empty space next to Lindsay. "Do you know who did?"

"They're gone." Erica shot to her feet. "They looked at each other, and they disappeared."

Lindsay rose and stepped toward the stage. "Let's play back the recording and see if we caught anything."

Erica crossed her arms to hug herself. "They didn't speak. Only nodded their heads like they usually do when I talk to them. You're not going to hear them."

Gage stood next to her, and she hugged herself tighter. "Probably not, but let's give it a listen anyway. Tech is our only means of communicating with ghosts, since we aren't gifted like you."

She chewed her bottom lip as Lindsay played the recording.

"I don't hear anything." Lindsay handed the device to Gage.

He held it against his ear and listened. Other than their own voices and the low hum of the air conditioner, he couldn't hear a thing. Not a trace of the supernatural. Shaking his head, he handed the recorder to Lindsay.

Erica huffed. "I told you it was nothing."

"Okay. All right." He placed a hand on the small of her back, hoping his touch would calm her. "I think we're done anyway, right guys?"

"Yeah." Richard shook his head. "Let's pack it up."

As they gathered their supplies and Lindsay and Richard said goodbye, Erica's shoulders moved away from her ears into a more natural position. She locked the theater and held Gage's hand as they strolled toward their cars in the parking lot, but her eyes still held a tightness as if she were worried…or keeping a secret.

He shoved his bag in the passenger seat of his Jeep and put a hand on Erica's hip. "Thanks for letting me check the place out. I'll sleep better knowing no sinister spirits are hanging out in there with you." None that made themselves known, anyway.

She met his eyes, but only for a second. "You're welcome."

"I still worry about what happened, though. Are you sure everything is okay?" A strand of hair had come loose from her braid, so he tucked it behind her ear.

She rubbed her arms as if she were cold. "Yeah. Fine. It's…" Her breath came out in a huff. "I've had this secret all my life, and telling you…I was okay with that. But talking about my ability to see spirits and actually doing it in front of Lindsay and Richard didn't feel right." She chuckled. "You're so open about everything. That probably doesn't make any sense to you."

A little pang shot through his chest. He hadn't been entirely open, but he didn't want to steer the conversation toward his little un-truth. "It does, actually. You don't have to do it in front of them anymore."

"I don't think having a secret or two is such a bad thing."

He rubbed the back on his fingers down her cheek and rested his hand near her neck. "It's not. I agree. The world doesn't need to know everything about us."

She smiled, and the tightness in her eyes released. "Thanks, Gage."

"Anything for you, sweetheart." He pulled her into a hug. "Let's get out of this parking lot. Want to go to my place? I never did get to inspect what's beneath this lovely, pink shirt."

"Only if you promise a thorough investigation."

CHAPTER FOURTEEN

"Try it again," Erica said as her cast finished the scene. "Amber, remember your character is doing something she thinks she shouldn't be doing. She'd be looking around, afraid she's going to get caught. Make sure that comes across as emotion."

Amber nodded and scurried off stage to reset the scene. Erica looked at her notes. Colette's insight into the nuances of these characters was amazing. With her advice, Erica had taken her cast of teenagers to an almost professional level in only three weeks.

She couldn't give the ghost all the credit, though. The show was coming together under her own direction, but the little bits of advice Colette offered made a big difference.

She glanced at the empty light booth and sighed. Gage, still worried something in the theater might be affecting her, had come to rehearsals after he got off from work every night for two weeks. He'd made himself useful, trying out different lighting effects for the show until he was satisfied Erica and the kids were safe. She'd been teaching her classes on her own for a week, but she had to admit she missed him hanging around.

"Ms. Miller? Did we do okay?" The concern in Amber's voice pulled Erica out of her daydream.

Had the kids already run the scene? What had she been thinking about to miss the whole thing? She pretended to write something on her notepad to hide her confusion. "That was great." She looked up and smiled.

"I told you something's wrong with her," Caitlyn whispered. "She's got that blank look in her eyes again."

Jason stepped toward the front of the stage. "You're okay, right, Ms. M?"

She rose to her feet and made her way toward the students. "I'm fine. I've had a lot on my mind lately."

Daniel snickered. "I'd have a lot on my mind, too, if I had a hot boyfriend like yours. Why'd he stop coming to rehearsals?"

She shook her head. "Daniel…"

He raised his hands. "What? It's true."

Her student had a point. And if it moved the focus away from her apparent black out, all the better. "He is easy on the eyes, isn't he? Anyway…I think we've done enough today. Go home and get those lines memorized. I don't want any more stumbling tomorrow."

The kids left, and Erica locked the front door and then plopped into the chair in front of the mirror. The kids were doing fantastic, but the stress of pulling this together before the summer ended seemed to be affecting her brain. And with no advertising budget, how would she even get the word out that they'd be performing this grand production? "I'm still not sure this is the way to go."

The ghost appeared in the mirror. "You can't back out now, dear, the show is next month."

Doubt gnawed in her gut. "I know. I've sunk my entire savings into this." And if this show didn't bring in the kind of revenue Colette swore it would, she'd have to find a real job. Maybe even sell the place.

Colette's image faded, her form becoming more transparent as she spoke. "If you want to get the return you deserve, you need to make a change to the cast."

"What kind of change? We only have a month until opening night."

"Caitlyn should be the lead. She has the look. She has the voice. I've kept my mouth shut about you casting your little pet in the star role, but she's going to ruin the show."

Erica crossed her arms. With her attitude, Caitlyn was lucky she even got a role. Not that Erica could afford to let any of her students go. Even though the kids had managed to draft a few of their friends to dance in the ensemble, there weren't enough cast members to do the show justice. "Caitlyn is not playing the lead."

Colette crossed her arms, mirroring Erica's posture. "Give me one good reason why not."

"Attitude."

"What's wrong with her attitude?"

"She's spoiled and entitled, and sometimes downright mean. The lead should go to someone who's going to work for it. Not to someone who thinks it's owed to her."

"She has the guts to go after what should be hers. Caitlyn deserves the lead."

"Not in my theater."

"*Your* theater? I have just as much say as you. You'd still be wasting your money advertising a juvenile show that was sure to flop if it weren't for me. When I agreed to help you, you promised to follow my advice to the T. You can't stop now." The spirit narrowed her eyes as the shimmering mist undulated around her until it almost seemed seep outward from the glass.

Erica rubbed her eyes, and the mist disappeared. Colette was right, she had promised to do everything the ghost told her to. But she drew the line at changing the cast this late into rehearsals, especially since it was Caitlyn she wanted her to promote. "That's a neat little trick you do when you're angry, but I'm not afraid of you. You're trapped inside the mirror, and I'm done doing everyone else's bidding."

Aside from the live orchestra, she'd done everything her spirit mentor had advised so far, most of it against her better judgement. Hell, everything she'd done in her life had been for someone else. She'd followed Carter to Hollywood even though she'd been so sick about it she'd stayed up the night before puking her guts out. When she'd finally decided to give up acting and go to college, she'd wanted to become a teacher. Her dad had convinced her to get a degree in technology, saying schools were dangerous and teachers had no potential to earn a decent income. Her stupid graphic arts degree had been a compromise she regretted making. Sure, it allowed her to be a little bit creative, but she couldn't spend her life trapped inside a cubicle.

Then, three months after she'd moved back to Michigan, she'd taken on the theater and all the debt that came with it because Mrs. Spencer had wanted her to have it. But what about what Erica wanted? It was time she started living life for herself. Doing what she wanted to do. If only she could figure out what that was.

Colette's lips tightened as she regarded Erica through the glass. "I see how it's going to be." The scowl on her face said she wasn't happy being disobeyed, but honestly, what could she do?

Erica put her hands on her hips. "The cast stays as-is. We'll put on the show because I've sunk my life savings into this, but if it doesn't at least pay for itself, I'm selling the theater."

The spirit's mouth hung open. "And what will you do with me?"

She threw her arms in the air. "You can stay here and bug the next owner. I don't care."

"What if they can't see me?"

"That won't be my problem."

Colette's expression turned steely. "You won't sell this theater. Julia wanted you to run it."

Erica squeezed her hands into fists so hard her nails bit into her palms. "Mrs. Spencer is dead, and her spirit has moved on. It doesn't matter what she wanted." She stood and picked up her purse. "I didn't want to run this place to begin with, and at first I didn't think I *could* run it without your help. Having you here has been a tremendous blessing, but I'm confident enough to make decisions on my own now. I'll see you tomorrow."

She marched out of the building and locked the front door. Her phone chimed on her way to the car, a message from Gage lighting up the screen: *Want to come over? I've got something you might want to investigate.*

She couldn't fight her smile as she slid into the driver's seat. A romp between the sheets with her favorite IT guy would relieve some stress, but her argument with Colette had drained her. It had felt good to stand up for herself, but now she wanted to crash. And she'd already promised her dad she'd stop by his house for dinner.

She replied: *I would love to see what comes up during the investigation, but I have to go to my dad's. Maybe tomorrow?*

Her phone buzzed with his response. *You could stop by after…*

His offer was tempting, but… *I'm exhausted. Rain check?*

As she buckled her seatbelt, the phone rang. Gage, of course. She pressed the phone to her ear.

"Are you okay?" His voice oozed with concern.

Not really. But she didn't want to get into the details with him. "I'm fine. Tired. I need a good night's sleep." Her conversations with Colette had been getting more heated lately, and every night she seemed more tired than the night before.

"Yeah…I guess you wouldn't get much sleep if you came to my place."

She laughed. "Probably not. Why don't you come over tomorrow around seven-thirty? We can order take-out and see about that investigation."

"That sounds like an excellent idea. If there's anything I can do for you in the meantime, let me know."

A warm, tingly sensation spread through her body. Gage would drop everything to come and help her if she needed him. She was a lucky woman. "Thank you. See you tomorrow."

Erica woke the next day more tired than she'd been the night before. After she showered and dressed, she poured a cup of steaming-hot coffee and curled up on the couch with her box of memories.

Her dad had been cleaning out the garage when he'd

come across her old keepsake box. He'd given it to her after dinner last night, but she'd been too exhausted to go through it. Now, she rummaged through the remnants of her high school years, tossing aside newspaper clippings, concert tickets, and old playbills from her days in the theater.

She smiled as her fingers brushed an old photograph. Pulling it from the box, she examined the image, running her thumb across the smooth, glossy paper. In the picture, Gage leaned against the stage in the high school auditorium, his lanky arms crossed, a goofy smile lighting up his face. Though his body had changed in the ten years she'd been gone, he still had the same sweet eyes. She sat next him in the photo, leaning an arm on his shoulder as she grinned at the camera.

The picture had been taken senior year, right before the second performance of her final high school show. Gage had asked her to go to dinner afterward, but she'd politely declined, opting to hang out with Carter and his friends instead. Her boyfriend had ignored her the entire night.

Gage wouldn't have ignored her. Why had it been so hard for her to realize the perfect man was right there all along? At least she'd finally figured it out.

She shuffled to her closet and rummaged around for the frame she'd gotten at a work Christmas party last year. Glittery red and green ornaments adorned the sides and bottom of the wood, but it would hold a picture, and that was what counted. She slipped the photo inside and set it on a shelf in her living room.

Returning to the box, she dug to the bottom to find a little, silver flash drive. Gage had given it to her shortly before she'd left for California, and it contained a file she'd never been able to open. Maybe he could open it now. Or at least tell her what it was about. She set the drive behind the picture frame and put the box in her closet. She'd have plenty of time to reminisce after the show was over. Right now, she had work to do.

Hoping to avoid another confrontation with the ghost, she opted to spend the day at home, working on her budget and figuring out what the hell she was going to do about her sinking theater.

She could sell the place. She didn't know the first thing about running a business. Entrepreneurship just wasn't in her blood.

But she'd promised her students a show, and she planned to follow through. Once it was done, though… well, what would she do? If she sold the theater, she'd have to go back to work. A nauseating sensation churned in her stomach at the thought of spending the rest of her life in a dead-end job like her last one. She needed to be able to move, to express herself, to help people. Designing advertisements didn't help anyone but the business owners.

Taking on this theater may not have been the best decision she'd ever made, but she would stick with it. Somehow, she would make it work.

She shut down her computer and headed out the door. As soon as she stepped through the threshold, a frigid sensation ripped through her body like shards of ice clawing at her insides. She shivered and turned around to find Sandra standing in the doorway. The ghost had the same sad expression she'd had for weeks, but she gave Erica a curious look.

Erica rubbed her arms to chase away the chill. "Please don't stand right in front of the door."

Sandra tilted her head to the side. "She's getting to you."

"Who?"

"The other ghost. She's affecting you."

She closed and locked the door. "Other than annoying the hell out of me, she can't do much. She's trapped behind the glass."

Sandra shook her head. "She's inside your mind."

Colette had been trying to get inside her head. Attempting, through manipulation and guilt trips, to convince her to make decisions she didn't want to make. But she wasn't letting the ghost get to her anymore. "I'm fine." She headed down the stairs.

The spirit followed. "Why can't I leave here?"

"I've told you, I don't know. Maybe you're attached to something, like Colette is attached to the mirror. Did you die in this building? Or…" Erica paused. She'd been so wrapped up in her own issues, she hadn't thought to ask the spirit about herself. "How did you die? I'm sorry I never asked."

"Breast cancer." Sandra hovered over the sidewalk, her brow creasing in concentration. "I don't think I'm attached to anything. I lived in the neighborhood half a mile up the road, and I've been wandering since my death…until I felt you."

"I'm sorry. I wish I could help you." She wished Sandra had *felt* someone more capable. Erica opened her car door and tossed her purse inside. "If I ever figure out a way, I'll let you know. I have to go."

On the drive to the theater, her mind drifted to her conversation with Gage about his psychic friend, Allison. If she really was as gifted as he'd said, maybe she could help Sandra cross over. Maybe she could even free Colette from the mirror…if Erica were willing to admit she'd lied to Gage about the ghost. That was another issue entirely.

She inhaled deeply, waiting for the flush of jealousy to claw its way through her insides, but it didn't come. Why had it bothered her so much when he'd talked about Allison before? If Gage thought they'd get along, they probably would. Maybe she'd ask him to introduce her to his friends when they got back in town. It might be nice to have another girlfriend to talk to. Especially one that shared her ability to see spirits.

Erica waited outside the theater in her car until the first student arrived. She wasn't afraid of the ghost in the mirror, but she didn't have the energy to deal with another argument of who should be lead.

Running the rehearsal her way, she ignored Colette's image when it appeared in the glass. She walked the stage, putting the actors into their proper positions, choreographing the scene the way *she* thought it would look best. Then she stood in the wing as they took their places to run through their lines with the new choreography.

"Ms. Miller?" Amber put a tentative hand on her shoulder. "Are you okay?"

Erica blinked. "I'm fine. Go ahead and run the scene."

"We just did. Twice." Caitlyn crossed her arms and looked at Jason. "She's doing it again. I'm telling you, there's something wrong with her."

Twice? How had they run the scene twice? She'd walked off stage, turned around, told them to run through the scene, and…what? Where had the time gone? What had she been thinking about? "There's nothing wrong with me. I want to see the scene again. Places, everyone."

She ground her teeth, wracking her brain to remember

the first two run-throughs. Nothing. She held her eyes wide to make certain to see it this time.

As Amber shuffled toward stage right, Caitlyn stuck her foot out and tripped her, sending Amber stumbling into a chair. Jason caught her by the arm before she could hit the floor.

"Be careful," Caitlyn said. "I'd hate for you to hurt yourself right before the show."

"Caitlyn!" Erica marched onto the stage. "What do you think you're doing?"

"Just what you told me to do."

"What I...I didn't tell you to trip her!" She rushed to Amber. "Are you okay?"

Amber smoothed her shirt down her stomach. "I'm fine."

"Take five everyone." Erica pinned Caitlyn with an angry gaze. "You and I need to talk." She jerked her head toward the wing and waited for her student to follow her off stage.

The fog in her brain was starting to lift, and she vaguely remembered the first two run-throughs of the scene. Sort of. But she definitely did not tell Caitlyn to trip Amber.

Or did she?

She stepped toward her student and spoke softly, trying to mask her worry with anger. "What exactly did I say that you interpreted to mean you should try to hurt your fellow actor?"

Caitlyn let out an annoyed-teenager sigh. She was good at those. "You told me that if you were me, you'd do whatever it took to get what you wanted."

She had no memory of saying those words. It sounded like something Colette would say, though. Could Caitlyn see the ghost? No, that was ridiculous. Maybe Erica had told her to do what it takes to get what she wants, but she would never suggest violence. "If I said do 'whatever it takes,' I meant work hard. Hurting someone is never the answer."

"Whatever." Caitlyn rolled her eyes and returned to the stage.

Erica glanced into the mirror to find Colette smiling smugly. Her stomach sank. Could the spirit be the one responsible for the brain fog and causing her to act in a way she normally wouldn't?

No, she was trapped inside the mirror. But maybe she could influence the other ghosts to…

She shook her head. This was crazy. Ghosts couldn't get inside someone's mind, could they? That kind of thing only happened on television.

Anyway, she had more pressing matters to deal with, like the fifteen teenagers staring at her like she was crazy. She'd have liked to kick Caitlyn out of the show and be done with the silly rivalry all together. But this close to the opening, she'd never find a replacement.

She straightened her spine and raised her voice so everyone could hear. "This is my first and only warning to all of you." She said it to the group, but she focused on Caitlyn. "If anything like that happens again, you'll be out. I will not tolerate violence or nastiness in any form. Are we clear?"

Caitlyn lowered her gaze to the floor. "Yes, ma'am."

"Now, let's run the scene again from the top."

Erica made it through the rest of the rehearsal with a clear mind, but she couldn't ignore the nagging feeling that what she was experiencing wasn't all in her head. She rarely saw Leroy or Stanley anymore, and neither ghost seemed capable nor interested in mind control. That left two options: either Colette was somehow affecting her brain, or she really was going crazy.

Neither option was a good one.

As the students left the theater, she shuffled backstage and approached the mirror. "Colette?"

The spirit image manifested in the glass.

"Were you listening when I told Caitlyn to do whatever it took to get the lead?"

"I was, and I am so proud of you, dear. I knew you'd take my advice. Smart not to just pull Amber for no apparent reason. Now you'll get none of the blame if her parents get upset."

"What..." She inhaled deeply. She needed to stay calm. Making accusations would only make things worse. "Did you...you didn't happen to *influence* me to say that, did you?"

The ghost laughed. "I'm trapped inside a mirror. How could I have possibly influenced you?"

"Did one of the other ghosts? I don't remember telling her that. Well, I kinda do, but not clearly. It feels like someone's messing with my mind."

Colette cast a sympathetic look. "No one is messing with your mind, dear. I think your subconscious is finally breaking through. You're doing the things you really want, deep down in your heart."

"I don't think I wanted Caitlyn to hurt Amber." Nor did she want to order the scripts for the show and arrange all these rehearsals when she hadn't even decided for sure this was the route she wanted to go.

A sly smile curved the spirit's lips. "You certainly seemed to want Gage. And from the view I had of you two, he enjoyed it."

A fluttering sensation formed in her stomach. That time may have been her subconscious coming through, but she'd never act so forward on her own. At least, she didn't think she would. "And you haven't been whispering in my ear, persuading me to do these things?"

"I want what's best for you and this theater, dear."

"Of course you do." The ghost wanted the theater to thrive, anyway, and she seemed willing to do whatever it took. "I'm tired. I'll see you tomorrow."

Erica's mind reeled as she made her way to her car, the memories of her conversation with Caitlyn coming out of the fog. She had said those things, and now she was certain someone else had made her do it. But who?

Colette had become a thorn in her side lately, but that was because her drive to make the theater a success trumped any type of empathy she might have been capable of feeling. Hell, if Erica had been trapped inside a mirror for seventy-something years, she'd be ornery too.

The spirit was beautiful, and Leroy and Stanley had been men at one time. Could they be manipulating Erica to try to make Colette happy? Maybe one of them had fallen in love with her. She'd heard of people doing far worse in the name of love.

One thing was certain: she couldn't continue living with this brain fog and strange behavior. It was time to come clean with Gage. Hopefully he wouldn't be too angry with her for lying.

CHAPTER FIFTEEN

With a bag full of Thai food in one hand and a bouquet of yellow daisies in the other, Gage tapped on Erica's door with the toe of his shoe. She swung it open, throwing her arms around his neck before he could step inside. She pressed her lips to his and showered his face in kisses.

Warmth spread through his chest at the sudden onset of affection, but the thin handle on the Thai food bag dug into his fingers so hard he was starting to lose circulation. As she pulled away, he handed her the flowers and shifted the bag to his other hand. "If I'd known food and flowers would earn me that kind of welcome, I'd have been doing this all along."

She grinned, pulling him inside and running her gaze along the floor in the entry before closing the door. "The food and flowers are nice, but that welcome was just for you. I missed you."

"I missed you too." He set the food on the table. "Come here and let me give you a proper hug." He wrapped his arms around her, pulling her close to his chest and breathing in her intoxicatingly feminine scent.

Her body melted into his embrace, and…was that a sniffle he heard? He grasped her shoulders, pushing her away to look into her eyes. "Everything okay?"

She smiled, but a little glimmer of a tear collected on the inside corner of her eye. "Everything's great. What did you bring for dinner? I'm starving." She took the flowers from where she'd laid them on the table and put them in a vase in the kitchen. When she returned to the table, her eyes were dry. Maybe he'd imagined the sniffle.

They dined on Pad Thai and spring rolls, chatting about his day at work, but every time he tried to steer the conversation toward Erica's theater, she would change the subject, saying she'd been there all day and didn't want to think about it anymore tonight. Something heavy seemed to weigh on her mind, but he didn't want to push too hard.

After cleaning the dinner mess, which involved shoving everything into the trashcan—man, take-out was convenient—he shuffled into the living room and found a Christmas frame sitting on a shelf.

"It's a little early for Santa, isn't it?" He chuckled and stepped toward the frame, but his breath caught when he saw the image nestled inside the festive ornaments. "Where did you get this?"

"I had it in a box of high school memories." She wrapped her arms around him from behind, resting her cheek against his shoulder. "My dad found it when he was cleaning out the garage."

He picked up the picture. "Man, I was goofy. Look at that floppy hair."

"You were cute in your own way." She moved to stand

next to him and kissed him on the cheek. He could get used to this kind of affection.

"I swear you haven't changed a bit." Young Erica wore her hair in the same side-braid as she did now. Her smile lit up her features, but her hair cascaded down her shoulder, covering the side of her face. Her unscarred arm hung casually on his shoulder, but she'd whisked her damaged hand behind her back for the photo. She'd always been good at hiding.

Smiling, she took the photo from his hand and playfully rolled her eyes. "I've changed."

He turned to her, resting his hands on her hips. Tonight, her hair hung loose down her back, her scar blatantly marring her otherwise perfect skin. As he let his gaze wander over her face, down to her lips and back to her eyes, she didn't smooth her locks down the side of her face to hide from him. "You're right. You've gotten more beautiful."

"You are too charming for your own good." She gave him a quick peck on the lips and set the frame on the shelf.

He glanced at the photo and found a small, silver flash drive resting next to the frame. His heart gave a weak half-beat before slamming into his breast bone. "You still have this?" He reached for the drive and held it gingerly in his palm. "128 megabytes. That was top of the line back then." A nervous chuckle escaped his throat before he could stop it.

"You gave it to me a few days before I left for LA, remember? I never got the file open."

How could he forget? He'd poured his soul into the document on that drive. Told her everything. Exactly how he'd felt about her. Then, he'd coded it so she'd never be able to read it. "I encrypted the file. You weren't supposed to be able to open it."

She furrowed her brow. "Why would you give it to me if you didn't want me to open it?"

Memories of senior year rushed through his mind… the piece of his heart she'd torn from his chest when she'd left. Ten years later, she'd finally made him whole again. He closed his hand around the drive and swallowed the lump in his throat. "There were things I needed to tell you that you didn't need to hear."

"I don't understand."

He inhaled deeply, toying with the plastic device, sliding the lever to extend the USB plug and then sliding it back in again. "I never had the courage to tell you how I really felt about you. About us. I wanted you to know, but I waited too long." He pressed the drive into her palm and curled her fingers around it. "You were leaving. I didn't want you to think I was trying to change your mind."

"Can I see it now?"

"Now?"

"If I plug this into my computer, can you open the file?" She held his gaze, her expression a strange mix of anticipation and pleading.

Why not? Though he couldn't recall the exact words he'd used, he remembered the emotions. The way he felt about her back then was no different than the way he felt now. He loved her. He always had, and he always would. It was time he told her. He grinned and cocked an eyebrow. "I was eighteen years old when I encrypted that file. I could open it blindfolded with one hand tied behind my back."

Licking her lips, she returned his smile. "That gives me an idea for later." She ran a finger down his stomach and hooked it in the waistband of his jeans, tugging him toward the bedroom.

"I like the way you think."

Unfortunately, she hadn't dragged him to the bedroom to ravish him. Instead, she opened her laptop and plugged the flash drive into the USB port.

Holy hell, he was doing this. He would let her read the rambling words of his love-sick teenage self, and then she'd know he was in love with her. Hopefully, she felt the same. "Remember, I was a kid when I wrote this. Promise you won't laugh?"

She drew a cross over her heart. "I promise."

He took a deep breath and let it out in a huff. Hopefully he wouldn't regret this. With a few strokes on the keyboard, the file opened, and a text document occupied the screen. "Man, I had a lot to say."

"Let me read it." She sank into the chair at her desk and stared at the screen.

Gage's core tightened, a heavy fist twisting his heart as he read the words over her shoulder.

Dear Erica,

You're leaving soon, and I don't want you to go. But I'm not going to tell you that again. Our parents bark enough orders at us, and you don't need to hear them from me too. You don't need to hear any of this.

I'm not going to tell you going to LA is a bad idea. I'm not going to tell you Carter isn't good for you. That he doesn't love you. Not the way I do. It's because I love you that I'm not telling you any of this. Going to LA was your decision to make, and you've made it, and I will always support you. If I told you all this, you'd only think I was trying to make you change your mind, and I'm not. But I still need to say it. If I don't, I'll never forgive myself.

I'm going to miss you. I'm going to miss the way your eyes sparkle when you laugh at one of my stupid jokes. I'm going to miss seeing your smile lighting up your face. You are so beautiful. Always remember that.

I love you, Erica. I've been in love with you for a while now, and I've been too afraid to tell you. You don't feel the same way about me, and that's fine. I get it. Now you're leaving, and it's too late, but I'm telling you anyway. I love you.

My love for you is like an ocean, vast and deep. It rages through my soul like a river…

Gage scrubbed a hand down his face. *Holy hell.* Could he wax any more poetic? He couldn't bear to read the rest of his teenage heart bleeding all over the screen.

He took a step back and shoved his hands in his pockets as he waited for Erica to finish reading the letter. At least she wasn't laughing.

Her shoulders lifted as she inhaled deeply and closed the laptop. She rose to her feet and turned to face him, but she wouldn't meet his gaze. "That was…"

"Corny. I know." He chuckled. "Eighteen-year-old me had a lot to say."

She finally looked at him, and tears collected on her lower lids. "You loved me?"

"I still do."

"God, I was an idiot." She sniffled, and a fat tear splashed onto her cheek. "I'm *still* an idiot."

His heart ached at the sad expression in her eyes. "Don't cry, sweetheart." He pulled her to his chest. "We're together now. The present is all that matters, right?" Man, if he'd known this would be her reaction to his sappy love letter, he would've told her he couldn't open it.

"No." She let out a deep sob against his chest before

pulling from his embrace. "I'm a horrible person, Gage. Horrible. I don't deserve you."

"Hey, don't say that. I survived. Turned out to be quite a catch, if I say so myself." He winked, hoping to lighten the mood, but she didn't smile. This definitely wasn't the reaction he'd been hoping for.

Her bottom lip quivered. "I lied to you." She paced to the bed and sat on the edge. "I've been lying to you for a few weeks."

Coldness flashed through his veins, and he ran a hand through his hair. Shuffling toward her, he lowered himself onto the space next to her. "It can't be that bad." Unless she'd met someone new…or Carter was back in town. *Please don't let it be that bad.*

"It's bad. I must be going crazy."

"How so?"

She fisted her skirt in her hands and smoothed the material down her legs, then fisted it again and repeated the process. "I think one of the ghosts in the theater is affecting my brain. I'm losing periods of time, doing and saying things I normally wouldn't. Like when you were there. That was the first time, but it's still happening, and it's getting worse."

He scrunched his eyebrows, trying to understand what she was telling him. "You've been sleeping with other guys at the theater?" Maybe it *was* that bad.

"No!" She shot to her feet and paced in front of him. "I would never do that." She paused and tilted her head. "I would never *willingly* do that, but something in that theater is making me do things."

She wasn't making any sense. "Something *made* you sleep with another guy?"

Erica stopped pacing and held his face in her hands. "I haven't slept with anyone else. Only you."

He let out a slow breath. If she hadn't cheated, whatever lie she'd told him couldn't be that bad. He could handle this. "What's going on?"

"There's another ghost in the theater that I didn't tell you about." She continued pacing. "Her name is Colette DeVeau. She died in the 1940s, and she's stuck inside a mirror. The fancy one with the pewter frame."

He stiffened. That mirror had been in her bedroom the first night he'd spent with her. Lindsay had mentioned getting some blips on the EMF detector around it at the theater, but Erica had brushed the comments aside, not bothering to mention why it might have happened. He'd asked her specifically if she knew of any other spirits, and she'd told him no. Why would she keep this from him? "How long have you known she's been there?"

She plopped onto the bed and put her hands over her face. "I've always known. The mirror used to be in Mrs. Spencer's house. When I'd go for private lessons, Colette would help. Give me pointers." She laughed humorlessly. "She called me her protégé."

He rubbed his forehead. "You've been getting acting lessons from a ghost? I don't understand. Why didn't you want me to know?"

"She made me promise never to tell anyone. The same promise my mom asked of me."

What was it with ghosts not wanting people to know Erica could see them? She'd been a child when her mother's spirit made her promise not to talk, a teen when she'd met Colette. He could understand her hesitation when both ghosts were a secret, but now… "You told me about your mom. Why not Colette too?"

She picked at a loose thread on her skirt. "When she found out what you do…the paranormal investigations…she said you'd try to force her to cross over. She said people had done it before and that it was painful for her. Like she was being burned alive." She shivered and wrapped her arms around herself.

He rubbed a hand on her back. "That's why you were asking if it hurts the ghosts to cross them over." It made sense that she'd be willing to keep the ghost's existence a secret if she thought she'd cause her pain. Erica knew first-hand what it felt like to be burned alive.

"And when you couldn't give me a definitive answer…"

"You couldn't bring yourself to tell me about her."

More tears trailed down her cheeks, falling onto her skirt to darken the fabric. "I'm sorry."

He squeezed her shoulder. "This ghost is the *friend* who's been helping you? The one you told me about?"

The muscles in her neck contracted as she swallowed and gave a shallow nod.

His mind reeled. Erica's foggy memory. The way she'd acted out of character. The pieces of the puzzle began clicking into place, and the end result was not pretty. "The spans of time you're losing…how long do they last?"

She shrugged. "Usually a few minutes. Sometimes hours, I think."

If this ghost was strong enough to take over Erica's body, even for a minute or two, her life could be in danger. And by keeping it a secret for so long, there was no telling what kind of hold the spirit had on her. He clenched his hands into fists. If the mirror used to belong to Mrs. Spencer, could it have been responsible for her mental deterioration too? "You should have told me."

Another sob. "I know."

"You've been channeling her. She's using you. Manipulating you."

"No, Gage. It can't be her. She's helped me so much… with my acting when I was young, with the production I'm putting on now. She's like a spirit mentor."

"You've got yourself a real-life Phantom of the Opera."

She flashed a small smile. "Sort of. Yeah."

"You do remember how the story goes, don't you? When Christine stops following the Phantom's orders… when she tries to get away…"

"He locks her up." She shook her head. "Even if Colette wanted to hurt me, she's trapped inside the mirror. There's nothing she can do. I think one of the other ghosts is doing it. Trying to impress her, maybe? She is beautiful."

He laughed. "You think you were channeling Leroy or Stanley when we…I doubt it."

She slumped her shoulders. "I don't know. I'm so sorry I didn't tell you. I feel like a rotten human being."

"You're telling me now. That's something." Though he had to admit her lack of faith in him cut deep. "Sounds like we might have some trust issues to work on though."

"I know." She cast her shame-filled gaze to the floor. "I don't blame you if you never trust me again."

He wrapped his arm around her. "I was talking about you trusting me."

"I do trust you. I know you'd never lie to me, but I… haven't been myself lately. Whatever is happening to my brain is affecting my judgement."

His stomach turned. If she was coming clean, he should too. "I might have told one small lie."

She stared at her hands in her lap. "You did date Allison."

"No." He rested his hand on top of hers. "But I did kinda have a thing for her for a while."

She stiffened. "I knew you did."

"It never turned into anything. It was years ago, and the feelings weren't reciprocated." He squeezed her hand. "Once she told me she wasn't interested, I got over it. I swear."

She licked her lips. "Did you love her?"

"No." The answer came quickly. Easily. He'd never loved Allison. Not romantically. "But she is my friend. Is that going to cause a problem?"

Letting out her breath, she relaxed her muscles as she leaned into his side. "It won't be a problem. I'd like to meet her sometime."

The tension in his own muscles eased. "I'm sorry I didn't tell you."

"I'm sorry, too. I promise I won't keep any more secrets from you." She laced her fingers through his. "Are we good now?"

"Definitely." He pressed a soft kiss to her lips. They'd get through this. Whatever was causing her problems... whether it was Colette like he suspected or if it was something else...they'd overcome it. He dealt with the paranormal every day, and if he could vanquish demons, he could handle anything a human ghost threw at him. As long he and Erica were together, they could do anything. "I meant what I said in that letter, you know? I love you. Deep like a river."

She grinned. "Deep like an *ocean*. Can't you even remember your own words from ten years ago?"

"That's right. Vast and deep. And from now on, I promise total honesty."

"Me too." She took his other hand in hers and traced

her thumb across his palm. "And since we're being honest…there's one more thing I need to tell you." She pulled away to look into his eyes, her gaze more serious than he'd ever seen. "I love you, too." The corner of her mouth twitched, tugging her lips into a smile that lit up her whole face. "Just wanted to put that out there, so you know."

Her words slammed into his chest like a confetti cannon exploding in his heart. He took her face in his hands and kissed her forehead, her cheek, her lips. "You have made me the happiest man alive."

"You make me pretty happy, too." She leaned into him, taking his mouth with hers.

His entire body warmed with her kiss, and he pulled her into his arms, losing himself to the moment. To the woman. Erica loved him. The real him. Not some made-up version of who the dating experts told him to be. This woman knew him, and she loved him, and that was all that mattered.

She pulled away, pressing her lips together, her brow furrowing in concern.

"What's wrong?"

"Do you really think Colette could be controlling me from inside the mirror?"

He straightened his spine and held her hand. "I'm not certain a spirit can actually be *inside* a mirror. But I know someone who can help us."

"Allison."

"Do you mind if I call her?"

"It's almost ten. Do you think she'll be up?"

"It's only two or three in Fiji. She's not due home for a few more days." He held her gaze, searching for hesitation or any sign that she wasn't comfortable with involving his friend.

She nodded. "Call her."

He pulled his phone from his pocket and dialed Allison's number.

"Hi, Gage." Her voice sounded raspy from sleep.

"Are you okay?" It wasn't like Allison to nap in the middle of the afternoon. He switched the phone to his other ear and rested a hand on Erica's leg.

"I'm fine. Just jetlagged a little. Why are you calling so late? Is something wrong?"

"Isn't it afternoon there?"

She inhaled deeply, the sheets rustling as she moved. "We came home early."

"Oh, shit. I'm sorry to wake you then."

"It's okay. Did you need something?"

"Well, Erica…the one I told you about…she's having a problem with a ghost. I was hoping you could give her some advice."

She yawned. "Why don't you bring her over tomorrow around ten? We can talk then."

"Sounds great. Thanks, Allison."

"Bye, Gage."

He pressed the end button, and Erica looked at him expectantly. "What did she say?"

"How do you feel about meeting her tomorrow?"

CHAPTER SIXTEEN

Erica fidgeted with her seatbelt for the twelfth time since she'd gotten into Gage's Jeep. She had no reason to be nervous. They were going to meet Gage's friends for coffee at their multi-million-dollar mansion on Grayhaven Island. No big deal. Except for the fact that Gage used to have…what did he call it? A *thing* for Allison.

She stared out the window as they crossed the bridge. "You didn't have to take the day off from work for me."

He glanced at her, placing his warm hand on her thigh and giving it a squeeze. "I've got plenty of vacation days saved up. I don't mind using one on you. Besides, I don't want you going back to the theater until we talk to Allison."

She shifted in her seat to face him. "Can she really do all that stuff you talked about? Reading people and helping spirits cross over?"

They pulled into the driveway, and he cut the engine. "She can. But she won't read you without your permission."

"She can just turn it off?" She chewed her bottom lip as she unbuckled her seatbelt and let it slowly slide across her body. "That's a little hard to believe."

The passenger door opened, and Gage held out a hand to her. She hadn't even noticed him getting out of the car. *Fantastic.* Now she was talking to herself.

He smiled. "Are you nervous?"

"A little."

"Don't be. Allison's one of the nicest people you'll ever meet. Logan's not so bad either."

She took his hand and let him lead her up the porch steps. "I've heard of him. He's the one that organizes all those three-hundred-dollar-a-ticket fundraisers for local charities, right?"

Gage chuckled. "See? They're nice people."

The heavy oak door swung open, and a beautiful woman with long blonde hair and a perfect complexion smiled at them. "You must be Erica. It's so nice to meet you. I'm Allison." She held out her hand, and Erica had no choice but to shake it.

She readied herself for the psychic to close her eyes and start spouting off random things about her future... like she'd seen on TV...but it didn't happen. Allison's handshake was firm, her palm warm, and her smile so genuine, Erica almost forgot she was nervous.

"Come on in, guys. Logan's bringing the coffee to the living room." She motioned for them to follow before padding through the foyer.

Gage slid his arm around Erica's waist and guided her into the living room. A dark-haired man with bright blue eyes kissed Allison on the cheek as he set a tray on the coffee table. "Your decaf is in the Keurig. I'll be right back." He strode out of the room, and Allison perched on the arm of an overstuffed chair.

Erica sat on the sofa, and Gage settled in next to her, draping his arm across her shoulders. His outward display of affection in front of the woman he used to *have a thing* for eased her tension. The dark-haired man returned to the room, settling into the chair, and Allison introduced him as Logan.

Allison grinned, her gaze darting between Erica and Gage for a moment before she spoke. "Gage tells me you're a medium."

Erica sipped her coffee to give herself time to form an answer. "I wouldn't call myself a medium. I can sometimes see ghosts…when they feel like showing themselves to me."

She narrowed her eyes, studying her. "You probably have more power than you think. Would you mind if I did a quick reading on you?"

"Umm…" She looked at Gage, who smiled and nodded. "Okay, I guess."

Allison moved to sit on the sofa next to her and held out her hands. "Physical contact helps."

Erica swallowed the dryness from her mouth and slipped her hands into hers. Allison closed her eyes, rocking slightly from side to side, as a tingling sensation formed where their skin touched. The area around Allison seemed to open up, almost like a vacuum or a magnet, drawing Erica in. Her body swayed toward the other woman's, and a strange quivering sensation formed in her stomach.

As Allison's eyes fluttered open, she released Erica's hands and cast a conspiratorial glance at Gage. It was a mischievous smile, with a glint in her eyes that said *we'll talk later* without actually saying anything at all. "Your ability is quite powerful. You see spirits clearly and hear their voices."

Of course she heard them. How else would she communicate with them? "Don't you hear their voices?"

"Not with my ears. I'm an empath, so everything for me is about emotion. I *feel* what spirits are saying more than hear them speak."

"Hmm." What else could she *feel* about Erica? Did she pick up on her skepticism? Or that tiny shred of inferiority deep in her heart that she couldn't seem to squelch no matter how hard she tried? Gage idolized this woman's talents. Erica's ability could never compare.

Allison rose and returned to her perch on the arm of the chair, moving so gracefully, she almost seemed to float across the carpet. No wonder Gage had been hot for her. She was flawless, and Erica was nothing more than a failure.

"Your abilities have never been developed," Allison said, "but that doesn't make you a failure."

Erica's mouth dropped open at Allison's use of the same word that had just danced through her mind. How could she have known that's what she'd been thinking?

"Your mom asked you to keep your ability a secret because she couldn't be there to protect you. She doesn't blame you for what happened, and you don't have to hide anymore."

Erica's eyes widened, her breath catching in her throat as she turned to Gage. He must have said something to her about Erica's past. There was no way she could know all that.

He raised his hands in a show of innocence. "I swear I didn't tell her a thing."

"How did you? Is my mom here?" She scanned the room, but saw no sign of her mother's ghost.

"Her spirit has moved on, but she checks in on you from time to time. She isn't here, but she's sending me the message through the energy of the universe."

Pressure built in the back of her eyes. "Wow. That's… wow. I didn't know that was possible. Is there anything else you got from ten seconds of holding my hands?"

Allison tilted her head. "Why don't you tell me about your ghost problem?"

Gage rubbed Erica's back. "She seems to be involuntarily channeling something at the theater. A ghost that's attached to an antique mirror."

Erica let out a frustrated sigh. "I really don't think Colette is the one doing it. She's always been so helpful." She told Allison about her foggy memory and the lapses of time she'd missed, being careful to avoid sharing the incident with Gage in the wing.

Allison furrowed her brow as she listened, casting occasional glances at Logan, who'd remained quiet the entire time.

"So, that's what's happening." She leaned into Gage's side as the weight of the world seemed to lift from her shoulders. Sharing her ghostly encounters wasn't as bad as she'd thought it would be.

Logan leaned forward, resting his elbows on his knees. "You guys are the experts at this, but…can a ghost really be trapped *inside* a mirror?"

Allison shook her head. "I don't think that's possible. Gage?"

"In all my research, I've never heard of it. Not even with a demon involved." He squeezed Erica's shoulder. "If she's going to help, you need to tell her everything."

Her stomach dropped at the horrifying thought. She couldn't tell these people she barely knew that a ghost may have used her body to have sex with her boyfriend. "I, um…" The words died before they could make it past the lump in her throat.

Gage sat up straighter. "She came onto me, rather aggressively, in the wing. We ended up doing it in a chair."

Heat flushed her cheeks. She shrank into herself, bringing a hand to her forehead to cover her eyes. If it were possible to die of embarrassment, her demise would be slow and painful.

Logan chuckled. "Nice."

Allison elbowed him in the shoulder.

Gage grinned. "Yeah, it was kinda hot. Until she didn't remember doing it."

Erica groaned inwardly.

"I had a long conversation with Leroy and Stanley when we investigated." Allison's face turned serious. "I don't see either of them doing something like that. Not even to impress a lady ghost. If no other spirits are haunting your theater, it has to be Colette."

"But she's dead. Why would she try to manipulate me?"

"Have you ever tried to research her?" Logan asked. "Find out what she was like in real life?"

Her shoulders slumped. "I guess I took her at her word that she was a Broadway star." Why had that thought never occurred to her? If Colette were a living person making claims of stardom, she would have at least Googled her name. She shrugged. "I was a kid when I met her. My teacher told me her story, and I believed her."

"What's her story?" Logan asked.

"She was popular on Broadway, until a jealous understudy murdered her. She'd been sitting in front of the mirror when it happened, and that's why she got trapped inside it." She sucked in a sharp breath. If Colette had been murdered because someone wanted her part, would she have put Caitlyn up to hurting Amber? Could she be fueling that rivalry because of what had happened to her?

Gage squeezed her shoulder. "Things starting to make sense now?"

No, she wouldn't believe it. She couldn't. "I don't think Colette would do this. Sure, she's ornery sometimes, but she wouldn't hurt anyone." At least, she didn't *think* she would.

"But, babe." He shifted toward her and rested a hand on her leg, tightening his arm around her shoulder as if afraid she might bolt for the door. "If she was a manipulator in life, she'll be that way in death too. People don't change just because they lose their bodies."

"But she wasn't a manipulator; she was the victim."

"Maybe so, but from the way you've described her, it sounds like she's a woman who expects to get her way."

She shook her head. "She's done nothing but help for as long as I've known her."

"Help me out, Allison." Frustration sharpened Gage's voice.

"Her reaction is normal. If Colette is manipulating her...whatever her endgame may be...she's probably been grooming her."

"Grooming me?"

"Like when kidnapping victims bond with their abductors."

"Oh, my God." Erica leaned her head back on the sofa. Her hair fell away from her face, so she sat up quickly and smoothed it into place. A tornado of thoughts whirled through her mind. Betrayal. Disbelief. Fear. Bolting for the door sounded like a viable option, but Gage's hold on her was firm.

Breaking down now wouldn't help her one bit. She needed to focus. To stay calm and figure out how to stop whoever was taking over her body. She looked at Allison. "You can read people. Can you read ghosts too? Will you come to the theater and talk to Colette?"

Pressing her lips together, Allison cut her gaze to Logan. He took her hand, bringing it to his lips before holding it tight against his chest. "Allison is taking a break from spirits for a while."

A tiny smile lit on her lips as she glanced at Erica before focusing her gaze on Gage. "I don't think channeling would be good for the baby."

Gage straightened, excitement sparking in his eyes. "Baby? You're pregnant?"

Allison nodded. "That's why we came home early."

Gage shot to his feet, reaching Allison in two long strides and pulling her into a hug. "That's fantastic news. You're going to be a great mom."

He held on to her, rocking from side to side and gushing about how happy he was for her. Erica picked at a loose thread on her jeans, reminding herself he was congratulating Allison on the baby she was having with another man. No need for jealousy. Gage came from a huge family, so babies were probably a big deal to him. He probably wanted to have a few himself.

Warmth spread through her chest. Would she be the one to give them to him? Could she even have children? She couldn't think about that right now. Instead, she rose to her feet and shuffled toward the others. "Congratulations."

Gage finally released his hold on the other woman and shook Logan's hand. "Yeah, congrats, man."

Erica gave Allison a quick hug before settling on the sofa again.

"You definitely need to stay away from this ghost." Gage plopped down next to her and gave her thigh a squeeze. "Can you teach Erica how to cross her over?"

Erica grimaced. "Doesn't it hurt the ghosts to send them to the other side?"

"No, not at all. I've felt nothing but peace from the spirits I've helped. But if she truly is attached to the mirror, you'll have to free her first, then cross her over." She sighed. "And if the spirit is as strong as she sounds, that would require a form of energy manipulation that would take years to master."

Gage leaned forward. "What can we do then?"

Allison tapped a finger against her lips. "What about the PILFER machine? If you adjusted the energy output and attached it to the mirror, you might be able to create a frequency high enough to break the spirit's bond with the object."

Gage rubbed the scruff on his face. "You mean it won't take psychic powers to free this phantom?"

"When I clear objects, I'm practicing a form of energy manipulation. Maybe you can recreate it."

Erica rubbed her neck. "What's a PILFER?"

"It stands for Positive Ion Low Frequency Energy Resonator." Gage drummed his fingers on his knee, and Erica could practically see the gears turning in his mind. "Maybe. I'll have to do some research."

"Wait." Erica's heart raced. She didn't understand their technical jargon, and their casual discussion of vanquishing her friend sank in her stomach like a brick. "I want to talk to her first. We still aren't even positive she's the one doing it. And even if she is…maybe she'll stop if I ask her to."

"I doubt…" Gage blew out a hard breath. "Okay. I'll go with you though. I don't want you around that mirror alone."

"Don't forget to find out what she was like in life," Logan said. "That'll help you figure out how to handle her ghost."

Erica swallowed the sour taste from her mouth. "And if I do need to help her cross over?"

Taking a small crystal from a drawer, Allison handed it to her and explained her method of creating a portal with her mind. Erica tried to memorize every word. Even if she didn't have to use it on Colette, the ghost hanging around her apartment had been begging for help for weeks. Maybe she could try it for her.

They said goodbye to Allison and Logan and headed back to her apartment. Gage seemed lost in thought on the drive. She couldn't blame him; her own thoughts raced through her head so fast, she could hardly grab onto one. She needed time to process everything she'd learned from Allison, but the silence in the car was deafening.

She turned to Gage. "You seemed excited about the baby news."

His eyes crinkled with his smile. "I love kids. Hope to have a few of my own someday."

Another flush of warmth spread through her chest. "Me too."

Keeping his gaze on the road, he reached across the console and slipped his hand into hers. She rested her other hand on top of his. Then he looked at her, and her heart lodged in her throat. As Lindsay would have said, they had a moment. Words weren't necessary to convey the emotions that passed between them. He'd said it all with his eyes. Hopefully she'd be able to give him the family he wanted some day.

Returning his gaze to the road ahead, he held tight to her hand. "What time are rehearsals today?"

"Noon to two. The kids wanted their Friday night free."

His brow furrowed. "That doesn't give me much time to research."

"We can talk to her after rehearsal."

"I don't want you in there without me. Can you hold rehearsal outside? Maybe at the park next door?"

"It's not ideal, but I guess it will work. A change of scenery might be nice."

He pulled into the parking lot and stopped by the curb. "Okay. I'll do some research, see if I can find out anything about the woman the spirit used to be. I'll meet you at the theater at two, and we'll go in together."

"Sounds like a plan." She reached for the door handle.

He tightened his grip on her hand. "Promise you won't go in alone."

"I promise."

CHAPTER SEVENTEEN

Gage made his way to his favorite spot in the back of the research room and dropped a stack of books on the table. Situated in the corner where two massive windows met, the location normally provided a well-lit work space in the dim library, but thick clouds hung in the ominous sky, casting the room in shadow.

He'd scoured through his demonology books at home, which reinforced his absolution that the entity they were dealing with used to be human. That fact didn't console him. Sometimes human spirits could be as nasty as demons.

While he didn't know exactly how Allison used her psychic ability to detach spirit energy from objects, she had mentioned something about being a conduit and energy passing through her body before it's released. No way in hell was he letting her attempt a trick like that with this ghost. She may have been strong enough to handle it, but who knew how it would affect the baby?

A smile tugged at his lips. Erica had never said anything about wanting children until today. Her mention of wanting a family in the car this morning solidified his resolve to make her his forever. As soon as they took care of this ghost issue, he'd tell her so. Right now, he had work to do.

After two hours of research, he came up with a plan to use the PILFER machine to create what he thought would be the right frequency to free the spirit from the mirror. Unfortunately, he couldn't guarantee it wouldn't hurt. Once the spirit energy was detached, hopefully Erica could figure out how to create the portal to cross the ghost over.

If he could convince her Colette was actually the problem. Based on everything she'd told him, there was no way the old actress had Erica's best interest in mind.

He logged on to the library's account for access to the *New York Times* database. If Colette DeVeau really was a famous actress, there'd be records of her somewhere, especially if an understudy murdered her in a theater.

It didn't take long to find her, and the more he read about Erica's so-called mentor, the more his stomach churned with nausea. Colette had indeed been murdered, but her history had been far more sordid than she'd let on. Poor Mrs. Spencer hadn't known what she was dealing with when she got that mirror. He wouldn't let Erica meet the same fate.

He returned the reference books to the shelf and packed up his computer. As he exited the library, the bottom seemed to drop out of the clouds, sending sheets of rain pummeling to the ground. He darted to his Jeep and headed straight to the theater, saying a silent prayer to whatever gods might be listening that Erica sent the students home and was waiting for him in the parking lot. Or even better…at her apartment.

Rain sloshed against his windshield as he pulled up to

the theater. Erica's car sat alone and empty under the downpour. She'd gone inside without him.

"Goddammit." He shouldn't have let her come anywhere near this place until he'd researched the ghost. If anything happened to her, he'd never forgive himself.

He bounded through the parking lot, shaking the water out of his hair as he passed through the door. "Erica?"

Pushing open the lobby door, he found her standing in the middle of the stage, a single spotlight shining on her like she was the star of her own private show. She'd wound a red scarf around her neck, and she absently picked at the frayed end, ignoring his entry. As the door thudded shut behind him, she blinked, lifting her gaze. Her eyes were vacant, distant.

He stepped to the light board and turned on the house lights, shutting the spotlight off as the auditorium brightened. Still, she didn't look at him.

"Erica, we need to get out of here. I did some research, and Colette isn't who she says she is." He started down the aisle toward her.

She sucked in a breath and looked at him. "She wasn't supposed to tell you. She wasn't supposed to tell anyone."

"Who? Erica, what are you talking about?"

"I could have made this theater thrive. I could have found another protégé. One that would actually take me back to Broadway." She curled her hands into fists and made her way down the steps as her hungry, angry gaze devoured him. "You're not going to send me away. She's mine now."

Oh, shit. She was channeling. As she stepped into the aisle, he grabbed her shoulders and gave her a little shake.

"Erica, I know you're in there. You have to fight her. Don't let her control you."

She blinked, the anger in her eyes fading to confusion. "Gage?"

"Erica."

She yanked from his grasp, whirling toward the seats, dropping into one as she sighed dramatically. "Oh, Gage." Her laugh started out small, but the chuckle morphed into a maniacal cackle as her eyes rolled around in her head. "She really thinks you're in love with her."

He had to do something. The spirit was obviously insane and way more powerful than he'd thought. Erica needed to be grounded. She needed to hold on to something tethered strongly to this plane. She needed to hold on to *him*. He sank into the chair next to her. "I do love her."

She scoffed. "Men aren't capable of love."

"We are, Colette. I am." He took her hand in his, her cold skin sending a chill down his spine. "Look in my eyes. Can't you see the love there? I'm in love with Erica."

Her lips parted on a gasp. She blinked, furrowing her brow in an Erica-like expression. She was fighting the ghost, his touch giving her strength. Her eyes softened for a brief moment before she yanked her hand from his grasp. "She's mine now. It's time for you to go."

She moved like lightning, twisting the scarf around his neck and pulling it tight. He clawed at the fabric, scrambling to relieve the pressure on his windpipe. He couldn't breathe. When had she taken the damn thing off?

He wiggled from his seat, flopping to the floor and pulling Erica and the ghost inside her down with him. Her grip loosened enough for him to wedge his fingers beneath the cloth as he gasped for air.

She stood, dragging him backward, but she tripped and tumbled into the seats. He yanked the scarf from his neck and shot to his feet as she charged toward him, screaming. Stooping, he caught her around the waist and threw her onto his shoulder. With her hands beating into his back, a string of curses flew from her lips.

He had to get her out of the theater. The ghost could only stretch so far from the mirror before she'd be ripped from Erica's body. She yelled, her arms and legs flailing as he bounded up the aisle to the exit.

"She'll be back," the ghost used Erica's voice to scream. "She belongs to me; you can't keep her away."

He shoved open the door and trudged into the torrential downpour. As he crossed the parking lot, she let out a gurgled moan and went limp in his arms. He lowered her into the passenger seat and buckled the seatbelt around her before racing around to the driver's side.

Her head lolled to the side, her skin cold and pale. Her normally pink lips had turned an icy shade of blue, and her breathing grew so shallow he had to rest a hand on her chest to feel the miniscule rising and falling motion.

He dialed Allison's number and peeled out of the parking lot. "She was channeling. I got her away, but she's unconscious." He tried to suck in a deep breath, but he couldn't get enough air into his lungs. "She needs help."

Allison's words came out calm and steady. "Don't panic. Where are you now?"

"On the road. I'm taking her to the hospital." He made a sharp left and floored it through the intersection before the yellow light turned red.

"Is she breathing?"

He put his hand on her chest, feeling it rise and fall steadily, more deeply than before. "Yes."

"Don't take her to the hospital. As long as you're getting her away from the ghost she was channeling, she'll be okay."

He gripped the steering wheel tighter. "She's unconscious. She needs medical attention."

"What are you going to tell them? She was possessed by a ghost? Take her to your house, and I'll meet you there. She needs energy healing, not medical attention."

Hot tears brimmed in his eyes. "Thanks, Allison. I'll leave the door unlocked."

"I'll be there soon."

He tossed the phone in the cup holder and squeezed Erica's thigh. "I'm going to take care of you, baby. Just hold on."

Parking the car, he scooped her limp body into his arms and carried her into his house. He laid her in his bed and peeled off her wet clothes. Goose bumps pricked on her bare skin, so he got an extra blanket from the closet and covered her, tucking the fabric in around her body.

He changed into dry clothes, tossing his and Erica's wet garments into the bathtub. He'd deal with them later. He'd helped Allison through plenty of bad channeling experiences when they'd investigated together, and the one thing she'd always needed was physical contact. His grounding energy could always bring her back to herself. It had to work with Erica.

He slid under the covers, snuggling next to her and draping his arm across her body. The coolness of her skin felt far too corpse-like. He pulled his shirt off, wrapping his arms around her and pressing his chest against her side. Hopefully the skin-to-skin contact would be enough to bring her back. Twenty minutes later, a pale pink color returned to her lips, but still she didn't move.

A knock sounded on the door, followed by the sound of it opening and closing. "Gage?" Allison called.

"In the bedroom."

He sat up and pulled his shirt on as she and Logan padded into the room, and he carefully slid out of the blankets, keeping Erica covered. Sitting cross-legged in the center of the bed, he kept a hand on her shoulder. Her skin had warmed to a normal temperature, but he couldn't bring himself to break contact.

"What happened?" Logan asked.

"She went into the theater without me. She was already channeling when I got there." He gave them a condensed version of what happened. "I researched the spirit. Strangling is her M.O."

Logan shook his head. "That would explain your neck."

Gage glanced in the mirror. A deep purple bruise stretched across his trachea to curve upward toward his ears.

Allison leaned in to examine it. "I know you're worried about Erica, but are you okay?"

He fisted the blanket in his hand. "I'm fine. Just… please. Can you take care of her?"

She hovered her hands above Erica's head and smiled. "You didn't need my help, Gage." She nodded toward his hand on her shoulder. "How many times have you helped me through stuff like this? You know how to take care of her."

He shook his head. "It's different this time."

"It's only different because you're in love with her. You did everything right." She moved her hands to Erica's chest. "I'll do a full Reiki treatment on her, but you are the one who saved her."

He swallowed the thickness in his throat. "She's going to recover?"

"She already has. She'll need to sleep it off, but she'll be fine."

Relief washed through his body as he exhaled a shaky breath. "Thank you." He would never forgive himself for this. He knew how dangerous ghosts could be, and he never should have let her get near the theater. No production was worth risking their lives for, no matter how much Erica loved her students.

Allison finished her Reiki treatment and motioned for him to follow her out of the bedroom. She pulled the door shut and padded into the living room. "The most important thing when a medium is channeling a hostile spirit is grounding. Having that skin-to-skin contact with a grounded person keeps the psychic tethered to the Earthly realm. No matter how you decide to handle this ghost, hold on to Erica. She needs you."

She reached into her purse and pulled out an oval-shaped crystal the size of an ostrich egg. "Crystals aren't necessary for creating portals, but they help. The one I gave her was small. This one will amplify her power more." She handed it to Gage. "She has the ability to cross the spirit over; I felt it when I read her. She just has to believe in herself."

Allison and Logan left, and Gage set the crystal on the table and returned to Erica's side. Slipping off his shirt, he snuggled next to her, giving her as much skin-to-skin contact as he could without disturbing her rest. Warmth returned to her body, her cheeks turning a rosy-pink shade, and her breathing grew deep and rhythmic. Closing his eyes, he rested his head on the pillow next to her and tried to sleep. His mind wouldn't quiet. He held her for another hour, taking comfort in the steady rise and fall of her chest, but following an attack like that, she'd probably sleep until morning. Slipping out of bed, he put his shirt on and tip-toed out of the room, pulling the door shut.

He spent the afternoon preparing for what would hopefully be their final battle with the spirit actress. A combination of paranormal investigation equipment, a battery pack, and a set of jumper cables should do the trick for detaching the ghost from the mirror. All the positive ions his device would emit into the air would intensify Erica's portal enough to suck the spirit energy into it, whether it wanted to cross over or not.

He wired the equipment, using cables long enough to move the living person operating it at least ten feet away from the mirror before he activated the device. Who knew what kind of effect the massive amount of energy he'd be harnessing would have on them? The ghost would probably feel like it was being torn in half, but there was nothing he could do about that.

Too bad he couldn't test the device on an actual spirit. It would've been nice to know if this would really work before they went to battle. He clamped the cables onto a metal folding chair in his guest-bedroom-turned-office and ran the wires into the hallway. He turned the knob on the device, ramping up the energy to let it charge. The static in the atmosphere built, thickening the air until his skin tingled and every hair on his body stood on end. As soon as the green light flickered on, he flipped a switch, sending a pulse of electricity from the machine, through the cables, and into the chair.

A throb of energy radiated outward from the chair,

slamming into his chest. Blue bolts of electricity crackled across the metal surface, and red sparks showered down from the jumper cable clamps, glowing on the beige carpet.

"Shit." He stomped on the embers, extinguishing them before they could light the carpet on fire, but black burn marks dotted the rug in a circle around the chair. "Guess I won't be getting my deposit back." He disconnected the device and packed it into a duffel bag. As soon as Erica woke up, he'd tell her his plans.

Erica's head pounded as she struggled to stay asleep. Foggy memories and distant thoughts tumbled through her mind, fleeting in and out of her consciousness, teasing her brain with horrid images.

Soft cotton sheets draping across her body shielded her from the chill in the air, and the man snuggled next to her, breathing softly in her ear, gave her a sense of security. Of home.

She fluttered her lids open and gazed at the culprit responsible for the cool breeze on her forehead. The ceiling fan whirred above. She stared at the blades, latching onto one and following it in its incessant twirling motion. Around and around. Much like the thoughts spinning through her head, if she focused on one blade for too long, her stomach lurched.

She rolled onto her side and snuggled into the security of Gage's arms. He pulled her to his chest, placing a tender kiss on the top of her head, before starting awake.

With his hands on her face, he looked her hard in the eyes. "Are you okay?"

"I think so." Was she though? The last clear memory in her mind was of sending her students home as the rain began in the park. She'd dashed to the theater parking lot, and…then what?

Gage ran his fingers along her temple, brushing the hair away from her face. "Do you remember what happened yesterday?"

"Yesterday?" She sat up, and the blankets fell away. A hard chunk of dread solidified in her stomach. "Why am I naked?"

"Your clothes were wet. I washed them." He slid out of bed and retrieved a stack of laundry from the top of his dresser. He padded toward her, wearing nothing but a pair of blue flannel pajama pants, and she ached to have him crawl back into bed with her and hold her against his chest. To make the sickening feeling clawing its way through her entire body go away. To make whatever happened yesterday…and it couldn't have been good…be a dream that never really happened.

"Here." He handed her the clothes and rubbed a hand across the back of his neck.

His neck…

Her breath felt as if it were sucked from her lungs. An image flashed in her mind of the back of his head as she… "Oh, God. Did I…did I do that to you?"

"This?" He gingerly ran his thumb and forefinger across the bruise. "It wasn't you. I'm okay."

The fog in her mind began to recede, bringing the memories she'd so desperately hoped were only dreams into crisp focus. "I choked you." Her hands shook. She fumbled with her bra straps, finally managing to hook the damn things together on the fifth try. Yanking her shirt over her head, she swung her legs over the side of the bed.

Gage sat next to her and took her hands in his. "Baby, you didn't choke me. You were channeling Colette. The ghost did this."

"I could have killed you." She pulled from his grasp and finished dressing. This was her fault. Why had she gone into the theater? Was she trying to escape the rain? Why didn't she get in her car and drive away? "I'm so sorry, Gage. I don't know why I went in there."

"Hey, it's okay." He pulled her into his arms, and for a moment, her trembling subsided. For a moment, she allowed herself the comfort of his embrace. But she didn't deserve it. She didn't deserve him.

"It's not okay. I just…I don't remember why."

"She has a hold on you. She probably called you in. I don't know how far she can stretch from the mirror, but she may have even forced you. It's not your fault."

She pushed him away. "Yes, it is."

"No, it's not. Look, come with me." He took her hand and tugged her through the living room. A massive, black duffel bag sat on the couch next to his backpack, but he pulled her past it toward the kitchen table.

"What's in the bag?"

He flashed a cocky grin. "Everything we need to vanquish the ghost for good."

"Gage, I can't endanger you again." He may have fought off demons and all kinds of evil spirits in the past, but this was different. Erica had almost killed him herself, and she couldn't let that happen again.

He ignored her comment and picked up a manila folder from the table. "Look." Opening the folder, he spread the papers across the surface.

She scanned the pages: newspaper articles, obituaries, death certificates. "What is all this?"

"I did some research on Colette DeVeau. She was an actress on Broadway like she said, but she wasn't famous for the reasons she told you. She's a murderer."

Her breath caught at the accusation. "Not Colette." She backed away. Colette had been her mentor. She loved the theater. She loved helping, teaching. She wasn't capable of murder.

Gage grasped her hand. "Please, hear me out. Look at this." He passed her a photocopy of a newspaper image. The woman in the photo had long, dark hair piled on top of her head, with shiny ringlets framing her delicate features.

The paper shook in Erica's hand. Her heart stammered. "Where did you get this?"

"It's from an article in the *New York Times* on February 5, 1946. Is that Colette?"

She opened her mouth to speak, but words wouldn't form on her tongue. The paper slipped from her hands, floating down to the floor.

He handed her a copy of the article. A smaller version of the same photograph appeared beneath the headline: Broadway Starlet Murders Husbands, Killed by Jealous Lover.

"This can't be real."

Gage touched his hand to his neck. "She strangled her first three husbands. She had plans to kill the fourth when she discovered he was having an affair with the star for which she was the understudy. But the mistress got to her first."

Her head spun, and she grabbed the back of the chair for support. "How do you know it was she who killed her husbands?"

"She kept a diary. They found it after she was murdered."

She inhaled deeply, squeezing her eyes shut and trying desperately to make the room stop spinning. Though she didn't want to believe it, the pieces slowly began clicking together. The things Colette had said about Gage. That men were only good for sex and money. That he was trying to hold her back. She'd said the same thing about Mrs. Spencer's husband. She covered her mouth to stifle a gasp. "Mrs. Spencer."

"She strangled her husband too. Colette probably forced her to do it…like she tried to force you."

A cold heaviness formed in her chest like a block of ice expanding in her core. She'd screwed up, yet again, and this time it almost cost Gage his life. She needed to leave. To get far, far away from him before she did anything else stupid. "You almost died because of me. *My* hands almost murdered you."

"Hey." He wrapped his arms around her. "It's not your fault."

"But it is. I'm the one who got the mirror in the first place. I invited her into our lives, and then I hid her from you. You could have died, and it would have been my fault. I could have killed you." A sob lodged in her throat, but she swallowed it down. "Just like I killed my mom." She tried to pull from his embrace, but he caught her by the shoulders. She stared at the floor, unable to meet his gaze.

"Look at me." He hooked a finger under her chin, raising her eyes to meet his. "You did not kill your mom."

"Yes, I did. I mess up everything I touch. I need to go. Where's my stuff?"

He dropped his arms by his sides. "Your keys are on

the kitchen counter. That's all you had on you when I carried you out of the theater."

She marched to the kitchen and grabbed her keys. "My purse…my phone…" She squeezed her eyes shut as the memory returned. She'd taken shelter with the students under the covered theater entrance when the rain started. Her purse must've still been in her car. "Where's your phone? I need to call a cab."

"Please don't leave. I have a plan to fix this. We can fight her together."

"No, Gage. You need to stay away from me. I'm dangerous."

"You're not dangerous; the ghost is. But I know how to break her connection to the mirror. As long as you can follow Allison's instructions to make the portal, we can get rid of her for good."

Make a portal? She couldn't even think straight; there was no way she could focus enough to make a gateway to another realm. "No. She's put thoughts into my head. I don't trust myself." She paced to the front door and fumbled with the lock.

"Where are you going?"

"I'll walk to the theater. I need my car. I need to go." She unlocked the door.

"Wait." He sighed heavily and grabbed his own keys from the counter. "I will drive you to your car, if you promise to go home and not step foot inside that theater alone."

Pressure mounted in the back of her eyes as she took in his pained expression. She'd hurt him, but if he hung around her any longer, she might kill him. She could never live with herself if Gage lost his life for her. He couldn't help her vanquish the ghost. She had to do it on her own.

"I won't go in the theater. I just want to go home."

Gage opened the door, and she followed him through the parking lot and climbed into his Jeep. He gripped the steering wheel as if he wanted to strangle it and drove her to the theater without saying another word.

She stared out the window, unable to speak through the thickness of tears in her throat. Confusing thoughts clouded her mind like a tornado whirling through her head. Colette's words rang in her ears: *Men are only good for sex and money. He's holding you back; he'll try to get rid of me and it will feel like I'm being burned alive.*

Erica shuddered. Murderer or not, she wouldn't wish that fate on anyone. There had to be another way.

Gage stopped next to Erica's car and shifted into park. She reached for the door handle, and he caught her other hand. "We can fix this together."

"No, Gage. We can't." She pulled from his grasp.

"I love you."

"I know, but please…stay away from me." She slid out of the car before he could say anything else to make her change her mind. His gaze bore into her back as she unlocked her door and climbed into the driver's seat.

With trembling hands, she turned the key in the ignition and buckled her seatbelt. This was the right thing to do. He wasn't safe with her. No one was.

Gage clenched his teeth so hard a sharp pain shot through his jaw. That didn't go anything like he'd expected. He clutched the steering wheel and followed Erica as she drove to her apartment, keeping far enough behind that she wouldn't notice him. She'd promised not to go back inside the theater alone, but he'd heard that same promise dance from her lips before.

The ghost in the mirror had a hold on Erica's mind, and until they'd vanquished it, she couldn't be trusted to make sound decisions.

He stopped along the curb and watched as she climbed out of her car and plodded toward the staircase. She kept her gaze trained on the ground, her posture slumped, her movements heavy.

As she disappeared up the steps, he slammed on the gas and headed home. Damn it, he had to fix this. Erica needed his help…whether she wanted it or not. She needed *him.* And he needed her.

It was only a matter of time before she went back to the theater, and he planned to make damn sure he met her there when she did. Inside his apartment, he opened his laptop and hacked his way into the theater's video surveillance. When D.A.P.S. had done their investigation a few years ago, he'd tapped into the system to use the existing cameras to gather paranormal evidence…with Mrs. Spencer's permission. What he was doing now was highly illegal, but fuck it. Erica's life was at stake.

He found the feed for the parking lot camera and positioned the live image on a monitor in his office. The theater was a five-minute drive from his house. The second he saw her car pull in, he'd be out the door and on his way to meet her. His bag full of supplies sat packed and ready by the door.

Hopefully, between the charge he'd be emitting into the air around the ghost and Allison's crystal, Erica would be able to create the psychic portal beneath the spirit and force her into it. But with the mindset she'd had this morning, who knew? She wasn't thinking clearly. He needed a backup plan.

Portals were made of energy. The PILFER machine he planned to use to break the spirit's bond from the mirror would charge the air with positive ions. If he set up another device next to the crystal to create another energy field, all Erica would need to do was tap into the energy already there. Give it a psychic boost to connect it to the spirit realm.

He trotted to the living room and shoved the machine and an extra battery pack into his bag before racing back to the office to check the screen. The parking lot still sat empty. He let out a breath. He had a plan of attack, and the equipment to execute it. If he could send a shadow demon back to hell, he could handle a murderous ghost.

But what if Erica couldn't create the portal? What if she started channeling the ghost as soon as she entered the building and didn't have control of her mind? He tapped a pen against the desk and stared at the screen. He needed a backup for his backup plan.

Allison wasn't going anywhere near the evil spirit, and all the other mediums he knew would probably pass based on the danger factor involved. Well, all but one. He picked up his phone. Tina hadn't realized she had psychic tendencies until a year ago, when her fight with the shadow demon triggered her ability. She could see spirits...and demons...but she didn't have much more experience in mediumship than Erica. She would help him, though, and having two inexperienced mediums was better than nothing.

He dialed her number.

"Hey, Gage. What's up?" Her cheerful voice wouldn't stay cheerful once he answered her question.

No point in beating around the bush. "I need your help."

"Uh oh. That sounds serious."

"It is." He told her what had happened with the ghost. "Erica has the power to create the portal, but she's not thinking straight. I expect her to show up at the theater any time now, and I have to be there to help her. I know you said you wanted nothing to do with ghosts after what happened to you and Trent, but I'm desperate. Allison can't help."

Tina paused, inhaling deeply before she responded. "No, Allie can't. You know you can count on me, though. Trent too. You did save his soul from a shadow demon." The smile behind her voice was evident, but so was the apprehension.

"I can't take all the credit. That was a group effort."

"And this will be too. I don't know how much help we'll be, but we'll be there."

"Thanks, Tina."

He pressed the end button and ran through a mental checklist. He had the gear. He had psychic help for Erica. Trent would keep Tina grounded; Gage would ground Erica. But if he was holding onto her the entire time, he'd need help with the gear.

He dialed Lindsay's number. "Want to help me vanquish a murderous ghost?"

"Hell yeah. Let's do it."

Erica set the small crystal Allison had given her in the center of her living room. If she was going to help Colette cross over, she first needed to be sure she could create the damn portal to begin with. She stared at the stone and imagined a white light coming down from the universe, like Allison had told her to do.

She tried to focus on the light, but so many thoughts raced through her mind, she couldn't focus. Her stomach churned every time an image of Gage flashed behind her eyes. Pressure built in her chest until she thought her heart would explode.

Gage was the most amazing man she'd ever met. Her best friend. Her lover. But she couldn't be with him now. Not when she'd almost killed him.

She shook her head to chase the thoughts from her mind and refocused on the crystal. On the light. Every muscle in her body tensed as she willed the portal to open. Nothing happened. Her efforts were as futile as a kid who'd seen *Star Wars* and tried to use the Force to move things with his mind.

She needed to relax. How could the energy flow if she'd clenched and clamped down every aspect of her being? *Deep breaths. Inhale. Exhale.* Slowly, one by one, she relaxed each muscle in her body. She sat cross-legged on the carpet, ignoring the raging storm of doubtful thoughts in the back of her mind and opened her heart to the universe.

A beam of pale, white light formed around the crystal, extending up through the ceiling. Tiny flecks of silver sparkled in the light, dancing like dandelions in a spring breeze. Her stomach fluttered. She'd done it. She'd created a portal. A tapping sound on the window drew her attention away from the light. As soon as her focus shifted, the light dissipated, closing the gateway.

"Sandra." She shot to her feet and raced to the window. "I think I can help you. Come in."

The spirit shook her head, her sad expression tearing at Erica's heart.

"Why not? Oh! The salt." She grabbed her hand-held vacuum and sucked up the line of salt in front of the window.

Sandra drifted in through the glass, her excited gaze lingering on Erica's. "I felt the portal when you made it. It called to me, but I couldn't get in."

Erica's heart raced. "I did it right then. I'll make another one." She returned to a seated position, clenching her fists in her lap. "Are you sure this is what you want? I doubt I can bring you back once you cross."

"I don't belong here."

"Okay. Here goes." She tensed her shoulders, focusing her energy on the crystal, imagining the light.

The spirit cut her gaze between Erica and the stone. "I don't feel it. Are you sure you're doing it right?"

She exhaled and unclenched her fists. She had to relax or this would never work. "I'm too excited. Give me a second to calm down." She breathed deeply, relaxing her body, allowing her gaze to go unfocused on the crystal. The light shimmered and dissipated. The ghost looked at her expectantly.

With one more deep inhale and exhale, the portal grew, a beam of warm, white light extending up into the universe.

An ethereal tear rolled down Sandra's cheek as she placed a frigid hand on Erica's shoulder. "Thank you." She floated to the light and disappeared in a shimmering mist.

Erica gasped and pressed a hand against her chest. There had been no pain. The ghost didn't scream or appear to feel as if she were being ripped from the Earth. It had been a peaceful crossing. Sandra was finally at rest.

Could Erica do the same for Colette? After what the ghost had made her do to Gage—what it had done to Mrs. Spencer—she *had* to get rid of her. If she could convince the wicked spirit the crossing over would be painless, surely Colette would want to leave. She wouldn't possibly choose an eternity trapped inside…no, not trapped inside…*attached* to a mirror.

She still had a hard time believing the spirit she'd considered a trusted mentor could be so evil, but the evidence proved it was true. And since Erica was the one who brought her into their lives, she had to be the one to vanquish her. She wouldn't endanger anyone else.

CHAPTER EIGHTEEN

Gage stopped in the coffee shop parking lot across from the theater, in the space closest to the exit, facing the street. His friends would be showing up anytime, and then they'd form their plan of attack. Sure, between hacking into the security system and staking out the entrance, his actions could've been considered creepy. But he'd much rather be accused of stalker-like activity than face the consequences of letting Erica handle a serial killer ghost on her own. Even if she did figure out how to detach the spirit from the mirror and force her to cross over, the lasting effects a ghost that strong could have on her mind would be detrimental.

His heart raced as Erica parked at the theater and slid out of her car. His suspicion that she'd try to handle this alone had been spot-on, but he'd been hoping she'd prove him wrong. She scanned the parking lot, probably looking for his Jeep, and tiptoed toward the entrance. He followed, slinging his heavy duffel bag over his shoulder and darting across the street.

The front door shut behind her, and he let out a

breath. She hadn't seen him. Trent's Audi pulled into the lot, and his friends approached him as he stepped onto the sidewalk.

Tina's brow puckered with anxiety as she hugged him. "I thought we were supposed to meet you at the coffee shop."

"Erica's already here."

Trent shook his hand. "What's the plan?"

He grabbed the door handle. "She just went in. Lindsay's supposed to be here to help with the equipment, but we can't wait for her."

"I'm here!" Lindsay scurried toward them from around the corner. "I live two blocks away, so I walked. Sorry I'm late."

Gage looked at Trent. "Protect the women at all costs."

Trent nodded.

Tina scoffed. "I don't need protection."

"Me neither," Lindsay added, though the quiver in her voice didn't sound convincing.

The women could act as brave as they wanted. When it came to this ghost, he wasn't taking any chances. "Erica and Tina can channel, which means the spirit can take them over." He leveled his gaze on Trent. "She's already screwed me and tried to kill me. Be prepared."

Tina raised her hand. "I vote for screwing."

Gage didn't smile.

She let out a nervous laugh. "Not the time for jokes. Got it."

"Keep her grounded. Skin to skin contact, and don't let her go."

Trent slipped his hand into Tina's. "No worries there."

He handed his bag to Lindsay. "There's a PILFER device connected to a battery pack and a set of jumper cables. Attach the cables to the mirror in the wing near the curtain. It's an antique…pewter, oval-shaped. You can't miss it."

Lindsay unzipped the bag and peered inside as she made a whistling sound. "The ghost isn't going to like that."

"The shock should disorient her enough that we can catch her in the energy stream and Erica and Tina can create the portal right on top of her."

Tina let out a whimper. "No pressure."

This was dangerous. If their plan didn't work, any one of them could end up dead. He looked at Tina, offering her one last chance to back out. "You don't have to help."

Trent clapped him on the shoulder. "I wouldn't be alive and standing here if it weren't for you, man. We're in this together."

Gage nodded. "Good. I'm going to work on keeping Erica grounded. Everyone ready?"

Lindsay nodded. "As we'll ever be."

He pulled open the door and stepped into the lobby. The door to the auditorium stood closed, so he tip-toed toward it and slowly pulled it open before slipping inside.

Erica sat in an aisle seat facing the stage. "What are you doing here, Gage? I asked you to stay away from me." Though she sounded resigned, her voice was her own. Maybe.

Hopefully.

He took a few tentative steps toward her. "How'd you know it was me?"

"Who else would it be?" She didn't turn around.

"Where's Colette?" The door opened, and he held up a hand to stop his friends from getting any closer. They paused a few feet behind him.

"She's not showing herself, but she's here. I can feel her." She stood and turned to face him. "You shouldn't… oh." She cut her gaze over his shoulder and smoothed her hair over the scarred side of her face. "You brought reinforcements."

He hesitated, gazing into her red-rimmed eyes, trying to gauge whether he was speaking to the woman he loved or if the ghost already had control of her.

"Hey, Erica." Lindsay started toward her, but he caught her by the arm. Erica seemed to be herself, but he wasn't taking any chances until he was sure.

"This is Tina and Trent…some friends of mine." He took another careful step toward her.

Erica eyed his friends and crossed her arms. "I'm sorry Gage dragged you all the way out here, but you should go. This is between me and Colette."

"We want to help," Lindsay said.

"I'm just as involved in this as you are. Please, let us help." Gage reached for her hand, but she stepped away.

"Do you not remember what I did to you last time you were here?"

He inched toward her. "That's *why* I'm here."

"And you thought you'd throw their lives into danger too? Some friend you are."

Trent put a hand on Gage's shoulder. "He saved my soul from a shadow demon. I trust this guy with my life."

"Me too," Tina said.

Erica turned on her heel and marched toward the stage. "You being here is only going to piss her off." She stomped up the steps. "If you'll let me talk to her, I'm sure I can convince her to leave."

Gage followed her up the stairs and caught her hand

before she could enter the wing. "She's attached to the mirror. She can't leave."

"It has to be a psychological attachment. She was murdered while gazing into it. If she makes up her mind to be free, she will be."

"That's not how this works. It's an energy attachment; it will take energy to pull them apart."

She yanked her hand from his grasp. "I suppose that's what your friends are here for?"

"They're here to help." He took her hand again, but she pulled away. Her irrational behavior would spiral out of control if the ghost got a hold of her. She needed to be grounded if she wanted to stand a chance against the spirit. Damn it, she needed *him.* "Please, Erica. I don't ask you for much, but give me this. Let me hold your hand. Let me keep you grounded."

She opened her mouth as if to protest. Instead, she swallowed hard and slipped her hand back into his. "Thank you."

"Where's the mirror?" Lindsay set the bag on the stage and pulled out the equipment. Tina and Trent stood beside her.

"It's there." Erica pointed at the object in the wing. "But I don't think she's in it. I can't see her."

"Oh, my God." Tina's eyes widened.

Trent grabbed her other hand. "Do you see her?"

"She's really strong."

Erica tried to pull from Gage's grasp again, but he held her tight. "I can't see her. Maybe you're grounding me too much."

His heart hammered in his chest. "I doubt that. Lindsay?" He nodded toward the mirror. "Just like I told you."

"Got it, boss." She gave him a mock salute and put the

device together, clamping two claws of the jumper cables to the mirror and the other two to the device.

"This isn't funny, Colette." Erica's voice trembled. "Show yourself to me."

"No." Tina shook her head. "I'm not an actress…No, I don't want to be." She sucked in a sharp breath, her body shuddering for a split second before straightening.

"Now, this is a woman who knows how to get what she wants." Tina's voice turned smooth and sultry. All the playfulness drained from her eyes as she turned her steely gaze on Trent.

Gage tightened his grip on Erica's hand. "Shit. Hold onto her, man. She's channeling."

Tina flashed a wicked grin. It was the same expression he'd seen on Erica's face when the ghost had used her to seduce him. "You're a handsome man, Trent. Are you rich?"

"Fuck."

Her grin widened. "I'd love to." She twisted a hand from his grasp and grabbed a handful of Trent's crotch. "Not bad."

Erica gasped, clutching Gage's bicep and drawing him closer to her. "Is that what I looked like? We have to help her."

Though the vessel was different, the mannerisms and expressions were identical. The way Tina moved mimicked the fashion in which Erica had come on to him in the wing. He patted her hand. "They've got this."

"Tina." Trent grabbed her hands and pressed both her palms against his face, holding them there as he stared hard into her eyes. "You have to fight this, baby. For me. For us."

"Mm-mm." She shook her head. "I like this one. I think I'm going to keep her."

"Tina, please. We've been through worse than this. You're stronger than her." Confusion clouded Tina's eyes before she slumped into his arms. "I've got you, baby." He helped her stand. "Are you okay?"

She rubbed her temple. "I…what just happened?"

Trent kissed her forehead. "You were channeling."

"Damn."

"Damn, indeed." Erica straightened her spine and tried to step away from Gage. "This one's much easier to control. She's weak."

He took both her hands, turning her toward him and away from the mirror. "Don't listen to her, Erica. You're not weak; she's been grooming you since you were a kid."

He chanced a glance over her shoulder at Lindsay. The PILFER was set. All she needed to do was place the crystal by the mirror and set up the other device.

"You're not weak, Erica." Colette used Erica's voice to mimic him. "I should have killed you the first time." She yanked from his grasp and whirled toward Lindsay. "What are you doing to my mirror?" Hands extended, she darted toward her, grabbing her by the shirt and pulling her to the floor.

They tumbled, rolling over each other until Erica came out on top, her knees pinning Lindsay's arms to the stage. "You're not getting rid of me."

He grabbed the device and switched it on, sliding it into place next to the crystal.

"Damn, Gage, your girlfriend's strong." Lindsay struggled beneath Erica's weight. "Really strong."

"It's the PILFER machine. She's only going to get

stronger." He grabbed Erica from behind, lifting her from Lindsay's chest. "Tina, can you work on a portal?"

Erica kicked, her foot connecting with the side of Lindsay's head.

"Ow." Lindsay rolled and pushed to her feet.

"Sorry." He put Erica down, keeping his arms wrapped around her shoulders. He needed to ground her, and for that, she needed skin-to-skin contact. Her damn long-sleeved shirt blocked him, so he slid his hands down to hers, grasping them tightly. "As soon as we separate the ghost from the mirror she should get trapped in the device's energy field. We'll need a portal ASAP before she wiggles her way out."

Tina grimaced. "I'll try. I've never made one on my own before."

He struggled to keep his hold on Erica's hands. "Well, she's out of commission right now, so you're all we've got."

"Okay. Okay." Tina took a deep breath and stared at the crystal.

Gage hoped to hell she knew what she was doing. This exorcism wasn't going at all as planned. "Lindsay, flip the switch."

"If we turn the PILFER on now, she'll be electrocuted. You both will."

Erica stomped on his foot, sending a sharp pain shooting up through his kneecap. She tore from his grasp and hurled herself into his chest, knocking him to the ground. The air *whooshed* from his lungs as the back of his head smacked the floor. With her hands wrapped around his neck, she pressed, blocking his airway. Searing pain shot through his temples. He couldn't breathe.

Wrapping his arms around her waist, he rolled, throwing her to the floor. "Do it now!"

"No!" Erica scrambled toward the device.

Gage caught her by the legs.

"It won't turn on." Lindsay flipped the switch up and down. "The wires came loose."

Tina swayed on her feet. "It's not working."

"She's losing focus, guys," Trent called. "Hurry it up."

Erica flailed beneath Gage, kicking and clawing the floor. Lindsay jiggled the wires. Sparks shot from the device. "Gage…"

He jumped to his feet, hurdling over Erica, and grabbed the machine. She plowed into him again, knocking him down.

"Give it to me!" Her shrill voice echoed through the auditorium.

He turned the dial, charging the instrument. Static electricity built in the air until every hair on his body stood at attention.

Erica scrambled backward on her knees. "No. Please don't."

"I'm sorry, baby. This is going to hurt." He flipped the switch.

Erica convulsed on the floor, her body shuddering as she let out a blood-curdling scream.

A raging inferno ripped through Erica's body, seeming to pull her organs through her skin, turning her inside out. She jerked, her muscles involuntarily spasming about as she flopped on the floor. A scream echoed through the room, deafening her to the chaos around her. She covered her ears, but the sound intensified.

The scream was coming from her.

The burning, tearing sensation strengthened until death knocked on her door. Then it ceased. In an instant, the burning returned, but now it felt as if the heat came from somewhere outside her body. The strangled scream echoed in her ears, but it didn't resonate in her throat. With her hands still covering her ears, she curled into a fetal position and squeezed her eyes shut.

Footsteps. Shouts. Electricity crackling in the air.

She felt the sensation of being lifted. Her feet making contact with the floor. Being cradled against someone's chest.

Gage.

She pried her lids open. He said something incoherent, his chest vibrating against her cheek as he spoke. More shouting came from behind her. Why was it so hot? And that smell…

Her stomach turned. The unmistakable scent of fire and cinder assaulted her senses like a tidal wave crashing into her face. She peeled away from Gage's chest and peered at the debacle that once was her theater.

Lindsay clutched Gage's shoulder. Trent stood next to them, his arms wrapped around Tina as she stared wide-eyed at the electric display of sparks showering the stage. Gage's device sat on the floor, emitting waving beams of crackling, blue light like a giant plasma ball…only no glass sphere existed to hold the electricity inside.

Instead, the beams stretched upward like angry vines reaching toward to sun, suffocating their trellis as they climbed. Colette writhed within the electric beams, her once-delicate features contorting in anguish and rage.

Erica's heart hammered in her chest. Sparks from the electric storm had ignited the curtains, and the fire was spreading, reaching upward to the ceiling, traveling across the curtain rod toward them. Something above them popped. A light bar dropped, getting tangled in a loose wire that stopped its fall.

Ice flushed through her veins. Memories flooded her mind. Her bedroom. Her mom lifting her from the blazing bed and tossing her out the window. The screams. The agony.

All these people.

She gripped Gage's shirt in her fist. "Fire." Her raspy whisper barely rose above the noise. "It's on fire." She cleared her throat. "You have to leave. Everyone, you have to get out."

Gage tightened his arms around her. "We have to cross over the ghost. Can you focus? Can you and Tina create the portal together?"

"No."

"If you don't cross her over, she'll be free." He gripped her shoulders. "Do you understand? She'll be free to follow you wherever you go. You'll never be rid of her."

Better for her to suffer the wrath of a spirit than to be the cause of any more death. "You have to go." She'd make the portal. She'd get rid of the ghost or burn to death trying, but she would not allow Gage or any of his friends to stay inside a burning building. If they didn't make it out...

"Let's vanquish the spirit first."

"No!" She shoved Gage toward the stairs. "You have to leave. All of you." She pushed Trent and Tina to the edge of the stage. "The fire. I can't...please, you have to leave. Get out. Please!" Her voice cracked with panic. She'd barely survived the guilt of killing her mother. She couldn't be responsible for killing anyone else.

"It's the fire." Gage ushered his friends off the stage.

"She lost her mom to a fire when she was a kid. Get outside; call 911. I'll take care of her."

"Are you sure?" Trent asked.

"Yeah, man. Go. Get Tina and Lindsay to safety."

The flames grew hotter, traveling along the line of curtains like a freight train rushing toward them. Colette's strangled cries morphed into a maniacal laugh.

"You have to go too, Gage. I can't lose you to this."

The door thudded shut as the others left. Gage wrapped his arms around her from behind and pressed his lips to her ear. "We're in this together. I'm not leaving without you."

"But…"

He took her hands. "Focus on the crystal. I know you can do this."

She looked toward the stone, but all her eyes would focus on were the raging flames consuming the building. The thick, black smoke billowing across the ceiling like a monster ready to suck their souls from their bodies.

Her heart sprinted. Her head spun. She tried to imagine the light, but she could hardly breathe with the smolder in the air and the adrenaline coursing through her veins. Sweat rained from her pores. They needed to get out of there. The heat intensified until it felt like her skin would melt from the bone.

It was a feeling she was all too familiar with.

Gage's mouth moved against her ear. "Breathe with me, baby. You can do this."

She could. She had to. She inhaled deeply, nearly choking on the tainted air. Relax. She had to get her body under control in order to focus her mind. She allowed her shoulders to droop, her breathing to slow. Focusing on nothing but the crystal, she imagined the light. The portal stretched from the stage, up past the flames, and into the mass of smoke above.

The crackling energy intensified. Colette thrashed in pain.

Erica could no longer feel her heart in her chest. It was beating in her throat, threatening to rip it open with each pulse. "She's in the portal. Why isn't she crossing over?"

"Shit." Gage loosened his arms around her but hesitated. "Will you be okay if I let you go? The machine is holding her here."

"Yes. I've got this." Though her stomach churned with nausea, she sent another wave of relaxation through her body, loosening her muscles even more, focusing more intently on the light.

Gage released her and dove for the device. A booming *crack* sounded from above, but she didn't have time to worry about what it may have been. He flipped the switch.

The vines of electric blue light crackled and died, and Colette's contorted face fell slack. She raised her gaze to Erica's and cast her one last pleading look before disappearing into the portal.

Erica allowed herself to feel five seconds of relief that she'd defeated the so-called mentor who turned on the ones who'd trusted her. She was finally free.

"Let's go." She rushed to the stairs, her legs feeling fluid as pudding, but strong enough to run a marathon at the same time.

Gage rose to his feet as the culpable object that had cracked above crashed down on top of him. The curtain rod itself must've weighed fifty pounds, the heavy, red fabric doubling its weight. A mass of flaming curtain buried him.

"No." The memory slammed into her mind like a

sledgehammer. An eight-year-old girl, tangled in her bed sheets. The heat. The searing pain. The screams. "Gage!"

She darted toward him. He moved beneath the fabric. Hopefully he hadn't been burned yet. *Oh, please, dear God, don't let him be burned.*

Fumbling with the weighty cloth, she folded the unignited part over on itself again and again, tossing it aside until she found him. His foot protruded from the curtain, and she latched on to his ankle, pulling with all her might.

He gasped as she freed him, his wild eyes darting about the room as if he didn't see her. Linking her arms beneath his shoulders, she dragged him to his feet and down the stage steps.

As they made it to the aisle, his coherence returned. "Holy shit." He grabbed her hand, and they raced toward the exit. Shoving his shoulder into the massive lobby door, Gage pulled her through the exit.

She squinted against the bright sunlight as they stumbled into the parking lot. She needed to stop, to catch her breath, but Gage kept pulling until they reached the sidewalk across the street.

"Thank God you're okay." Tina threw her arms around Gage's neck and hugged him tight. Then she pulled Erica into an embrace.

The first bit of pressure built behind her eyes, but she would not cry now. Not here. Even though this woman, whom she'd only just met, was hugging her as if she cared for her. Tina had risked her life to help her. They all had.

Trent clapped Gage on the shoulder. "I was about to come in after you, man."

Lindsay blew out a hard breath. "That was intense."

"Tell me about it." Gage wiped the sweat from his forehead with the back of his hand, streaking soot across his skin. The hem of his shirt was singed, but he otherwise didn't appear burned.

Erica swallowed the thickness from her throat. "Are you okay?"

A slow smile spread across his face. "Never better. Come here." He pulled her to his chest, and this time, she couldn't stop the tears from flowing. His signature, musky scent peeked out from beneath the smoke smell as she pressed her face against his shirt. His arms formed a protective cage around her, silently reassuring her he'd be there for her. That everything would be okay.

But it wouldn't. He'd nearly died because of her. Again.

The blare of sirens pulled her from the edge of the deep, dark ravine of thoughts she'd almost fallen into. She wiped the tears from her ash-stained cheeks and turned to watch the firemen attack the blaze. Gage's hands felt heavy on her shoulders, but inside, numbness consumed her. The theater her former teacher and mentor had wanted her to run burned to the ground before her eyes, and she felt nothing. Not sadness. Not fear.

Nothing.

The police came. The paramedics. They questioned them. Examined them. Extinguished the fire. After what could have been hours or only minutes, she and all the people who tried to help her were free to go.

Tina hugged them both. "Call us if you need anything."

Trent shook Gage's hand and then hers. "I wish it could've been under better circumstances, Erica, but it was nice to meet you." He slapped Gage on the back. "Take care of this guy."

She flashed a half smile and averted her gaze. How could she take care of him? She'd almost killed him twice.

"My offer for a girls' night still stands," Lindsay said. "You have my number. Take care, guys."

"Well." Gage held both her hands. "The worst part's over. Now all we have to deal with is the clean-up, the rebuild, where to hold your classes while it's being rebuilt. Minor stuff." He chuckled, trying to lighten the mood.

A heaviness formed in the pit of her stomach as if she'd swallowed a brick. "There is no *we* in this, Gage. This is my fault. *I* have to deal with it."

He furrowed his brow. "I want to help."

"I know you do. You always want to help, but I need to do this on my own." She had to get her act together or she would continue screwing up other people's lives.

"I don't understand."

She cast a glance at the charred building. No flames leapt from the windows. No billowing smoke remained. A firefighter swung an ax onto his shoulder as he trudged out of the entrance. Tomorrow, they'd allow her inside to assess the damage. Right now, she needed to rest. To think. To figure out what the hell she was going to do with her life.

"I need space. I've spent my entire life doing what I thought I *should* do. Living for other people because I was too afraid to make a decision for myself. I went to LA for Carter. I became a graphic artist for my dad. I took on this theater for Mrs. Spencer. I almost killed you for Colette. But this…" She gestured to the burned building. "If this isn't a sign, I don't know what is. It's time to make my own decisions. To do things my way. I need some time alone." She shuffled toward her car.

"Erica." He caught her by the hand. "I've always supported you, no matter what decisions you've made."

The sadness in his eyes tore her heart in two, but she needed to figure out her life for herself. "I know. And I appreciate that. You've always been my best friend, and you always will be. But, right now…I need to be alone."

She pulled from his grasp and slid into the driver's seat. He shoved his hands into his pockets and stood there, watching her as she started the car and drove away.

CHAPTER NINETEEN

At their monthly brunch at Angelica's Café, Gage toyed with the last bite of omelet on his plate as his sisters chatted around him. Once he'd congratulated Deanna on *finally* getting an engagement ring from Mark, he'd only been half-listening to everything else they'd said. His mom was getting serious with her cop boyfriend. All of his sisters had someone. It seemed no one needed him anymore. Not even Erica.

"Gage? Did you hear me?" Chelsea tapped his plate with her fork.

He blinked his gaze into focus. "What? Sorry…I was daydreaming."

"I saw Erica when I went to visit mom yesterday."

"Oh?" His heart thrummed, but he lifted one shoulder in a dismissive shrug…trying to play it cool.

"She'd just been to see her dad when I pulled into the driveway." She gave him a pointed look, screwing her mouth up to the side as if she were waiting for him to ask for more. "Aren't you curious about what she said?"

He inhaled, lifting both shoulders this time and

drumming his fingers on the white linen tablecloth. Hell yes, he was curious. But if he let on about how much spending two weeks away from the woman he loved was eating him alive from the inside out, he'd never hear the end of it.

"She's selling the theater. Said she never should've taken it on in the first place and she had other plans for her life."

The news didn't surprise him. Though she'd never said it outright, owning her own community theater had never been her life's ambition. "Did she mention what those plans were?"

Chelsea folded her hands in her lap. "No. And she also didn't mention you. She didn't ask how you were…nothing. What are you doing, Gage?"

"What do you mean?" He folded his napkin and dropped it on his plate, preparing himself for the scolding his little sister was surely about to hand him.

"I thought you loved her."

"I do."

"So, why aren't you fighting for her? You should be calling her. Going to her house. Chasing her down. *Something.*"

He let out a dry chuckle. "What good would that do? She said she needed space, so that's what I'm giving her."

"You need to call her before she gets away."

"I'm giving her what she asked for. What else can I do?"

Chelsea sighed, defeated. "You always give. You give and give, and you take care of people, and you never ask for anything in return."

"I don't see a problem with that."

She rested her right hand on his shoulder, gripping his

bicep with her left as if to drive her point home. "It's okay to ask for what *you* need sometimes too."

He opened his mouth for a rebuttal, but his sister had a point. He needed Erica. Then again, if she didn't need… or want…him, his needs were futile.

"Here's the thing, Chels." He shifted in his seat to face her. "Erica said she's been living her life for other people. Doing things everyone else wanted her to do and not thinking for herself. If I pursue her…chase her down like you say I should…our relationship will be no better than any other decision she's made to please someone else. If Erica comes back to me, I want it to be because *she* decided to. Not because I wore her down or talked her into it."

Chelsea crossed her arms. "You're willing to sit back and watch her slip away?"

He spread his hands on the table. It was possible she'd already made up her mind. That she was already gone. He could've taken her silence as an answer, but he doubted he'd recover from the effect that would have on his heart. He wasn't ready to let her go. "If it's meant to be, she'll come back to me. The universe has a way of making things happen…if they're supposed to happen." Now all he could do was hope and pray that Erica was meant to be his.

"Wise words, little brother." Abigail winked.

He sat up straight. *Fantastic.* All three of his other sisters had been listening to their conversation.

"She'll be back." Becky emptied the pitcher of mimosa into her glass, dribbling a quarter of it onto the tablecloth. "Right, Deanna?"

Deanna tore her gaze away from the diamond on her finger and smiled at him. "It's meant to be."

Was she talking about herself or about him and Erica?

Hell, it didn't matter. He truly believed what he'd said. It was either meant to be or it wasn't, and he wasn't about to pressure Erica into a relationship she wasn't one-hundred-percent sure she wanted...even if it left him a broken man.

After brunch, he said goodbye to his sisters and spent the afternoon at the rock-climbing gym. He worked until his arms shook and his muscles burned with exhaustion. Using his body to its limits helped calm the storm of thoughts raging in his mind. His limbs felt like noodles as he gathered his things and headed home.

He tossed his sweaty clothes in the hamper and checked his phone. No missed calls or messages lit up his screen. He swallowed hard, unable to fight the lump of disappointment settling in his stomach. He'd been disappointed every goddamn day since the fire.

Wise words, his sister had said. Maybe his outlook on the situation was wise, but it had taken him a week and a half to get there...and it still hurt like hell.

He *had* tried calling Erica. He'd left her messages three days in a row until she'd finally texted him: *I'm fine. Figuring things out...on my own.*

He could take a hint. He hadn't tried to contact her since.

Dropping his phone on the dresser, he shuffled to the bathroom and stepped into the shower. The warm water gliding over his skin reminded him of Erica's soft hands and the intimate ways she'd touched him.

Fuck. What was he doing? It had been two weeks since the fire. Eleven days since she'd sent that text. Maybe he should check in with her. Make sure she was okay.

No. She wanted space.

He finished his shower and shut off the water. Ruminating on what might have been with Erica would do him no good. He'd wallowed enough the last two weeks. It was time he did something productive.

He dried off and threw on a pair of jeans and a T-shirt. As he reached for his sock drawer, in his peripheral vision, his phone screen seemed to have dimmed. Had it been lit with a message notification? He picked it up and pressed the home button, and his heart lodged in his throat.

A message from Erica lit up the screen: *Can we talk?*

He wiped his sweaty hands on his jeans, trying to get the damn thing to accept his fingerprint and unlock. Finally, it opened, and he entered his response. His thumbs felt so thick and clumsy, he nearly hurled the damn phone across the room. It took seven tries to type the words *of course.*

Her response came back almost instantly. *Are you home?*

Yes.

A knock sounded on his front door. His heart dislodged itself from his throat and tumbled into his stomach.

He ran through the living room, skidding to a stop before he could throw the door open. He needed to calm down. As much as he wanted to sweep her into his arms and make her his forever, he had to remember the talk she wanted to have might not be the same talk he wanted… needed…to hear.

Taking a deep breath, he tousled his damp hair and smoothed his shirt down his stomach. He opened the door. Erica stood beneath the porch light, wearing a lavender shirt and a long, deep-purple skirt. Her braid hung over her shoulder, and she clutched a bright-yellow sunflower in both her hands.

Her eyes brightened as she caught his gaze, and a sweet smile curved her lips. "Hi, Gage."

His heart thudded an irregular rhythm. "Hey."

"Can I come in?"

"Yeah. Of course." He widened the door and motioned for her to enter.

She set her purse on the table and offered him the flower. "There's nothing in the rulebooks on what gift a woman should bring a man when she wants to apologize. Guys have it easy."

He chuckled, taking the flower and pressing it to his nose before laying it on the table next to her purse. "Thanks. I don't think anyone's given me flowers before."

Stepping toward him, she ran a finger down his chest. "I like your shirt. How have you been?"

He glanced down to find a giant Captain America emblem blaring *nerd* on his chest. He'd worn a superhero shirt to win back his girl? *Smooth move.* "I've been okay. Worried about you."

She took his face in her hands and kissed him. And not a chaste *I've missed you* peck. She parted her lips and drank him in like he'd been missing for years.

His body responded before his mind caught up with what was happening, and he slid his arms around her and held her close, deepening the kiss, tangling his tongue with hers. God, he'd missed this woman. She tasted like a wintergreen Tic Tac, and her body felt so damn good pressed against him, he could've taken her right there on the kitchen floor.

But he couldn't. *Think, man. Get it together.* As much as he longed to let this play out—to undress her quickly and make love to her slowly—they had to talk. To establish their relationship and figure out the future because he was done playing the door mat. He enjoyed giving and taking care of people, but Chelsea was finally right about something…There was nothing wrong with asking for what he needed sometimes.

He pulled from her embrace and gave her shoulders a squeeze. "I thought you wanted to talk."

"Talking can wait." She leaned toward him.

"No." He stepped back, shoving his hands in his pockets. "No, it can't. If we're going to do stuff like this, there are some things I need from you."

She tilted her head. "Like what?"

Shit. What was it exactly that he needed? He should've made a list. Damn it, if he'd known they'd be having this conversation today, he would have. "For starters, I need to know what's going on with the theater. Chelsea told me you're selling it."

She opened her mouth to speak, but he held up a hand to stop her. His mind had finally caught up.

"And then I need to know exactly what you want from me. What *we're* going to be. Because I can't handle the back and forth. We're either a couple or we're friends. I'm not playing the friends-with-benefits game."

Her lips twitched as if she wasn't sure whether to smile or frown. "I'm sorry for shutting you out these past two weeks. I had a lot of soul-searching to do, and I thought I had to be alone to do it." She shifted from foot to foot like she was uncomfortable.

"Do you want to sit in the living room?"

She wrapped her arms around herself. "No, this won't take long."

Oh, hell. That could only mean one thing. She was planning a getaway. A clean break, and then she'd walk out the door. He steeled himself for the blow that would be.

"I have a bad habit of making decisions based on what other people think I should do. But this time, every decision I've made has been one-hundred-percent my own. I am going to sell the theater. It was a total loss; it would be cheaper to bulldoze the whole building and start from scratch than to try to restore it."

"That sucks. I'm sorry."

She smiled. "It doesn't suck, though. I never wanted to run my own business to begin with. I only took on the place because Mrs. Spencer wanted me to. The investigators ruled the fire an accident, so I'm getting the insurance money. That combined with the value of the property...as long as I can find a buyer...will pay off the mortgage and the renovation loan." She chuckled. "I'll be free from that nightmare soon."

"And Leroy and Stanley?"

"I helped them cross over when I went back to see the damage."

Swallowing the thickness from his throat, he nodded. He was running out of easy questions. "What about your students? They never got to perform."

"They're going to do a scaled-down version in the park next weekend." Her eyes glistened. "They're so sweet. Jason was trying to arrange it as a fundraiser to help me restore the theater. When I told him I was letting it go, they decided to make the show a free community event."

"Oh, I guess everything worked out then. But what are you going to do about a job? Graphic arts again?"

She laughed. "A cubicle job isn't my style. I'm putting my barista skills to work at my favorite coffee shop." She took a tentative step toward him, looking him hard in the eyes as if waiting for him to challenge her job choice.

"That's great. I'm glad you found something so quickly."

Her smile widened. "You wouldn't mind if I stayed a barista for the rest of my life, would you?"

Was that a trick question? A dozen different responses flitted through his mind, but he had no idea which one she wanted to hear. He settled on speaking the one in his heart. "If that's what makes you happy, why would I mind?"

"You don't think I'm capable of being more?"

"You're capable of doing anything you set your mind to. Your occupation doesn't define you."

The intensity in her gaze made his stomach flip. She searched his eyes for…he had no clue what, but he hoped she'd find what she was looking for.

Seemingly satisfied with whatever she'd found, she put her hands on her hips, her smile returning. "I'm going to get my teaching certificate. I want to be a high school theater director."

He smiled. That was the perfect job for her. "You'll make a fantastic teacher."

She inhaled deeply and let out a sigh. "Does that answer your first question?"

"Thoroughly. Thank you." He tensed. It was time for the important question.

"As for what I want from you…I want my best friend back. I want the boy-next-door who was always there when I needed a shoulder to cry on. The one who listened to me." She ran her hands up his arms, entwining her fingers behind his neck. "Who never judged me and who supported me no matter what stupid decision I made."

His heart sank. There it was…the friend zone. He'd seen it coming. It was how all of his relationships ended.

Why should this one have been any different? He pulled her hands from his neck and held them halfway between their bodies. "If you want to be friends, I can do that... but the touching...the kissing..." He gave her hands a squeeze and let them go, taking a step back to put some distance between them. "I can't handle that."

"I wasn't finished." She closed the gap between them, returning her hands to his neck. As she slid her fingers up into his hair a shiver ran down his spine. "I want my best friend, but I also want Gage 2.0."

"2.0?"

She chuckled. "Yes. The *man* standing before me with the muscles and the sexy smile and the intensely bright eyes that draw me in like metal to a magnet. The man in whose arms I have never felt safer. The man who sees past my scars and into my soul, and makes me feel things I've never felt before. I want the man who loves me...like I love him." She paused, allowing her words to sink in.

This would have been a good time for him to respond. To say something...anything. But he couldn't form words. It felt like a sock was wedged in his throat, sucking all the saliva from his mouth.

When he didn't speak, she continued, "I've realized our relationship has always been a little one-sided...you giving me exactly what I need, me gladly taking it. I want to give you what you need now. Will you let me? I love you."

Erica looked at him expectantly, her chest tightening as she awaited his answer. He took a deep breath, his gaze traveling from her eyes to her lips and back again.

Without saying a word, he reached for the band on the end of her braid, tugged it out of her hair, and tossed it beside her purse. He loosened her entwined tresses, brushing the strands behind her shoulder, and running his fingers through her hair to pull it away from her face… exposing her.

She fought the instinct to pull away. She was done hiding from him.

He brushed the backs of his fingers over her cheeks, down her neck, and across her shoulders. Goose bumps rose on the unmarred side of her body.

The intensity of his gaze pinned her to the spot, smoldering with a heat that threatened to consume her very soul. She wanted this man. She *needed* him with every fiber of her being.

He took her face in his hands and kissed her softly, gently. Pressing his forehead to hers, he ran his thumbs across her cheeks and inhaled a deep breath. "Say it again."

The thick, raspy sound of his voice turned her knees to pudding, and she inhaled a deep breath of her own to steady herself. "I love you, Gage."

"I love you, Erica."

Her heart thrummed in her chest. He slid his arms behind her back to lift her from the floor and carried her to the bedroom. As soon as her shoes touched the carpet, she yanked his shirt over his head and ran her hands over his smooth, firm chest. How had she gotten so lucky? This smart, sexy, hunk of a man loved her, and it was time she showed him just how much she appreciated him.

He started to pull her shirt up, but he paused. "I'll turn off the light."

"Don't." She swallowed the thickness from her throat. "Then I won't be able to see you."

"Are you sure?" He rested his hands on her hips. "I want you to be comfortable."

They could turn off the lights. She could continue to hide in the shadows, pretending...hoping he was pretending...that she was perfect. But she wasn't. No one was. All humans were flawed...scarred even. Erica wore hers on the outside.

She lifted her shirt over her head and tossed it aside. "If you love me, you love all of me. Scars and everything."

He pulled her close, his warm, musky scent spinning through her head, erasing her insecurities. "I love you fiercely. Every part."

He did. She could see it in his eyes. Feel it in the vibration of his chest as the words flowed from his lips. Those soft, kissable lips.

As he dipped his head to kiss her neck, she unhooked her bra and let it slide off her arms to the floor. The feel of his skin against hers had her aching with need, but this time would be all about him. He'd given her so much already.

She pushed her skirt and panties to the floor and slipped out of her shoes, standing naked before him in the bright overhead lights. There were no shadows to conceal her, no fabric to hide her scars. She felt exposed and exhilarated at the same time as his passionate gaze took in her form.

"You are so sexy, Erica."

A shudder ran through her body at the sincerity in his words. She popped the button on his jeans and slid down his zipper.

As his clothes fell to the floor, the corner of his mouth tugged into a heart-melting grin. "Why don't you lie down, so I can have my way with you?"

She pushed him onto the bed. "This time, let me do for you."

Moving to the center of the mattress, he lay on his back. "What are you planning to do for me?"

She crawled on top him, straddling his legs, lowering her lips to his chest. The fresh scent of soap mixed with a deliciousness unique to Gage teased her senses, making her mouth water to taste him. She trailed her tongue down his stomach, stopping above his navel, reveling in the way his muscles contracted with her touch. "What would you like me to do?"

"This is good." He was breathless already, and she'd barely begun.

She moved her lips lower, grazing her teeth along his hip bone. His dick twitched as he sucked in a sharp breath, and she giggled.

He rose onto his elbows. "What's so funny?"

"Nothing." She pressed a kiss to his stomach. "I'm enjoying the fact that you're enjoying this."

"You have no idea how much I'm enjoying this."

She took his length in her hand. "I have a pretty good idea."

He closed his eyes and let his head drop back on the pillow, moaning as she stroked him. His voice seemed to vibrate through his entire body, and as she lowered her head, her hair brushed across his skin. He held his breath.

She paused, her lips a scant centimeter from his sensitive flesh, letting the anticipation build until he fisted the sheets in his hands so hard she though he might tear them from the bed. She flicked out her tongue, gliding it from base to tip, and he exhaled a long, slow hiss.

As she took him into her mouth, he released his grip on the sheets to instead tangle his hands in her hair. But he didn't push her nor try to force her into a rhythm. He simply held her, his fingers gently massaging her scalp as she slid her mouth up and down his shaft. She started slowly, enjoying the taste of him, the feel of his soft touch. But as his hips started to move in sync with her own rhythm, she couldn't help but quicken her pace.

"Erica..."

The hoarse sound of her name on his lips made her tremble. She loved that she could do this to him. Make him feel this way.

"I need to be inside you. *Right now.*" The last part came out as more growl than words.

Releasing her hold, she rose to her knees. She fought the instinct to pull her hair over her shoulder, and instead, flipped it behind her back. His pupils dilated as he swept an approving gaze across her body. She didn't need to hide herself from this man. She never would again.

Straddling his hips, she took him in her hand and guided him to her center. She held his gaze as she sheathed him, his thickness filling her completely, every nerve in her body firing on overdrive.

She ran her hands across his stomach, up his chest to his face. He was such a beautiful man. His exquisite body. His kind, loving soul. And he was hers. Her stomach flipped, and her heart pounded.

Gage was hers.

She moved up and down his length, delicious friction sending electricity shooting straight to her womb. He watched her as she moved, his intense gaze devouring her, a satisfied smile playing on his lips. Gliding a hand up her thigh, he found her sensitive nub and rubbed it with his thumb. Fire shot through her veins.

With her hands on either side of his head, she could

barely hold herself upright as the orgasm ripped through her body. Her legs trembled. Her elbows gave out, and she pressed her chest to his, nuzzling into his neck as he gripped her hips.

"I love you, Gage."

"I love you, too." His voice was rough, thick, as he continued thrusting, sending wave after wave of pleasure rocketing through her body.

"Take me."

A deep growl resonated from his chest, and never breaking their union, he rolled her onto her back and made love to her. He kissed her fiercely, his lips and tongue searing her with passion.

She gave herself to him completely. There was no other man for her. Her body had been an unforgiving reminder of the mistakes she'd made. An ugly prison. In loving her, Gage had found the key. As she finally allowed herself to be loved, he set her free.

His pace quickened, and he gripped her shoulders and moaned as his orgasm overtook him. He gasped for breath, the most beautiful sound she had ever heard. His climax thrilled her as much as her own. As he relaxed on top of her, she traced the contours of his sweat-slickened back with the tips of her fingers.

Soft skin. Hard muscle. The contrast on the outside mirrored the man on the inside. He was kind, sweet, and gentle, yet brave enough to battle demons and save her from a murderous ghost. Wise enough to recognize she couldn't do it alone. That she needed him, even as she'd refused his help. She tightened her arms around him. She would never let him go.

He inhaled deeply, his breath tickling her ear, sending a warm shiver running down her spine. Rolling to his side, he pulled her close. Face to face, legs entwined with hers, he held both her hands in his. "We may suck at dating, but I think we excel at love-making."

"I agree, and I think I know why."

He kissed the back of her hand. "Do tell."

"When we make love, we can turn our brains off and *be* together. There's no overthinking or trying to play by the rules. We just...*are.*"

"We *are*, aren't we?"

"Very much. We always have been. I'm sorry it took me so long to figure it out." Gazing into his kind, blue eyes, she reveled in the warm feeling of safety his presence provided. There would be no more second-guessing. No more doubt. They belonged together. She trusted him with her life and her heart, as he did with her.

He lifted his head to press a soft kiss to her mouth, his lips lingering near hers, his breath warming her skin. "I'm glad you finally let me love you. It's all I've ever wanted to do."

"I'm glad you finally told me you did."

He smiled. "I did, I do, and I always will. Forever."

She snuggled into his chest. "Even when we're ghosts?"

He chuckled. "Forever never ends, so...yeah. Even then."

EPILOGUE

Erica held tight to Gage's hand as they ascended the steps to the mansion. The first time she'd come here, she'd been nearly sick with anxiety over meeting Gage's friends, especially Allison. She'd been fully prepared to dislike the woman for the simple fact that Gage used to have feelings for her, but she'd turned out to be one of the nicest people Erica had ever met.

Gage paused at the front door, taking the frilly pink gift bag from her hand and pulling her into an embrace. "What are you smiling at?"

"Am I smiling?" She snaked her hands behind his neck, sliding her fingers into his hair. "I'm married to the sexiest man on the planet. I've got plenty of reasons to smile."

"We both do." He pressed a kiss to her lips. "You ready for this?"

"Absolutely." She rang the doorbell.

Logan swung open the door. "Hey, guys. Glad you could make it." He took the bag from Gage. "Come on in."

She expected the gift bag, with its giant pink ballerina bear and overflowing green tissue paper, to look awkward in Logan's hands. Instead, he looked completely at ease as he tapped the bear's pompom nose with his finger and set it next to the other gifts in the living room.

"There's the birthday girl." Gage's eyes beamed with excitement as Allison approached, carrying a chubby-cheeked, blue-eyed toddler on her hip. "How are you, little Jade?"

Jade squealed and clapped her hands then nearly fell out of her mother's arms as she dove toward him. Gage caught her beneath the arms and tossed her gently in the air. She let out another squeal and patted his cheeks.

Erica's chest tightened, her throat thickening at the sheer joy the baby brought her husband. They'd decided to wait a year, to give Erica time to get her teaching certificate and settle into her new job at the high school, before they tried for their own baby.

She'd never given much thought to becoming a parent before. After her mom died, it had been just her and her dad. The idea of family didn't mean a whole lot. Then Gage came along with his four sisters, and his nieces and nephews. Even as adults, he was still close with his family, and his tight-knit group of friends was an extension of that.

Seeing his face light up at the kids in the room made her palms sweat. If she couldn't give him children, she'd be devastated. He swore it didn't matter. He'd spent countless evenings assuring and reassuring her that as long as he had her, his life was complete.

She'd been to the doctor. Had ultrasounds and myriad blood tests. She might have issues with the scar tissue on her abdomen stretching, but she was otherwise perfectly capable of conceiving and carrying a baby. She'd taken her last birth control pill two months ago. Now, all they could do was wait.

Gage set Jade on the floor, and she toddled toward her dad. "She's getting so big." He hugged Allison and dropped to his knees to greet the other baby lying on the floor.

"I'm so glad you could come." Allison hugged Erica and pulled back to give her a curious look. She glanced at Gage. "He sure does love babies."

The tightness in her throat thickened again. "He does."

"Not yet, Jade." Allison scurried away to stop her daughter from tearing into the presents.

Gage stood, holding Tina's baby in his arms. Her dark mop of hair fell across one of her eyes, and Erica gently brushed it aside.

"Hi, Diana. How are you?" The baby gripped her finger and giggled.

Tina stood between them, wrapping an arm around each of them. "If you two ever want to get in a little practice, you can babysit any time."

"We might take you up on that." He handed the baby back to Tina and shook Trent's hand. "How's it going?"

"Good. Tina hitting you up to babysit?"

Gage chuckled. "Yeah."

Trent shook his head and grinned at his wife. "I told her you're probably busy trying to make one of your own."

"Maybe." Gage wrapped his arm around Erica, pulling her to his side. "Time will tell."

Her chest gave another squeeze.

Logan introduced them to his mom and sister. His niece and nephew sat in front of the television, watching a Disney movie, and Jade plopped into the little girl's lap.

"If I could have everyone's attention, please." Logan raised a hand, and everyone quieted down. "First, I want to thank you all for coming out to help us celebrate Jade's first birthday. We'll get to the cake and presents in a second. But I also want everyone to know that my lovely wife, Superwoman that she is, has not only been raising our daughter this year. She's also completed her bachelor's degree and is one step closer to becoming a licensed clinical psychologist. I'm so proud of you, babe."

"This calls for champagne." Logan's mom pranced to the kitchen and returned with a tray filled with glasses. Allison whispered something in her ear, and she smiled. "Lisa." She handed a glass to Logan's sister and said something to her. Lisa disappeared into the kitchen.

"Congratulations, Allison." Erica smiled at her friend.

Lisa returned from the kitchen and handed a glass to Erica before helping her mother pass out the rest of the champagne.

"To Allison." Logan raised his glass. "She never ceases to amaze me."

They all raised their glasses, but when Erica sipped her champagne, the sweet tang of apple juice surprised her. Gage took a long drink from his glass and slipped his hand into hers.

She furrowed her brow at her glass. "Is yours apple juice?"

He took another sip. "It's champagne."

"They gave me apple juice. Taste it."

He sipped the juice. "Hmm… Maybe it was meant for Logan's niece. I hope they didn't give her your champagne."

Allison put a hand on Erica's elbow. "Can I talk to you guys for a second?" She motioned for them to follow her to the next room.

Gage rested his hand on the small of Erica's back. "I think Logan's sister gave Erica one of the kids' drinks."

Allison clamped her lips together as if suppressing a smile. "She got the right drink. I'm sorry, Erica, I didn't mean to read you. But when you hugged me, it kinda jumped out at me."

Her heart pounded hard against her chest. "What jumped out at you?"

Allison's smile widened. "You're pregnant."

Her heart seemed to burst inside her chest, sucking the air from her lungs. "Really?" She could barely force the whisper over the lump in her throat.

Gage set the glasses down and gripped Erica's shoulders. "Are you sure?"

Allison nodded and looked at Erica. "I can read you if you want me to double-check, but the energy I felt earlier was undeniable."

Her heart sprinted, and she leaned into Gage to steady herself as she held her trembling hands out to Allison. She trusted her friend's psychic abilities. She'd helped Erica develop her own over the past year, but this news was too exciting to be true. "Read me. Just to be sure."

"Of course." Allison took her hands and closed her eyes. The moment seemed to stretch into an eternity as she swayed slightly from side to side and Gage's grip on Erica's shoulders tightened.

Allison opened her eyes and smiled. "Definitely pregnant."

Erica turned to Gage, and the light in his eyes took her breath away. "We're going to have a baby."

His smile beamed. "You're going to be a great mom." A tear rolled down her cheek, and he wiped it away with his thumb. "Are you okay?"

"I'm so happy."

"Me too, baby. I love you so much." He pulled her into a hug and pressed his lips to the top of her head.

Logan stepped into the room, eyebrows raised. "Everything okay in here?"

"Everything's fantastic." She wiped her eyes and kissed Gage on the cheek. "Does this mean I get two pieces of cake?"

Gage chuckled. "You can have anything you want." Taking her by the hand, he led her back to the living room. "Can we tell them?"

She looked at her friends and straightened her spine. "We're having a baby."

"This calls for more champagne." Logan's mom refilled everyone's glasses while they hugged and congratulated them.

When everyone was topped off, Allison gave a toast. "Everything that has happened in our lives…the good and bad, triumphs and failures…every struggle has led us to this point, and we are all exactly where the universe wants us to be." She raised her glass. "To the universe."

Tina lifted hers. "To hot husbands and beautiful babies."

Erica grinned and raised her apple juice high in the air. "To happy endings. We all deserve them."

ALSO BY CARRIE PULKINEN

New Orleans Nocturnes Series

License to Bite

Shift Happens

Life's a Witch

Santa Got Run Over by a Vampire

Finders Reapers

Swipe Right to Bite

Batshift Crazy

Collection One: Books 1-3

Collection Two: Books 4-7

Crescent City Wolf Pack Series

Werewolves Only

Beneath a Blue Moon

Bound by Blood

A Deal with Death

A Song to Remember

Shifting Fate

Collection One: Books 1-3

Collection Two: Books 4-6

Fire Witches of Salem Series

Chaos and Ash

Commanding Chaos

Claiming Chaos

Mayhem and Ember

Mending Mayhem

Mastering Mayhem

Haunted Ever After Series

Love at First Haunt

Second Chance Spirit

Third Time's a Ghost

Love and Ghosts

Love and Omens

Love and Curses

Collection One: Books 1 - 3

Collection Two: Books 4 - 6

Stand Alone Books

Flipping the Bird

Sign Steal Deliver

Azrael

Lilith

The Rest of Forever

Soul Catchers

Bewitching the Vampire

ABOUT THE AUTHOR

Carrie Pulkinen is a paranormal romance author who has always been fascinated with things that go bump in the night. Of course, when you grow up next door to a cemetery, the dead (and the undead) are hard to ignore. Pair that with her passion for writing and her love of a good happily-ever-after, and becoming a paranormal romance author seems like the only logical career choice.

Before she decided to turn her love of the written word into a career, Carrie spent the first part of her professional life as a high school journalism and yearbook teacher. She loves good chocolate and bad puns, and in her free time, she likes to read, drink wine, and travel with her family.

Connect with Carrie online:
www.CarriePulkinen.com

Milton Keynes UK
Ingram Content Group UK Ltd.
UKHW020225250424
441687UK00001B/15